ONLY LOVE CAN BREAK YOUR HEART

KATHERINE WEBBER

SCHOLASTIC PRESS
NEW YORK

FOR MY BROTHER, JACK, AND MY SISTER, JANE

SPRING

CHAPTER 1

SHE STILL WAKES ME TO watch the sunrise.

Not every morning, but often enough. There are so many things we can't do together anymore. But this, we can still do this.

"Reiko," my sister, Mika, whispers in my ear. "Reiko, wake up. We'll miss it!"

My room is already filling with that hazy pre-dawn light that means the sun will be peeking out over the mountains in a few minutes.

"Hurry," Mika says, bouncing on her toes. She's wearing the same yellow cotton dress she always wears. No matter what time it is or what the weather is like. She's always in the same yellow dress.

I groan but get out of bed, pulling on the blue silk robe hanging on the back of my chair. I open my window, and then, glancing back to make sure Mika is still there, pop the screen out and slip onto the roof of my garage.

Mika crawls out after me, and we sit at the edge, her legs dangling off, mine tucked under me, and watch the sunrise over the mountains. The golden red light turns the palm trees into silhouettes across the desert.

Mika scoots closer to me and rests her head on my shoulder. She's more affectionate in the mornings. Less sassy, more snuggly.

I yawn and put my head on hers.

"I'll never get sick of watching the sunrise," Mika says softly.

"Me either," I say.

"It's like magic every morning."

I nod, watching the sky change color right before my eyes. Then I yawn again. "There are few things I'd wake up this early for, but a desert sunrise is one of them."

Mika pulls back to face me, her dark, wide eyes unblinking. "But you'd wake up for me, right? It's not the sunrise that gets you up?"

It's early May in Palm Springs, so the morning is warm, but her words send a chill through me. I wrap my arm around her thin shoulders. "Of course, Mika," I say. "Always."

"Good. Because I'd do anything for you."

This is the truest thing in my life.

And all I can do in return is smile and squeeze her hand. I love her so much it makes my heart feel like a balloon that's about to burst. It hurts, how much I love her.

Mika stands, pulling me up with her. She lets go of my hand and tiptoes along the edge of the roof, balancing like a tightrope walker. Then she glances over her shoulder at me with a mischievous grin. "Dare me to jump?" she says, lifting a foot and leaning precariously over the side, arms out like a scarecrow.

"Mika!" I say, grabbing her wrist and pulling her back toward me. Back toward safety.

She laughs. "Oh, come on, Reiko. It isn't that high. You climb higher, right? When you go rock climbing?" Her eyes are curious and hungry. Hungry for a world that she can't exist in anymore.

Because she can't go anywhere with me. Can't even leave our house.

Because my sister, Mika—the Mika I see, the Mika I'm standing next to, the Mika I love with all of my heart, the Mika I'd do anything for—is dead.

CHAPTER 2

AT SCHOOL, NOBODY KNOWS I still see Mika.

Nobody knows that I watch the sunrise with her almost every morning.

Nobody knows about the holes inside of me.

I put on concealer, hiding my dark circles. I paint on bright lipstick.

And I smile.

All day long.

In class, I say everything my teachers want to hear. At lunch, I sit with my girls, leaning in to hear the latest gossip about who did what over the weekend or who hooked up with who. I flirt with boys I'm not interested in but who are socially acceptable to flirt with. I laugh and I preen because that's what is expected of me.

I hold my head high under an invisible crown as I glide from class to class, still smiling all the while, and when I feel myself about to stumble, I remind myself who I am.

I'm Reiko Smith-Mori. I shine the brightest.

But sometimes I wonder if it will ever be enough.

If I'll ever be enough.

If I can be good enough as one when there should have been two.

I have to be.

The days are melting in the heat, and it isn't even summer yet. When this weekend comes, I barricade myself at home. I give my friends fake excuses for why I can't go to this or that party, and then I tell my parents I've got studying to do. But I'm not studying. I'm in my room with Mika. Trying to be a better sister. The kind of sister she deserves. I put the blinds down to keep the sun out and blast the air conditioner to keep us cool. Not that Mika ever gets hot. We paint each other's nails (I even let her use my expensive nail polish) and play hours and hours of Monopoly.

By the time Saturday night comes around, I'm itching to get outside. Aching for an adventure. This happens when I spend too much time inside with Mika now. Sometimes the guilt tying me to her gets so heavy I can't move, can't breathe—and then I need to get out. I have to take advantage of every breath I have. To make it count. For me and for Mika.

Tonight is one of those nights.

So even though it is almost two in the morning, I slip out of the front door and into my red Jeep. I've never told anyone, but the reason I wanted a Jeep is because it makes me feel like an adventurer. Like someone brave who never needs to be rescued.

I drive, and I drive, on and on, until I get to the edges of Joshua Tree. It's a national park, about an hour from Palm Springs. In the moonlight, the spiky branches of its namesake trees look alien, like something out of a Dr. Seuss book. I've been here a few times before, but tonight it feels like the park is calling me. There's a boulder out here that's great to climb. I feel safe with it, even at night, even alone.

Last year, I started rock climbing, and I love the way it makes me feel: strong, like I can do anything, but also small, like I'm this infinitesimal, inconsequential thing on this earth, in this universe. When your fingertips are gripping rock and there's a long drop below you and the sky up above, you can't focus on anything but being alive. Especially at night.

I park and hop out of my Jeep. My climbing shoes are already on my feet. I just need to attach the little pouch filled with climbing chalk around my waist and I'm ready to go.

The moon is bright enough that I don't even need my flashlight. I go up to my boulder and pat it, the way someone would pat a horse. "Hi, pretty," I coo. Then I laugh quietly at myself, imagining how my friends would react if they saw me talking to a rock. Everyone expects me to be a certain way, but here, in the dark, on my own, I can be however I want to be. I don't have to worry about looking cool or being cool or anything at all. I can just breathe.

"Here we go," I whisper, both to the rock and myself.

My fingers slip into the familiar crevices, and my feet find the almost invisible clefts in the rock, just enough for me to start to climb up. Toward the stars.

The final stretch of the climb is tricky. I take a deep breath, and I swear the night breathes back. Then I swing my legs up, grab hold of the top ledge, and start to haul myself up the last bit with my arms. I'm sweating hard and breathing fast and with a jolt I realize—

There is someone here.

Someone on my boulder.

We lock eyes, and the air fissures. In the same moment I find his gaze, I lose my grip. With a small cry, I scramble against the boulder, fingers digging for purchase in the granite, feet slipping out from beneath me.

His eyes widen and he reaches out for me, but he is too far away, and I'm already sliding, and then I'm back on the ground with a thump.

"Shit," I hiss through clenched teeth.

There is a shadow above me and then a voice:

"Are you all right?"

I tilt my head back to see who is talking to me.

To see who is out under my sky, on the top of my boulder.

CHAPTER 3

THE BOULDER BOY CROUCHES NEXT to me. He's white and tall with long, wiry limbs. He looks around my age and vaguely familiar.

"Do I know you?" I say, frowning.

He smiles wryly. "I know *you*," he replies, pushing back a piece of light brown hair that has slipped out from behind his bandana. He has long hair for a boy, past his ears, almost to his jaw. The fact that he knows me doesn't help narrow down who he is. That just means he could be almost anyone at my high school, or even the school across town.

"That isn't what I asked," I say, my voice as sharp as steel wire.

"I'm Seth Rogers," he says. "We go to the same school. And *you* are Reiko Smith-Mori."

Now I remember him. We're in AP physics together. He sits in the back and never says anything. One of those quiet loner guys who disappear into the background.

"You're lucky you fell the way you did," he says. "You could've really hurt yourself."

"You distracted me!" I lift my chin to gesture at the top of the boulder.

He makes a small barking sound, like a seagull. I think it might be his laugh, but I'm not sure.

"What?" I say, scowling. People don't normally laugh at me.

"Just a strange thought. That *I* would be the one distract-ing *you.*"

Now I *know* that he's laughing . . . but then I'm grinning, too, even laughing a bit, at myself and at him and at this whole ridicu-lous situation, because he's right. Nobody at school would ever believe that someone like Seth Rogers could get *my* attention, let alone distract me.

"But seriously, are you okay?" he asks.

"I'm fine," I say. But for a second, I almost wish I could play the damsel in distress and have him whisk me away on a white horse—take me out of my life and into another one.

I look away from him, feeling unsure. Behind him, the moon is so large and so low I could scoop it out of the sky like a gyoza out of soup.

"What is it?" he says, following my gaze.

"Do you see the moon? It's beautiful." It is glinting and glowing—one second pure gold, the next, ivory white. After a moment, I lie down to get a better view of it, hands behind my head. It should be weird, lying down next to Seth Rogers to look at the moon, but for some reason, it isn't. Maybe because it's the middle of the night, or maybe because of that dark desert sky, I almost feel like I'm in a dream.

I scoot a tiny bit away from Seth, giving myself more space to get comfortable, more space to breathe. He lies down, too, his head close to mine, but his body going the other way so our heads make the top of a triangle.

"There's nothing like it, is there?" he says, and I know he doesn't mean the moon but the desert at night. I'm surprised, because that is how I feel, too, and who knew that Seth Rogers and I would have anything in common? Because the desert in the dark is the only place I'm able to breathe a little easier.

I don't need to tell him that, though, or that I'm out here to forget about Mika. Mika, who takes up so much of my heart that it feels too big for my chest, like it's pushing all the air out of my lungs. It strikes me that out here, even with Seth Rogers, I can be exactly who I want to be. And it's strange, because I barely know him, but lying under the same sky, breathing the same air, I feel closer to him than I have to anyone but Mika for a long time.

"Shooting star!" Seth says, and points.

I see the tail just before it disappears. "Did you make a wish?"

"Same wish I always make these days."

I don't ask. Everyone knows wishes don't come true if you say them out loud.

I see another shooting star; this one looks like it is shooting off the moon, and it dances across the sky.

I don't say my wish out loud either.

The stars start to pop like popcorn, until I lose count of how many shooting stars we see, how many wishes I make.

"It must be a meteor shower," says Seth in a soft voice, and

I notice that he's scooted closer to me, closing the gap between us like a minute hand moving toward midnight. Each minute that passes brings him closer to me.

"I wonder where that expression 'thinks he hung the moon' comes from," I murmur. Watching the stars is making me sleepy— like they are singing me a lullaby. "I wouldn't want someone to hang the moon for me; I'd want them to get it for me."

"Like this?" Seth reaches up into the sky and plucks the moon out, offering it to me. It shimmers in his palm like a pearl. "Without the moon, there won't be any tides."

My mouth goes dry. No tides means no waves, no waves means no—

Wet, coarse sand . . . in my nose . . . in my mouth, and water, so much water, my lungs a bubble about to burst . . .

"Do you want it? Reiko?" Seth's voice wakes me, brings me out of my memory, and I'm grateful. My view of the moon is blocked by his face. He's leaning over me, and in the darkness I can barely make out his features. "Are you all right?"

"Did you get me the moon?" I ask.

"I can if you want me to," he says in his husky, hoarse voice that doesn't match him at all, and I smile up at the moon, but Seth thinks the smile is for him, because the one he gives me back is brighter than the stars falling all around us.

When he lies back down next to me, he's so close that I can feel the hairs on his arm and I can hear his every breath.

We watch the sky until the sun rises and the moon fades away.

CHAPTER 4

AT SCHOOL THE FOLLOWING MONDAY, I find myself looking for Seth. I know I'll see him in AP physics, but I watch out for him between classes and at lunch, too. I want to know if he'll look different, if we'll say anything to each other or just continue on like normal, as the Seth Rogers and Reiko Smith-Mori everyone knows.

I don't have a crush on him or anything like that. God, no. Even if we shared this weirdly romantic bonding moment out under the stars, he's still Seth Rogers and I'm still me.

I don't see him anywhere, and I wonder where he hangs out. Then I wonder why I never thought about where anyone goes but my group of friends, who are always in their same spot in the back parking lot, holding court.

"Distracted much?" my best friend, Andrea, says after fourth period, nudging me with her hip.

"Just tired," I say, giving an exaggerated yawn that quickly turns into a real one. It's true. I am tired. I haven't been sleeping well (but that's nothing new), and I didn't have time to go to Starbucks this morning. "I'm going to grab a Diet Coke before class."

Dre nods, and I head toward the vending machine on the other side of campus, keeping an eye out for Seth as I do.

Of course the vending machine is out of Diet Coke. "How is there none left?" I mutter.

Someone taps my shoulder. It's a girl in my grade. At least, I think she's in my grade. I'm not sure—she might be a year below me. I recognize her face but don't know her name.

"I actually just got the last one. Do you want it?" She holds out a bottle of Diet Coke.

"Are you sure?" I really do want it.

"Yeah, absolutely," she says.

"Thanks," I say, taking it.

"You're welcome," she says. And then she just kind of stands there. Like she's waiting for something.

"I should probably get to class," I say, my smile stretching into something more awkward.

"We're in the same class?" she says, and it comes out like a question.

Is she asking me?

"I've got art history," I say. "In the Humanities building."

"I know. I'm in it with you. I'm Penny Collins."

She's in my class? I pretend like I knew that. Like I know who she is.

"So, um, we should probably head over," I say, still smiling.

We walk in silence, but she keeps looking at me like she's expecting me to do something. Or say something.

"Thanks again for the Diet Coke," I say. "I, uh, I owe you one."

"Great!" she says, beaming at me like I've just given her a present.

I watch her sit down and try to remember if I've ever noticed her before. Then I look around the rest of the class and try to see how many other classmates I don't know by name.

Finally, in physics, my last class of the day, I see Seth. I notice him in a way I've never noticed him before—how he folds himself into his desk, eyes down, knees jittery, fingers twirling a pen. I think about going up to him, but what would I say? Inside the walls of our real life, our desert encounter seems like an alternate universe. So, instead, I sit at my own desk and wonder if he's looking for me, too.

Near the end of the lesson, our teacher, Ms. Crawley, asks why stars twinkle but planets don't.

I raise my hand. "Because planets don't emit their own light. Not the way that stars do."

"That's not it," says a voice from behind me.

I whip my head around. It's Seth. He's leaning back in his chair, and he's smirking. This is the first time I've ever heard him speak out in class, and I can tell from Ms. Crawley's expression that she's just as surprised as I am.

"What do you mean?" I say. I know I'm right.

"Well," he says, in a bit of a drawl, "it's about the refractive index of the earth's atmosphere changing." I like his voice. It's all gravelly and low and raspy. He sounds like Liam Neeson or a young Willie Nelson or something. I noticed it at Joshua Tree, but it suits him better out in the desert than in a high school science classroom.

"That might be part of it," I admit, "but I'm still right."

"It also has to do with the distance of the stars and the planets," he goes on. "Stars appear to twinkle because they are so far away. Everything always looks better from a distance."

"Not everything," I say with a wink, getting a laugh from the class.

Seth grins at me and, to my surprise, I find myself grinning back.

"Maybe," he says.

"You're both right," says Ms. Crawley. "Now can someone else explain to me the refractive index of the atmosphere in more detail?"

We're still smiling at each other when the bell rings.

CHAPTER 5

AND THEN LIFE GOES ON, and it's like Seth and I never spoke, like we never found each other out in the desert. I stay in my sparkly orbit with my friends—the one that all other planets are drawn to—and he goes back to the outer reaches of the social galaxy. I catch him looking at me in class sometimes, and sometimes I look back, but that's it.

Then I come down with the flu and miss a week of class. Dre gets all my assignments for me from my teachers, but I need the lecture notes from AP physics.

"There's got to be somebody you can call who can share their notes with you," my mom says. She's got her blond curls pulled back in a bun, and she isn't wearing any makeup, which is rare for her. Right now, you'd never guess that she used to be a famous supermodel, *the* Suzie Smith. Right now, she's just my mom, and she's stressed out about me getting these notes in case I miss key information about what's going to be on the final.

"Well," I say, "there's this one guy I could call." That's a lie. I could call anyone in class. But it feels like . . . an opportunity.

I look up *Seth Rogers* in the school directory, but when I call, nobody picks up. I'm not surprised. Who even uses landlines anymore?

"No answer," I say.

"Well, darling, do you want me to drive you over there? I really think you need to get the notes this weekend, so you can prep for finals."

I groan because I know that she won't let up unless I get these notes. Both of my parents take my grades very seriously. They take everything about me very seriously. If Mika were here, the pressure on us would be split, the expectations divided. There is still my little brother, Koji, but it's not the same. Mika was the oldest, and all their hopes for her have been crushed onto me, the next eldest. And I hate to disappoint them. It's why I try so hard to be the best, to be everything they want me to be. To be everything they wanted Mika to be. It makes me wonder what high school would have been like with Mika. We would have been the Smith-Mori sisters.

We would have been legendary.

"I can drive myself," I say. If I've got to go over there, I'm at least going on my own. It'll be weird enough for me to just show up at Seth's house. I don't need to make it weirder by having my mom there with me.

I put the address into my phone and drive off into the darkness. He lives farther out than I thought. I'm practically in the high desert, and the dark is the kind of desert dark that can swallow you whole if you aren't careful.

"Well, shit," I say, starting to wish I *had* let my mom drive me.

Finally, I pull up in front of a small trailer, tucked next to a low mountain. No neighbors. No nothing. I wonder if this is the right place. But the number on the mailbox matches the one in the school address book, so it has to be.

I knock on the gray door of the trailer, and a small woman with graying curls opens it a fraction and peers out at me, like she's scared who might be on the other side. "Who are you?"

I blink, her rudeness taking me by surprise. Most people aren't rude to me. "I'm Reiko Smith-Mori."

"Smith-Mori? What kinda name is that?"

I bristle. My last name is double-barreled. My mom's American surname meets my dad's Japanese one. And it is a name that I'm proud of. To me, my last name perfectly represents who I am.

Seth appears behind this small, sharp-tongued woman. "Reiko?" he says.

It's the first time I've heard him say my name since we met out in the desert, and it does something funny to my insides.

"Hey," I say.

"Who are you?" His mom is still glowering at me.

"Just a girl who goes to my school," Seth says.

"We're in the same science class," I explain, going on full charm offensive. "I've been out sick for the past week, and I wanted to find out what I missed."

"Was I supposed to be taking notes for you?" Seth asks.

"Um. No. I just thought I could copy yours?"

I'm still talking to them through a crack in the door.

"I could come back tomorrow?" I'm starting to wonder if showing up unannounced at night like this was a bad idea. I just assumed Seth would say yes and get his notes, because that is what most people do when I ask them for something. It doesn't matter what time it is.

"No, no. Now's fine," says Seth, but his mom doesn't move.

"Now isn't a good time for guests," she says in a tight voice.

Seth sighs. "It's fine, Mom—Reiko won't care." He opens the door. "Come on in."

The trailer is small, and it looks like the sofa is in the kitchen, but that isn't what makes me blink and squint in the dim light. The floor, the table, the couch, every available surface, are covered in scraps of metal, glinting gently. Seth steps over a pile of it and makes a space on the couch.

"Welcome to our castle," he says, stretching his arms out wide above his head. "It's small but shiny!"

The whole trailer could fit inside the swimming pool in my backyard. I've never seen a home this small. Even the apartments in Tokyo that we used to stay in were bigger than this. I feel like I've fallen into a documentary or something. That this isn't reality.

I wonder what Seth would think if he saw my house.

"Thank you for having me in," I say. Then I crouch to get a closer look at all the shining scraps gleaming on the floor. "What's all this?"

"You'd be amazed what people lose in the desert," says Seth's mom. Now that we're inside, she's friendlier.

21

"Mom, you sound like you're some kind of pickpocket. Or a hustler." Seth looks up at me. "Before her shifts, my mom goes hunting for treasure."

"What kind of treasure?" I ask.

"Any kind! All kinds! I search with my trusty metal detector and haul home my finds and sort it."

"How'd it go today, Mom?" says Seth, and the tenderness in his voice hurts my heart, because I know what it is like to feel tender and protective of your parents. "Find any diamonds?"

"Maybe," she says, inspecting something that looks like a melted watch, like out of a Dali painting. "But then again, you never know until you look," she says with a wink. "Especially near the casino."

"My mom works at Morongo," Seth explains.

"What do you do there?" I ask. Morongo is a nearby resort with a casino and a nightclub. Dre and I have been known to sweet-talk our way in on occasion. Then we dance all night, and I turn into yet another Reiko, one who doesn't give a damn about anything but having a good time. When I go dancing, I feel alive. It's like when I go out in the desert and explore on my own. Sometimes I feel like I have to grab hold of anything I can, *everything* I can, and live live live.

"She's a server on the floor," says Seth, his voice spiked with defensiveness.

I nod and smile to reassure him that I'm not judging his mom. At least, I don't think I am. I'm trying not to.

"I'm also an occasional blackjack dealer!" his mom declares.

"Yes, that, too. Treasure hunter, cocktail waitress, and blackjack dealer," Seth says. But his tone has softened; his earlier defensive spikes have melted away like icicles in the spring.

"The boss doesn't like when I play because I always win," his mom whispers, like her boss might be right around the corner.

"I thought the house was always supposed to win?" I say, because that is what my limited experience of gambling (from watching James Bond movies) has taught me.

"House has gotta let the little guy win sometimes. Just enough to give him a taste. Just enough to make him keep coming back."

I smile politely. "I've never played blackjack."

Seth's mom's eyes widen. "Never played blackjack! Well, sit down then. And then Sethie can give you those notes. Oh, Sethie, you should show her your games, too. He's got so many. He's been collecting them since he was a little kid. He's a bit of a hoarder, just like me!" There's a pride in her voice. She smiles at me, and it transforms her face.

"Games? Sethie?" I mouth at Seth.

"Don't you dare," he mouths back as his mom starts dealing out cards on the table.

I smile. It's funny that this is only the second time we've ever really hung out; it already feels like we have inside jokes.

I copy Seth's notes quickly, because I'm more excited than I want to admit about playing games with Seth Rogers. We play cards for hours, and while we do, we talk about silly things like what our favorite flavor ice cream is (salted caramel for me, Oreo for Seth, mint for his mom) and what Harry Potter house we are (we're surprisingly both Slytherins, and his mom is definitely a Muggle) and what we think our Patronus would be (mine is an eagle or an owl, something with wings, something that flies, and he thinks he'd have a stag, like Harry. I try to tell him he can't have the same Patronus as Harry, but he insists). I can't remember the last time I talked about Hogwarts houses with my friends, and I like it. But then my phone buzzes, and it's Dre, and I suddenly wonder what she, what everyone would say if they knew I was hanging out with Seth Rogers.

I close my eyes for a second and remind myself who I am at school and who I have to be. I'm going to be a senior this fall, and it means so much to my mom for me to make homecoming court. No, not just court. Homecoming queen. Like she was. And I want it, too. I know Mika would have been, and I owe it to her and to my mom to make sure I am, too. And disappearing into the night with a guy like Seth Rogers is not the kind of thing a homecoming queen would do.

I stand up, my folding metal chair scratching against the linoleum floor. "I should get going," I say.

"But we haven't even finished this hand," says Seth's mom. "And Sethie still needs to show you his board game collection!"

Seth blushes, and I smile, and then it's like I can see all my friends, my group, right in front of me, brows raised, giggles muffled, and I can taste their judgment in the air.

"I'm so sorry," I say, and I am, but I also need to get out of here now. "I really need to get home." I smile at Seth's mom. "Thank you for having me."

Seth walks me to my car, and I pause before I get in, remembering something he said earlier. "Why did you tell your mom I wouldn't care about . . ." I struggle to find the right words.

"The trailer? The junk everywhere?"

"It's not junk," I protest. "It's like buried treasure."

"Exactly. I knew you'd see it like that."

"How did you know?" I say, feeling suddenly *seen* out in the desert dark. But not in a bad way, in the best way.

He shrugs. "I could just tell. I don't know. Maybe it was from that night . . ."

His voice trails off, and I know he's been thinking about that night, too, and I know that he saw me the way I saw him. Different from how anyone else sees us.

And I like it.

"So . . . what is the deal with this mysterious game collection your mom mentioned?" I ask, grinning.

"If you wanted to see it, you should have stuck around," he says, smiling back.

"Well"—my words come out before I've thought them through, before I know if I mean them—"I guess I'll have to come back."

"Really?" And he's so eager, so hopeful, I almost can't bear it.

"Really."

You know the expression "they lit up"? Seth really does light up when I say we should exchange numbers. It looks like someone has lit a match inside of him—no, more than a match. It's like a bonfire is alight inside of him, and the light is just pouring out of him.

It makes me light up, too.

CHAPTER 6

MY SISTER IS SITTING IN her favorite spot, at my vanity table, when I walk into my bedroom after getting back from Seth's.

"Where have you been? I've been waiting for you," she asks, her dark eyes full of hurt. "You said you'd play chess with me."

"Sorry." I flop down next to her.

"You never spend time with me anymore."

"What are you talking about? We spend plenty of time together." The lie tastes sour in my mouth.

"I always had time for you." The past tense of her comment, and the bitterness of it, startles me.

"Mika-Mouse," I say, but she turns away.

"I don't want to be Mika-Mouse anymore. That's a baby name. I'm fourteen, not a baby anymore."

Forever fourteen. It's so painful to think about how she's gone from being my older sister to my younger one.

"You'll always be Mika-Mouse to me. But I'll call you Mika if you want." Her name is pronounced *Mee-ka*. My mom wanted to spell it *M-e-k-a* to make it easier for people to know how to pronounce, but my dad said she meant easier for American people to pronounce, and Mika should be proud of her Japanese name.

And then Mika died and it didn't matter how her name was spelled or pronounced.

I told Dre once, years ago, that I still see Mika. And she didn't laugh at me. She did something worse. She told her sister. Who told their mom. Who told my mom.

And then I had to go to a therapist, who told me over and over that Mika is dead.

I know that.

After all, I was there when it happened.

But that doesn't mean I don't still see her. I just don't tell people that I do.

I haven't said Mika's name to anyone after that conversation with Dre. Her name has become some sort of unutterable curse.

Now I only say it to her.

"Hang out with me, Reiko," she says now, getting off my bed and twirling around the room. "You promised you would." She's switched into Japanese. We used to always speak Japanese together. It felt like our secret sister language. We were going to move to Japan together and study at our dad's alma mater, the University of Tokyo. She would have gone two years before me, of course, but I was going to follow her, and then we'd get an apartment in Tokyo. We even had a scrapbook with pictures of all the places we were going to go to in Asia together and what our dream apartment would look like. Mika would spend hours online, looking up maps and cool furniture, and then print everything and painstakingly cut it out and put it in our Japan scrapbook. We'd planned it all out.

After Mika died, I stopped speaking Japanese out loud, and this year I'm applying to UCLA with Andrea. I won't go to Japan without my sister and I won't speak Japanese with anyone else. Even if I wanted to, I can't; the words won't come. They died with Mika. And when she speaks Japanese to me, I answer in English.

But I still look at the scrapbook sometimes.

Mika walks away from the bed and absently picks up a small blue stone on my dresser. "Is that guy Seth your boyfriend? I think he looks weird."

"He's not my boyfriend," I say. I don't try to figure out how Mika knows about Seth and what he looks like. I don't question anything with Mika. I'm scared that if I look too hard, she'll disappear forever.

And then her voice drops to a whisper. "I've never had a boyfriend. Not a real one. Nothing that really counts."

And for what feels like the millionth time, my heart breaks for my sister. Sometimes I wonder if it will ever heal or just keep breaking and breaking.

I pull her toward me. "Boyfriends are overrated," I say. "You're not missing out on anything. Now come here. I'll braid your hair. Do you want fishtail or French braids?"

She looks me straight in the eyes and smiles sadly. "I think I'm missing out on everything."

CHAPTER 7

THE NEXT MORNING, I STAY in my room with Mika. We watch YouTube beauty tutorials and I let her do my makeup. I stay in all day until it is time to help my dad with dinner, and then I leave Mika reading in my room.

She isn't there when I come up to grab a hair tie, but I know she'll be back.

She always is.

I set the table for dinner with four bowls of salmon donburi—sliced salmon sashimi over white rice. In the middle of the table is a simple salad of cucumber, carrot, and daikon. Both of my parents like to cook, which means we always eat well at our house. My mom sits next to me at the table, her blond curls piled on top of her head. She glances at me and then does a double take, raising a perfect eyebrow. "I haven't seen you wear this much glitter and blue eye shadow since you were about fourteen. I didn't even know you still had that neon stuff."

I furtively wipe some of it off with a napkin. I can't tell her that Mika did my makeup and that is why it looks so ridiculous.

"You look like a clown," says my brother, Koji, from across the table.

I throw the balled-up napkin, now smeared with blue, at him.

"Hey!" he says, but he's laughing. He throws his own napkin back at me.

I laugh, too. And it hurts a little, laughing with Koji, because Mika used to laugh with us, too, and now she's disappeared to wherever she goes when I can't see her. Koji was only nine when Mika died. He's fourteen now, so he's the same age she was. I don't know how much he remembers about her because I never talk about her with him, or with anyone.

I wipe the rest of the blue makeup off, putting Mika out of my mind.

"All right, settle down," says my dad, sitting next to Koji. But he's grinning, too. Nothing makes him happier than seeing us happy as a family. We weren't happy for a long time. And even now, it feels like a performance. At least it does for me.

My dad doesn't know that my happiness is like this blue eye shadow, easy to put on and easy to wipe off and never lasting long. Koji's happiness is real and bright and tattooed onto him in indelible ink that glows and makes the whole room shine.

My mom passes me the plate of salad, smiling at me, smiling at my dad, smiling the smile that made her famous. I learned from my mother that no matter what is happening on the inside, you can always put on a good face, and always keep on smiling. Sometimes I wish she didn't smile so much. I never know if she's smiling on the inside, too. I know she misses Mika. She cried a lot when it happened, and sometimes I catch her sniffling now, but most of the time, she puts on her happy face. Her brave face. I hear her and my dad talking about Mika, in quiet voices, when they think I can't hear them.

"Dinner is delicious, thank you, sweetie," she says now to my dad.

He raises a wineglass in return.

My parents are so perfectly matched, even if they came from such different places. My father grew up in a fishing village in Japan, and my mom has always lived here in Palm Springs, in the desert. Maybe that's why my mother loves the desert and my father loves the sea.

My dad used to try to convert my mother to becoming a sea person. We used to go on family trips to the beach, to the coast of Japan, to Hawaii, to Maine, all along California.

We actually aren't too far from the sea. But you'd never know, since we haven't been in years.

The last time I saw the sea, I was twelve. I'm seventeen now. Five years is a long time. But the sea is a hard thing to forget. I still remember how it smells. How it's everywhere. You can't get away from it. And I still remember how the tide comes in and out, in and out, no matter what.

But mostly what I remember is this:

That the ocean is deep and dark and dangerous.

It might sing you soft lullabies to lure you, to soothe you. But I know what it is really like—

. . . water slamming me into the sand, tumbling me around like a sock in a washing machine, rolling me over and over . . .

I'm a desert person, like my mom. Dad will never convert us now. Not after what happened. And even before that, I loved the sand and the sun of the desert, the dry air, the endless sky, and the electric colors. It's funny because most people think that the desert is dead. Devoid of color. Ask a kid to draw the desert and they'll just draw sand. But you'll never see brighter colors than in the desert. The pink of bougainvillea and the yellow of a cactus bloom against the blue, blue sky.

If you cut my father open, he'd bleed saltwater. My mother would bleed desert sun. Like me. We're forever landlocked now.

It's a voluntary sentence.

"I want to get a guitar," Koji announces without preamble.

I roll my eyes. Koji's birthday was just last month and he got an Xbox, but of course now he wants a guitar.

"Really?" says my mom. "Since when do you play the guitar?"

There is a tendril of unease creeping up my spine. Mika had been the musical one in our family. I used to go to all of her piano recitals. I loved cheering for her and giving her a standing ovation at the end. What would she think about Koji getting into music, without her here?

Koji takes a bite of salmon. "Well, I don't play yet. But I'm going to. Ivan has been letting me practice on his. And"—he starts to grin—"I'm pretty good."

"Music does run in our family," my mom says softly, looking down with a sad smile, and my unease sprouts wings and envelops me because I'm scared someone will mention Mika. How can we talk about music without mentioning her?

And I don't want to talk about her. I can't talk about her being gone when she's so very alive to me. My parents don't know I still see her, but they know I don't like to talk about her. The grief counselors and therapists said to let me grieve in my own way. So, like in so many other things, they indulge me.

I wonder if Koji remembers that Mika used to play the piano. He has to, *he has to*. How could he forget? But maybe he was too young. Maybe he's blocked it out. And maybe it doesn't matter: The piano and the guitar aren't the same.

But still. I feel like he's somehow betraying Mika's memory. That we're all somehow betraying her.

"You know, I used to play the guitar. I could show you a thing or two," my dad goes on. He doesn't say that he also plays the piano. He taught me and Mika both, but she took to it more than I did, till she was better than my dad and needed professional lessons.

I'm angry at him for not mentioning it, and it isn't fair because I know I'm the reason he won't.

My mom smiles, and I wonder if she's smiling on the inside, too, or if she's hiding the hurt the way I hide it. "It's true. On our first date, your dad played the guitar for me." Then she laughs, and it's her real laugh, so I know she must mean it. "He was terrible."

My dad puts his palm on his chest, mock affronted. "I was not terrible. Why did you kiss me, then?"

"Because you were handsome," my mom says, leaning toward him and kissing him on the cheek.

"*Were* handsome? Why the past tense?"

My mom runs a hand through my dad's dark hair and kisses him again. "Oh, quit fishing. You're still handsome."

Koji groans. "You guys," he says, covering his eyes like he always does when our parents are affectionate in front of us.

My parents have the kind of love that burns so bright and strong that even Mika's death couldn't put it out. If anything, it made them more determined to love each other, to love us.

I know I'm lucky my parents are so in love, but sometimes it puts them in an impenetrable glass bubble that only they live in. I can look inside, I can see all that warmth and joy, but I can't feel it. I can't get in.

"Anyway," I say loudly. "Why the sudden interest in the guitar, Koj?"

"Because I'm destined to be a rock star, obviously," he says. He's being flippant, but he's deflated, and I feel like it's my fault, for not being more supportive. For not being the kind of big sister he deserves. For not being more like Mika.

"How do we know you'll practice?" asks my mom. I don't know why she's pretending that Koji isn't getting the guitar; of course he's getting the guitar. Ever since Mika died, my parents have given us everything we've asked for. I got the red Jeep I wanted; Koji gets every video game he wants, and he'll get the guitar. As if all the stuff could make up for a sister. Or maybe they wish that they'd never said no to Mika, that they'd given her everything she'd asked for while they could.

"I swear I'll practice," says Koji. "You can trust me."

"We'll see," says my mom.

"Sweet!" Koji says with a fist pump in the air. "Oh, and by the way, I want an electric guitar."

"Let's start with acoustic and go from there," my dad says. "Maybe for Christmas you can upgrade to an electric guitar. Speaking of," he goes on, in his extra-loud, extra-jovial voice that means he's got some sort of announcement, "I was thinking, this Christmas, we could go to Japan! What do you think? Go visit Obaachan?"

I choke on my rice. I can't believe my dad is just casually dropping this suggestion in over dinner.

My mother downs her glass of white wine. "Obaachan will visit us," she replies, without looking at him.

"I want them to know Japan," my dad says, almost pleading. "Just think about it. It's time . . . Isn't it?"

It will never be time.

My mom sighs, a long, raw sound that makes my own throat ache. She doesn't want to go to Japan either, not without Mika.

"We can talk about it later," she says, pouring herself another glass of wine. And even this is a concession too much for me. This isn't something that can even be considered.

"Reiko?" says my dad, reaching out and taking my hand. "What do you think?"

"Ken," my mom says, a warning in her voice.

I can't talk about this. I push my chair back and stand, my chopsticks clattering to the table. Koji's eyes are wide.

"I'm not feeling well," I say. "Please excuse me."

I hurry up the stairs, back into my room, and collapse into bed. I'm shaking.

There is a knock at my locked door. "Reiko?" says my mom from outside my room. "Are you all right?"

"I'm fine," I call back. "I just need to lie down for a minute. I'll come back in a little bit."

My mom hesitates. "Okay," she says. "I'll be downstairs if you need anything."

But my mom can't give me what I need. She can't bring Mika back, and she can't make me forget. She can't fix this.

She can't fix me.

Later Mika crawls into bed with me.

"I can't go to Japan," she says.

"I know," I say. "I know."

And that means I can't go either. How can I leave my sister behind?

"You're all doing stuff without me," she says. Her eyes are huge. "And what if he's better than me? Koji? What if he's better than me at music and everyone forgets me? He'll do concerts like I used to."

I stroke her hair. "Mika, that would never happen. Nobody would ever forget about you."

"Then why doesn't anybody talk about me?"

I take a breath. "Mom and Dad do. But I . . . I don't think I can talk *about* you, and still talk *to* you, like we are now, at the same time, you know?" I don't tell her my deep fear is that if I start talking out loud about her in the past tense, she'll disappear and I'll never see her ever again. This is better.

She nods, like she understands.

"I'm here now, here with you," I say.

"I don't want you to go away," she says, voice trembling. "Ever. Not to Japan, not anywhere. I want you to stay with me."

"But Mika . . . I—"

"Please," she says. "Please stay with me."

I can't say no to her. I can never say no to her.

So I stay. I stay and play chess with my sister, and I let her win. Like always.

CHAPTER 8

I'M ON MY WAY TO the kitchen the next morning when my dad calls out to me. "Reiko, can you come into my office for a second?"

My dad's office looks like an engineer's studio crossed with a library. It's got big tables covered in notes, whiteboards with equations scrawled all over them, huge monitors hooked up to computers that he's built himself, and wall-to-wall bookshelves.

Then there are the dioramas. My dad loves dioramas. He loves the real ones the most—the professional ones at the Museum of Natural History in New York—but he loves making small ones, too. He makes them the way some people make model planes. All along the bookshelves are dioramas he's made throughout the years, from different eras. He even has the first ones Mika and Koji and I made as kids. They are proudly displayed the way some people would display their kids' artwork. I guess to my dad, it *is* art.

He sits at his desk and motions for me to sit down next to him in his big leather armchair. He's nervous about something. I can tell because he keeps toying with his glasses. "I wanted to ask you something, but"—he looks down at his hands, folded in his lap—"I need it to just be between us. Okay? It might upset your mom."

Since my father's primary goal in life is to make my mom happy, I can't imagine him wanting to say or do anything that would upset her.

He's also a terrible secret-keeper.

"Okay," I say, suspicious but intrigued.

"I want you to apply to the University of Tokyo."

I'm stunned. I don't know what I thought he was going to say, but it wasn't this.

"But it's in *Japan*," I tell him, stating the obvious.

And I was supposed to go there with Mika.

He nods like he understands, but I know he doesn't. "I just don't want you to miss out on the opportunity. After all"—he points up at his diploma mounted on the wall—"I'm an alumni. You'll be a legacy applicant. But you could also . . . perhaps consider going to Temple University in Tokyo, too." He pushes a Temple University brochure toward me. I do not believe he's gotten *brochures* sent in. Without my mom noticing. This is the sneakiest he's ever been.

"But, Daddy . . . *they are both in Japan*," I repeat, in case he hadn't understood. "Across an *ocean*. And you know I want to go to UCLA. With Andrea."

"I know, I know, sweetie." He looks up at me, eyes wide behind his glasses. "Could you at least just apply, for me?" His eyes dart to a picture on his desk that I know is of me and Mika. "I think it might be good for you. Just to . . . consider it."

He reaches across his desk and takes my hand in his own. "I just want you to have all the best opportunities and options, Reiko. I don't think you should shut yourself off from anything. You used to love Japan." He looks so hopeful. "Remember your scrapbook?"

He's teetering very close to talking about Mika. My mom wouldn't have let this conversation get so far. No wonder he didn't want her to be a part of this discussion.

I close my eyes and take a deep breath. "Okay," I say. "I'll think about it."

"Wonderful!" My dad beams. "Thank you, Reiko."

"I just said I'll think about it."

"That's the first step!"

A step toward a future I'll never want. But I don't want to disappoint my dad.

CHAPTER 9

I'VE BEEN LYING IN BED, looking at the brochures and considering downloading application forms for the University of Tokyo and Temple, when headlights illuminate my driveway. I sit up, wondering for a wild moment if it's Seth. Maybe he's shown up at my house unexpectedly, just like I did at his.

It's not him. Of course it isn't. Why would it have been?

"Reiko! Andrea's here." My mom's muffled shout comes through my closed door. I hear Dre coming up the stairs and stuff the brochures under my pillow just as she bursts in. She flops down next to me on my bed. "Move over," she says, and I do.

Andrea bosses me around in a way that nobody else does. Not even my parents. The only person who used to boss me about like this was Mika.

Dre and I go way back. We have been best friends since we were four. She knows almost everything about me.

But the gap between *almost* and *everything* is a wide one.

Dre knew Mika, too, of course. She'd loved her like a sister. Dre's older sister, Tori, had even been Mika's best friend.

Sometimes I see Tori and I imagine Mika next to her. Not Mika how I see her now, forever fourteen in her yellow dress, but Mika at seventeen, eighteen, nineteen.

Dre knows what losing Mika did to me, even if we never talk about it. But sometimes I wish she didn't know so much, because when I get that suffocating feeling, Dre is wrapped up in it, too.

My whole friend group knows what happened, even if they didn't know me at the time, even if they never knew Mika. Having a dead sibling is the kind of thing that one friend whispers to another, not in a malicious way, but still. Then they know. And then when they look at me, they aren't just seeing me, they're seeing Mika, too.

Since she died, Seth is the first person I've met who is completely separate from Mika.

"Where have you been all weekend?" Dre asks. "You've been MIA! Last weekend, too! And don't you dare"—she waggles her finger at me—"try to tell me it is because you have so much home-work. I picked up your homework for you, remember, so I know exactly how much you have."

"Oh, I still haven't been feeling that great," I say.

Dre rolls her eyes so hard she looks like a cartoon character. "Mmm-hmm."

I'm trying not to smile, but I can't help it. Outraged Dre always makes me laugh. "Seriously!" I say.

She throws a pillow at me. "I know you are lying about some-thing, but I just don't know what."

"Honestly," I say. Now I'm full-on grinning like the Cheshire cat. "But! You know what I did do while I was out sick?"

"What?"

"I watched all eight Harry Potter movies."

"No way! Without me?"

"What do you mean, without you? I thought you were too cool for Harry Potter."

"Nobody is too cool for Harry Potter."

"Then how come we never talk about Harry Potter anymore?" I ask.

"Girl, I don't know! You know I love Harry Potter! We can talk about Harry Potter any time you want. The only reason we stopped talking about those books is . . ." Her voice trails off. It's the same reason I don't talk about music with my family. It's because it makes me think of Mika.

And I realize why I could talk about Harry Potter with Seth but not Dre. Because with Dre, it isn't just the books. It's the memories, and they are Mika-drenched.

"We used to go to the marathons down at the old movie theater," Dre goes on. "Remember?"

"Yeah," I say softly. We did. Mika and Tori would take us.

Dre is watching me closely. "I could look it up and see when the next marathon is going to be. It's been forever since we did that!"

I force a smile and nod. "Yeah, that could be fun." But it won't be. Not without Mika.

"We definitely need to do a big movie marathon at the theater at least one more time before we go to college," she says.

I turn over on my back, relieved the conversation has taken a different turn. "Why are you talking about graduation? We haven't even finished junior year."

"Yeah, but it is going to sneak up on us. Tori says time flies in your senior year. And that we gotta make the most of every moment."

I'm always trying to make the most of every moment.

"I don't believe this is our last real summer," I say.

"What do you mean? We'll have next summer, too. And you know what I heard?" Dre lowers her voice in a mock whisper. "Colleges have summer vacation, too!"

"You know what I mean! Like, the last high school summer. Next summer, we won't be coming back to Palm High in the fall. Who knows where we'll be going?"

"Um, I know? We'll be going to UCLA. Just like we've always planned."

But we haven't always planned that. I had a plan before that.

"My dad wants me to apply to schools in Japan," I blurt out.

Dre's eyes widen. "Oh, man," she says. Because she knows what that means to me. "How . . . how do you feel about that?" Her tone is measured and careful.

"I mean, it is ridiculous. Like you said, we're going to UCLA." Even though I'm the one who brought it up, I don't want to talk about it in detail.

"Exactly," she says. "But . . . maybe you should apply anyway? For him? I mean, who can say no to Ken? That smile? Those eyes? Those dimples?"

I groan. "Shut up, Dre." She's always teasing me about how handsome my dad is.

"No, but seriously, you should apply. I think it might be good for you."

"That's what he said."

"Well, he is a very smart man. And did I mention how good-looking he is?"

"ANDREA."

A low, loud laugh bursts out of her and bounces off the walls of my bedroom. It is so contagious that I start laughing, too.

"You've been cooped up at home for too long," she says, and I almost tell her that I was out on Friday night, at Seth Rogers's place, but then I realize how weird that would sound. "Let's get some ice cream," Dre goes on. "We can go to Freeze and pick up Libby on the way."

Dre pulls up to Libby's house and honks. Libby jogs out of the front door with her blond hair pulled up in a high ponytail. She clambers into the back seat.

I think Dre and I must have always been popular, even when we were little and people would pretend there was no such thing as popularity, but it didn't start to really matter to me until we got to high school. I'd seen Mika being popular in high school, and I knew I had to be like that, too. So when Dre and I got to huge Palm High after going to tiny Vista Mountain Middle School, we started hanging out with Libby and Megan and Zach and Peter and Michael, and we became a crew. Not just a crew. *The* crew. But Dre is still my only best friend.

I wonder if Libby sometimes still feels a bit third wheel to Dre and me. Probably she doesn't care. She's got Megan and the rest of our friends. Also Libby mostly just seems to care about Libby. She's pulled some shady stuff over the years, like when she made out with Dre's date at winter formal last year. Dre and Libby didn't speak for a few weeks after that, but it's hard to stay mad at Libby. Once you look past her flaws, she can be a lot of fun. And after all, nobody's perfect. I should know.

"I'm *so* hot and *so* bored. There is literally nothing to do here," Libby says.

"Not literally," I point out, thinking about the sunrise I saw this morning with Mika. And the tiny owl I saw on my way back from Seth's place on Friday. And the way the stars shine in the desert at night. But I don't tell Libby any of that. Because best-case scenario, she just wouldn't get it. Worst-case scenario, she'd laugh at me.

"I'm just *so* glad I'm going to Hawaii in a few weeks. Like, thank God. I'm going to get some island sun, maybe get an island *boooooy*," she trills in a singsong voice.

"We get plenty of sun here. And it'll just be other tourists at your hotel," I say.

"Maybe. Or maybe I'll meet a hot Hawaiian guy." She does what I think is her impression of a hula dance.

"With those moves, nobody will be able to resist you," says Dre dryly, but she's smiling.

"Hey! I'm a great dancer." Libby swats Dre's arm. Then she leans back into her seat and sighs. "Well, if I don't meet a hot Hawaiian surfer, at least I'll get tan. Maybe I'll even come back tanner than you two!"

Dre snorts. "Sure, babe. Good luck with that."

Dre's Mexican American, and I've got my dad's complexion, so we're always naturally more "tan" than Libby.

"Just you wait. I'm going to come back with a Hawaiian lover and a tan."

Dre shakes her head, her shoulder-length bob waving from side to side. "Whatever you say, Libbs."

"Where are we going anyway?" asks Libby.

"Freeze," says Dre, as she turns down South Palm Canyon Drive.

"Ohh! Free ice cream then." Libby bounces in her seat.

"Free ice cream?" Dre asks. "Are they having some kind of promotion?"

Libby tosses her ponytail over her shoulder and adjusts her cleavage. "If you call 'Libby always gets free ice cream at Freeze' a promotion."

"Since when?" says Dre.

"Since Jake Campbell started working there." Libby gives a sly smile.

"Jake Campbell, as in, 'the guy who got expelled last year for having weed on campus' Jake Campbell?" I ask.

"Jake Campbell, as in, 'the guy who Libby was totally hooking up with all last summer' Jake Campbell," says Dre with a smirk. "I should have known you were doing it for the ice-cream perks."

"How did I not know about this?" I say.

Libby, to her credit, doesn't even blush. "You don't know everything, babe. And you guys are just jealous I'm getting action *and* free ice cream. Reiko, when was the last time you even kissed someone?"

Dre fans herself in mock shock. "Holy Father, Mother, and Son, our baby Rei once kissed someone?"

"All right, all right," I grumble as we pull into a parking spot in front of Freeze. "It's been a while. I'm just picky. You guys know that."

"A while? Rei, you haven't hooked up with anyone since Ryan. And that was months ago," says Dre.

"Well, it isn't like there is anyone new. And unlike some people"—I raise my brows at both of them—"I don't like sharing what has been around the Palm High conveyer belt. But I bet I can get free ice cream from Jake Campbell, too. And *just* free ice cream, nothing else. Come on."

When I put on my best smile and stride into Freeze, my girls on either side of me, I'm fully expecting us to have to wipe Jake Campbell up off the floor. And to get complimentary ice cream, of course.

What I'm not expecting is to see Seth Rogers standing behind the ice-cream counter, staring at me like he's seen a ghost.

CHAPTER 10

IT TAKES ALL OF MY willpower not to spin on my heel and walk back out the door. I try to remember if he mentioned that he had a job at Freeze when I was at his place. Maybe he did and I forgot about it? Libby, oblivious, saunters up to the counter and leans against the glass case. "You're not Jake Campbell. But you look kind of familiar."

Seth's pale blue eyes dart to me. I know he is waiting for me to jump in and say, *This is Seth. Seth Rogers. I know him.*

I stay silent.

"What can I get you?" Seth says, finally.

"He speaks!" Libby gasps in false astonishment, twirling around. She's waiting for me to play my part because it always works better when we do this together.

Seth's eyes are still on mine, a silent plea there. Even though the sun has gone down and the air conditioner is blasting, I'm starting to sweat.

Acknowledge me, Seth is silently screaming.

I take a deep breath and step forward. Seth visibly relaxes.

"So what happened to Jake Campbell?" I ask, and Seth wilts like he's a marionette and his puppeteer has dropped the strings.

"Got fired," he replies, eyes down.

"God, you're boring, aren't you?" says Libby.

I flinch at her tone, but I know why she's being so harsh. She's unsure why he's not responding the way boys usually do and is thrown by it. And she's irritated that he hasn't really looked at her, not once, since we walked in.

Because he's been watching me.

"Libby," Dre chides.

"What? It's the truth," says Libby petulantly.

"We go to the same school," Seth says in a cold voice.

Libby laughs. "It's a big school, sweetie. No need to get all butt-hurt that we don't know your name."

As Seth's eyes find mine again, I try to remember if Libby is always like this when she wants something—if *I'm* usually like this.

"I'll have salted caramel," I say, keeping my voice steady.

"Your favorite," Seth says, and I wince.

Dre and Libby exchange a look, and Libby starts to snicker. It hurts more when Dre joins in.

"Lucky guess," I say to Seth.

But that isn't what I want to say. What I want to say is: *Guys, I actually went to Seth's house on Friday. And I kind of want to hang out with him again.* And then smile at everyone. I know I could do this, I could make it better.

But the words are trapped inside of me, and I don't know how to let them out. I try, I really do, but it feels like trying to turn on a faucet that has been rusted shut.

Because I know what my friends, what everyone thinks about him. And I know what they'll think of *me* if they know I've been hanging out with him.

"Well, my favorite flavor is chocolate-chip cookie dough," says Dre in her normal voice, not her flirty, trying-to-get-free-ice-cream voice. She has suddenly caught on that I'm uncomfortable, really uncomfortable, so she's stopped snickering and teasing and stepped in to smooth things over.

Seth scoops my salted caramel, then scoops Dre's cookie dough, and hands us our cones.

"For you?" he asks Libby, who is still trying to figure out what the hell has happened to our usual routine.

"Strawberry," she says.

"That'll be six dollars," Seth says as he passes the strawberry ice-cream cone to Libby.

"Oh, Sam—"

"Seth."

"Do you think you could give us, like . . . the student discount? Since we go to the same school and everything." Libby is still giving this her best shot.

Seth's face is stony. "Six dollars, please," he says.

"I mean, nobody will ever know. It isn't like they do a weigh-in with the ice cream each night. I know because Jake used to give me free ice cream all the time."

"Maybe that's why he got fired," Seth says, deadpan.

Dre snorts. And I start to think that maybe, just maybe, she'll get why I like spending time with him.

Libby sighs. "Fine," she says, clearly bored. Then she turns to me and Dre. "I left my wallet in the car, so one of you bitches can buy me ice cream."

"I've got it," I say. "I'll meet you guys in the car."

Dre and Libby exchange another look, and for a second it looks like Libby is going to say something, but a short headshake from Dre stops her, and they both go outside.

"Well, that was . . . enlightening," says Seth. His gaze is cutting.

"Just run the card, Seth." My voice is tense.

"You are unbelievable," he says, but he runs the card.

"Look, I didn't know you'd be here—"

He gives me a sardonic smile that stops my words. "Of course you didn't. Because if you'd known, you wouldn't have come. Wouldn't want to inflict me on your friends."

"It's not like that," I protest, but he raises his eyebrows.

"Whatever you say, Reiko." Then he gestures out of the window. "Don't keep your friends waiting."

"Seth—" I try again, but he turns away and goes into the storage room behind the counter, leaving me alone with the ice cream.

"Well, that was weird," Libby says as I climb into the back seat. "Reiko, why was he . . . watching you like that?"

"He wasn't," I say.

"He totally was. And how did he know your favorite ice cream?" She shivers. "What a creep."

"That's not a very nice thing to say," I say, feeling my cheeks start to flame.

"Since when are you Miss Congeniality?" Libby says with a snort. "Why are you defending *Seth Rogers*? He looks like one of those guys who is going to end up with a girl locked in his basement or something."

"Libby!" snaps Dre, turning to swat Libby on the leg.

"What?" says Libby, eyes wide with faux innocence.

"Oh, for God's sake, Libby," says Dre, scowling.

"I'm bored of talking about Seth Rogers." I keep my voice steady, like I really don't give a damn. "Dre, can you turn on the radio?"

Dre does what I ask, but I can tell she's watching me. I feel bad. I'm her best friend, and best friends are supposed to tell each other everything.

But I don't know how to explain me and Seth.

CHAPTER 11

I CAN'T STOP THINKING ABOUT what happened at the ice-cream store with Seth. And I don't want to feel guilty about it, but I do, and then my guilt gets bigger, until it isn't about Seth anymore, until it has morphed into something else entirely, and it is so big it is going to devour me. That night in bed, thoughts that I keep locked up in a corner of my brain come to life. They slide out of my head and surround me, pressing on me, pulling on me until I can't sleep. My sheets are soaked in sweat, and my long hair is tangled around my throat like seaweed. I untangle it and push it back off my face and neck.

Then I lie back down, trying to ignore that I'm trembling, and close my eyes. I should sleep. I should sleep. I should sleep.

But whenever I close my eyes, I see Mika. Not as she is now, in her yellow dress, but as she was the last time I saw her alive.

She was wearing a bikini. It was yellow. My mom sang when she saw her in it. *"Itsy bitsy teenie weenie . . ."*

"Mom, it doesn't have polka dots!" Mika protested, but she was smiling.

"Yeah, but it's itsy bitsy! And yellow!" My mom stood back and admired my sister. "You look beautiful."

"What about me?" I demanded, twirling in front of her.

She laughed. "You look beautiful, too. My beautiful girls."

. . . slamming into the ocean, tumbling around like a sock in a machine. Sand under my fingers. Another wave smashing my face. Water rushing down my throat . . . Mika. Mika!

My heart hammers hard in my chest and my lungs start to burn. I bolt upright, gasping for air.

I have to get out of my room.

I have to get out of my house.

I have to get outside.

My car is quiet; my car is free of ghosts. I sit for a minute in the front seat, under the gaze of the moon, head on my steering wheel. For a minute, I think about calling Dre, but I don't want to be the Reiko she knows.

I want to be someone else.

After a few minutes, I do text someone. But not Dre.

Can I come pick you up? I'll be outside your place in 20 min.

Seth is already waiting outside his trailer when I pull up. He didn't reply to my message, but I drove here anyway, just in case. I had a feeling he'd come outside, even after what happened at Freeze. Maybe even because of what happened.

He gets in the car without saying a word, and we drive in silence for a minute.

I break first. "Look, I'm sorry. I just wasn't expecting to see you."

He stares out of the window. "That was pretty crappy." Then he turns toward me, eyes sharp and bright like the stars above us. "Is it that unimaginable to you that we could be friends? Am I that unimaginable?"

I lock eyes with him. "Forgive me?"

He sighs, and it sounds like he's letting his frustration and irritation with me out, too. "Yeah," he says, then he shakes his head, but it is more at himself than at me. "Of course I do."

I drive into the deep desert dark a while longer. Neither of us says anything, and then I pull over. "Hey. Want to go on a walk?"

"Yeah," he says, eyes on mine. "I think I do."

We walk in the desert, side by side, mostly in silence, using our phones to light the way when the moonlight isn't enough. We find a coyote skull, picked clean by birds and bleached by the sun. It's smaller and more fragile than you'd think, and so bright it practically glows under the stars. I feel like we've found something magical. And then we get back in the car and drive and drive and talk.

After a while, I ask Seth what he wants to do after college.

"If I could do anything?" he asks. "Design board games. Or video games. Some kind of game design. How do I even get into that, though?"

"The same way you get into anything. Look at a company website. Email them. Call them. Get an internship."

Seth makes a derisive sound in the back of his throat. It takes me a second to realize he is laughing.

"What?"

He shrugs. "I don't even know if I'll go to college."

"What are you talking about? You are one of the smartest guys in our grade. And you would have the highest score in AP physics if I wasn't beating you." I grin and toss my hair over my shoulder. "Anyway, I bet you can qualify for some financial aid or something. You absolutely have to apply for the UC schools. It's just one application for all of them: UC Santa Barbara, UC Irvine, UC Riverside." I pause. "Maybe you'll even get into UCLA."

He rolls his eyes. "Okay, Reiko. Whatever you say."

"I'm just trying to be helpful."

"It's not like that for everyone, Reiko. Not everyone can make their dreams come true with a snap of their fingers."

"What is that supposed to mean?"

"You know you're pretty privileged, right? You can get whatever you want."

"I work my ass off," I say, frowning. But I think about where he lives and where I live, and I wonder if he has a point.

"And I don't?"

"Seth, all I'm saying is you have to prepare yourself for success."

He shakes his head. "You have no idea." But he smiles at me. "Maybe if I hang out with you enough, some of that luck will rub off on me."

"I'm not a four-leaf clover," I tell him, but I'm smiling, too.

On the drive back to his place, when the sun is just starting to turn the sky pink, Seth suddenly says, "Hey, pull over! I think there's something here." I slam on the brakes, and at first when we get out of the car, I think we're surrounded by these huge rocks. But then one starts *moving*, and I realize they are giant desert tortoises. There are at least eight or nine of them, and they are stretching out their old wrinkled necks and turning their faces to greet the sun. We sit down in the middle of their gathering, staying as still as we can. It's like watching the sunrise with dinosaurs.

Later, Seth tells me that desert tortoises are solitary, so there was no reason for them to be in a big group like that, and I say there doesn't always need to be a reason. Sometimes things just happen, even if they don't make sense.

Just like there is no reason for me and Seth Rogers to start spending all our time together.

It just happens.

SUMMER

CHAPTER 12

THERE IS NOWHERE TO HIDE in the desert.

Our shadows are long and lean and bigger than us. They stretch out across the sand, mimicking our movements before taking on lives of their own.

We aren't touching, but our shadows are.

I watch Seth's shadow reach for mine.

"It's hot," I say, turning away from his shadow. Turning away from him.

"You were the one who wanted to come here," Seth points out, scooting imperceptibly closer to me. He's been doing this more and more recently. Ever since we saw the sunrise with the tortoises, we've been hanging out on the weekends. Sometimes studying, but mostly roaming the desert. It's a Saturday, and we've come out in the heat of the day to shadow dance in the sun.

I see all his furtive glances, how his eyes slide down my body when he thinks I'm not looking. I notice how his fingertips linger when he has an excuse to touch me.

I wonder if it's the heat. I wonder if it's getting to him. Or to me.

Sun-touched, they call it. Air over 100 degrees can make any-one do crazy things. You breathe it in, all that heat. Can't escape it.

And this summer is even hotter than last. Out here, every degree makes a difference. Makes you feel like you are cooking to a crisp. My thin, silky shift dress is sticking to me, and it feels as snug as a second skin, like I'm a snake waiting to shed.

I want to peel it off.

I imagine what Seth's reaction would be.

Suddenly, I want to get out of the sun. Get out of the heat.

"Come on," I say, standing up and stepping away from him. "Let's go to my house and cool off in my pool."

"All right," he says after a slight pause, as if he had even considered saying no.

I smile, and when he grins back at me, I smile even bigger in return, and then there is this rapid back-and-forth between us with no words, only grins, like some kind of smile Ping-Pong, until it isn't just my mouth smiling, or even my face, but my whole body.

I smile more with Seth than I do with anyone else I know.

CHAPTER 13

WHEN WE GET TO MY house, I see Seth taking it all in. Despite hanging out so much, this is the first time he's been here, and he is so taken aback by it all that he barely says a word, just stares and stares till I think his eyes might pop out. It makes me see my house, my life, through new eyes. Through his eyes.

My house both blends in with the desert and stands out. It's two stories, long and low enough to snuggle up against the mountains.

We have a front lawn and one in the backyard. It's expensive to keep the grass green, but my mother insists and my father shrugs and says he doesn't mind paying. Because he likes to make her happy. Because if she is happy, so is he, and then that happiness will trickle down and fill our home and we will all be happy. Or something. Happiness is something that used to come easily to my family, but now it is something we work hard at. And while I'm sure my parents know that money can't buy happiness, they're trying their best.

We have a pool, too, but almost everyone I know has a pool. Except for Seth—and that's because he lives out in a trailer with nothing but rocks for company, where even the sand is scarce.

By the time we get inside, he is managing to keep his eyes in his head and has finally started to relax. A little bit.

"Whoa," he says, slightly under his breath.

"What?" I nudge him with my shoulder.

He lets out a low, appreciative whistle. "It's just . . . really nice."

"It's all right," I say with a shrug. It's all I've ever known. But I remember when I first saw his trailer, how it felt unreal. And suddenly I get that this is the inverse moment of that—that my house, my life, everything about me, might not feel real to him.

"Reiko, it's more than all right. I've never even seen a house this nice." He gives me a sheepish grin. "Sorry, I sound like some sort of hick from the sticks." And something about his sheepish smile makes me smile, too, like a reflex, like the corners of our mouths are connected by two invisible strings.

Thinking about having a mouth connected to Seth's makes me flinch. It's not that I've never thought about it. Because I have. In a casual, curious way. The same way I think about kissing lots of people I know I would never kiss. Like Tony at the deli or my art history teacher, Mr. Flynn—just a curious thought, a wonder about what their lips are like, nothing I'd ever act upon.

But for some reason, my mind keeps returning to Seth's mouth. His too-wide mouth with thin, chapped lips. It shouldn't be appealing, and yet . . . I can't stop thinking about it.

"You all right?" Seth asks. "You're looking at me funny."

"Sand on your cheek," I lie as I reach out and brush the imaginary particles away, the tips of my fingers feather-light on his skin.

Seth freezes under my touch—he stops breathing, and I wonder if even his heart has stopped beating.

"Got it," I say, relieved because I felt nothing more than I would feel if I touched Dre or my brother. That's good, that's normal. As much as we've been hanging out, I shouldn't be thinking about kissing Seth Rogers.

"Come on," I turn and call over my shoulder. "I'll show you the rest of the house." We head into the kitchen, which opens up to the living room. Koji is sprawled on the couch in front of the television, playing a video game.

"Where are Mom and Dad?" I ask.

"Out," he says without looking up. Koji used to be so cute. When he was tiny, Mika and I loved playing with him. He'd even let us dress him up. But since she died, it seems like the gap between us has grown. I spend more time with Mika as she is now than I do with Koji. He's always playing video games or practicing his new guitar, anyway.

"I gathered they're not here. But where are they?"

He doesn't respond, so I go and stand in front of the screen, meaning he can't see what he is blowing up or shooting at or whatever it is he is doing with the controller.

"Hey!" he says.

"Mom and Dad?"

"Hendersens', I think. Barbecue? Dinner party? Luncheon?

Something. I don't know. I wasn't listening. Text Mom. And move, please."

I flop next to him on the couch and wave Seth over. He's standing in the kitchen, behind a marble island, still looking a bit stunned by it all. "Koji, this is . . ." I pause. Not sure what to call Seth. I guess we're friends? But "friends" simultaneously seems both too intimate and too distant to describe us. So I just say, "This is Seth. Seth, this is my brother, Koji. Koj, can Seth borrow a pair of your swim trunks?" It is a slight dig at Seth, that he's my little brother's size.

"Sure," Koji says, still staring at the screen in front of him. "They're in the bottom drawer in the dresser next to my bed."

"Do you want to come swimming with us?" Seth asks, coming to sit on the arm of the couch.

"Um, you know my sister doesn't actually swim, right?" says Koji.

I flinch, wondering what he's going to say next. I haven't been swimming since Mika died. I can be in the pool on a raft, but I can't bear to be submerged in water. I don't want Seth to know this. I don't want him to ask why I don't swim.

"She just lounges," Koji goes on, and I relax. He glances away from the screen for a second to scrutinize Seth. "Who are you again?"

"I'm Seth."

"And you know Reiko how?" Koji sounds strangely protective of me, and I find it a little bit adorable. He looks back and forth between us, his video game forgotten for the moment, trying to piece it together.

If even my brother can't figure out how Seth and I fit, can't see why we hang out, there is no way my friends are going to. I want to run out of the house, pulling Seth with me. We can only exist in the desert.

"From around," Seth says.

Koji shrugs and picks up his controller again. "Cool," he says.

I let out a breath. I'm starting to realize that Seth and I only make sense when it is just the two of us.

"All right, man, good luck getting to that next level," Seth tells Koji. Then he shakes his head. "But there's always another level, isn't there?" He's not looking at my brother now, or even the television screen. He's looking at me. It makes me feel weird. I don't understand what he's getting at, but then he smiles, and he's Seth again, and it's all right.

He follows me up the stairs.

"My brother's room is at the end of the hall," I say. "Just grab any pair of swim trunks from the bottom drawer in his dresser."

"Got it," he says. But then he moves toward a door that isn't to Koji's room; it's the door to Mika's room.

I lunge at him and swat his hand away from the doorknob. "No!"

Seth jerks back.

"That's not . . . not Koji's room," I explain. "His is there, at the end of the hall." I point in the correct direction.

"What is it?" Seth's hand is straying toward the door again like he might open it. And I notice his eyes flicker to the framed picture on the wall of Mika, Koji, and me.

I step in front of it. "It's nothing," I say. "Storage. Go get changed."

I stand in the hall until he goes into my brother's room. And even then I wait a moment, just to make sure he's not going to come back out and open this door.

Open Mika's door.

I wonder if he knows. If he's figured it out from looking at the photo. Or maybe someone at school has already told him.

I don't want that. I don't want him asking questions about Mika. So even though I'm perfectly capable of tying my own bikini top, I wait for Seth in the hall with only the straps around my neck tied, holding the bikini to my chest, my back bare, the straps dangling at my sides. The bikini is new and maraschino-cherry red. I know it looks good on me.

Seth's eyes go wide when he sees me. I'm glad. I want him to think about me, just me, and nothing else.

"Help me tie this?" I say, turning around.

I can feel his fingers trembling as he fumbles with the straps.

"Double or single knot?" he asks, his voice barely a whisper.

"Single is fine," I say. And then, voice pitched feather-soft, "Just don't tug on it or it'll come off."

He makes some sort of noise that might be a laugh or a groan.

"Come on," I say, slipping away from him and back down the stairs.

And with that, Mika's closed door is banished from both of our minds.

I sit on the steps of the swimming pool, only my legs submerged in the water, like a mermaid sunning herself. I flinch at the thought of mermaids. It was a game Mika and I always played in the ocean together when we were little: diving under, like our dad taught us, and popping up again. I shake the memory away, then tilt my head back and close my eyes. I can feel Seth watching me. I keep my eyes closed so he can keep watching.

The seconds move slow, lazy in the sun. When I open my eyes, Seth is on the other side of the pool, floating on his back.

Maybe he wasn't watching me after all.

Maybe it is all in my imagination.

CHAPTER 14

AFTER IT GETS TOO HOT to even be in the pool, we towel off and go back inside to study for finals.

Whenever we hang out, I can tell Seth's a little more comfortable with me, like he's peeling off another layer of himself. There is something strangely intoxicating about feeling like I am really discovering someone. A someone that nobody else knows. A someone that is just mine.

Seth gets his books and note cards out of his backpack. "Doesn't your brother have to study for finals, too?" Seth asks as Koji plays the same chord over and over again on his guitar. He's switched from video games to guitar practice. Which is equally as loud and annoying.

"Koji! Go practice in your room!" I shout.

Seth and I look back down at our note cards.

"A mirage is due to: *a*, unequal heating of different parts of the atmosphere," Seth asks, "*b*, magnetic disturbances in the atmosphere; or, *c*, depletion of the ozone layer in the atmosphere."

I think for a minute. "*A*," I say. "I'm sure of it."

"Correct," says Seth with a smile. "Have you ever seen a mirage?"

"Of course. Haven't you?"

"How would you know if it was a real mirage or just your eyes playing tricks on you?"

"Because I know what a mirage looks like," I say.

"You ever wonder if what you see—like, what you think is a mirage—looks totally different to someone else?"

"Next time I see a mirage, I'll point it out to you and we can compare notes."

Seth grins. "What makes you think I'll be with you the next time you see a mirage?"

I roll my eyes. "It's the desert. We won't have to wait too long."

Seth's feet keep knocking against mine. I tuck mine under my chair. He probably thinks he's kicking the table leg. I don't want to embarrass him. I don't know why I care—it's just Seth Rogers.

"I'm going to get some water," he says, standing up. "Do you want anything?"

"No, thanks," I say, copying out another question from our textbook onto a flash card.

He pauses by the giant ceramic sculpture of the eagle in our kitchen. He's been looking at it since we came in. Not that I blame him; it's hard *not* to look at it. The thing has a wingspan of five feet and looks like it is about to fly out of the window. It sits on its own special podium, watching everything.

"This is cool," he says, running his fingertips across the eagle's wings. "Like, how cool would it be to be a bird? That's why I climb, you know? Closest I can get to flying."

I'm surprised by how wistful he sounds. "Mmm. I guess. Used to scare me to death when I was little. When my parents would leave us with a babysitter, I'd make the sitter cover its face with a dish towel because it scared me so much. Mom loves it because it belonged to her mom, my grandma Gloria. I never met her, but people say we're alike. It was a wedding present from this artist Ruth Setmire who lives way out in the desert. She's pretty famous now. She even knew Georgia O'Keeffe." I can tell Seth doesn't know who that is.

"It is so majestic. So lifelike."

"Have you ever seen an eagle up close?"

"No."

"Then how do you know it's lifelike?"

"I've seen pictures. And *Animal Planet*," he says with a hint of wounded pride. "I even know what they sound like." He starts flapping his arms like he's flying and makes some sort of cawing sound.

I snort. "You sound like a crow."

"I'm a majestic eagle!" he shouts, still flapping his arms and cawing. He looks ridiculous, and I feel a laugh, a real laugh, bubbling up.

He sees me laughing, and it sparks something in him. He starts to leap around even more, cawing and flapping like crazy. And then he loses his balance and he spins toward my mother's prized Ruth Setmire eagle. I get up to try to stop him, but I'm too slow, and he smashes into the eagle and it topples. For an instant it looks like it is going to take off in flight, but then it crashes to the ground and—oh oh oh . . .

The eagle is broken. Its head has shattered and the wings have cracked.

I think of all the times Mika and Koji and I ran by the eagle. All the times we ducked behind it and around it and were scolded by our parents. How it seemed unbreakable.

But apparently it isn't.

Seth is standing frozen, like he's turned into a statue himself, his mouth open and eyes wide.

Koji comes running in. Of course *this* would be the thing to tear him away from his guitar.

"You killed the eagle!" he says, sounding years younger than he is.

"We didn't kill it," I say, not meaning to implicate myself by saying *we*. "It isn't actually alive. It's just broken." I don't know how this is better, but I feel like I need to make the distinction clear.

"Mom is going to freak out," Koji says in a matter-of-fact tone. "That was Grandma Gloria's eagle."

"I'm so sorry," Seth says, running his hand through his hair. "I'm such an idiot." He doesn't offer to pay for it. Not that it matters. He couldn't anyway.

"Koji, help Seth clean it up," I say. "I'll be right back."

I need a moment to myself, a moment to calm down. I go up the stairs and into my room and collapse on my bed. After a moment, my bedroom door squeaks open, and Mika comes and sits on the edge of my bed.

"Did you break Mom's eagle?" Her eyes are wide. "The one that belonged to Grandma Gloria? What are you going to do?"

"I don't know. Mom is going to kill me."

"Oh, she won't kill you," says Mika, "but she'll be upset."

That's worse.

"Shit, shit, shit," I mutter.

Mika tilts her head to the side. "Aren't there two?"

"Two what?"

"Two eagles. Isn't that why this one was so special? Because it was one of a pair?"

I snort. "You think I should get the other one from Ruth Setmire? How? She never leaves her house."

"But you know where she lives. We visited once, remember?"

We did. It was years ago. That wasn't the last time I saw Ruth, though. The last time, the last time was . . . I don't like to think about it. It was at Mika's funeral.

"Mom will have Ruth's address in her book," Mika says.

I grin at Mika. "You little genius! What would I do without you?"

She grins back. She knows I need her.

I reach out and squeeze her hand, once, twice, and then three times fast. Our handshake.

"Nerd," says Mika, but she squeezes back.

"Look what I found," I say, standing at the top of the stairs and holding out Ruth's address like a trophy. There's no phone number, but hopefully what I have will be enough. If Seth is surprised that I have the personal address for a famous reclusive artist, he doesn't show it. He *is* surprised that we are just going to go to her house without calling or anything to see if she's there.

"Isn't Ruth pretty old?" he says.

"So what?"

"Well . . . what if she's . . . you know . . . ?"

"What if she's what?" I retort, even though I know what he's going to say next.

"Dead?"

"Yeah!" Koji chimes in, looking up from his guitar. "What if she's dead and her body is festering and rotting and you guys are the ones who find it and then, when you go into her house, you discover she's been turned into a zombie and then she turns you guys into zombies and then . . ."

"She's not going to be a zombie, Koj!" I say.

"But what if she . . . really is dead?" says Seth.

"We won't have any trouble getting the eagle then, will we?" I say.

Seth's eyes bulge. "I'm not breaking into a dead woman's house."

"One, we're not breaking in anywhere. And two, what are you so afraid of?"

"I'm not afraid . . ." Seth says.

"Sounds like you are. Sounds like you are afraid to go on an adventure. Sounds like you are afraid of a little old woman—"

"A little old ZOMBIE woman," Koji interrupts.

"I don't know why I'm even trying to argue," Seth says. "You always win."

"Of course she does," Koji snarks. "Have you met my sister?"

I tousle his hair. "Says you."

He swoops his head away. "Watch it! You're messing up my hair."

I look back up at Seth, who is still staring at me. I wonder if he's even blinked.

"So are you coming or not?" I ask, hands on hips.

He smiles, really smiles. "Of course I am." And something small fizzes between us, like a firefly buzzing from his hands to mine.

I text Mom and casually ask when she'll be home with Dad. She says late, close to midnight, which is exactly what I was hoping for. My plan is to get to Newberry Springs and be home with the replacement eagle before they even know it was missing.

"Koj, if Mom calls, tell her I've gone to Andrea's," I say. "We'll be back in a few hours. There's some pizza in the fridge from last night, okay? Don't forget to eat."

"I won't," he says.

"You will. You always forget to eat when you are playing guitar these days. Forget to do anything." Mika had been the same when she'd practice piano, but I doubt he remembers that.

"I'll eat, I'll eat," Koji says, eyes glued to a YouTube video of someone explaining how to do something that sounds complicated with guitar chords. "Good luck getting the eagle. If anyone can convince a cranky artist who has probably turned into a zombie to part with one of her most prized possessions, it'll be you."

"Thanks for the vote of confidence," I say.

"That *is* me being confident! Jeeeeeez," says Koji. "I'm confident you'll either come back with the eagle or you won't come back at all, because, you know, you'll be zombified."

"Koji! Don't be morbid."

"Worse things than being a zombie."

"Okay, that's it, I'm going. We're going," I say, tugging Seth's arm toward the door.

"BYE-BYE, ZOMBIE SISTER!" Koji calls out after us.

CHAPTER 15

SETH SETTLES INTO THE FRONT seat as I start my car. "So your brother is really into zombies, huh?"

I shrug. "Apparently. Last week, it was some other video game thing—assassins, maybe? This week, it's zombies. And guitars, of course. I don't know. I can't keep up."

"What about ghosts?" he says.

I tense. "What about ghosts?"

"I really like Japanese horror films. You know, like *The Ring*?"

"My brother isn't into ghosts. Or into Japanese horror films." I don't tell him that we have enough ghosts in our house without inviting fictional ones in. Instead, I toss my phone at him. "Here, I've put the address in. You navigate." Then the only sound is from my tires rumbling on the road and the hum of the car engine.

Neither of us speaks until we turn onto old Route 66. Then Seth clears his throat. "I've always wanted to drive down here," he says.

"Well, here you go," I say, turning up the air conditioner. I'm being terse, but I'm still angry with him for breaking the eagle— even though it was an accident.

"I've never really been . . . anywhere."

I glance at him. "What do you mean?"

"I don't have a car, and my mom needs hers to get to the casino for her shifts, and we don't ever take vacations or anything like that."

"So you've never been . . ."

"Out of the desert. This desert," he says, gesturing out of the window at the sand all around us. "I've never even been up the tram." The tram, officially known as the Palm Springs Aerial Tramway, takes people up from the desert into the mountains.

"If you wanted me to drive you somewhere, you could have just asked. You didn't need to break my mom's priceless eagle that belonged to my dead grandma."

"I can't tell if you are kidding or not," Seth says in a flat voice. "I'm sorry. I said I was sorry."

"I'm sort of kidding, but I'm not." I don't know why I'm being so honest with him. I'm rarely this honest with anyone.

"What if . . ." Seth's voice trails off and out the window, eaten by the desert wind.

"What if what? It drives me nuts when people do that."

"When they do what?"

"When they start a sentence and don't finish. What if what?"

"What if . . . someone else had broken it?"

"What do you mean?"

"One of your other friends. Like Libby Carter or Andrea Torres. Would you be mad at them?"

I would be, but I wouldn't show it. Not the way that I'm showing it with him.

"That's different," I say.

"Why?"

"Because they are my best friends! And you aren't." A half-truth. Dre is my best friend. Libby is Libby.

"Shouldn't it be easier for you to be mad at your best friends than someone you barely know? You know, the way people always say how the people you are closest to see your worst self?"

He's right. For some reason, I'm more comfortable admitting that I'm mad at Seth. Maybe because we don't have a history the way I do with my best girlfriends. Maybe it's because I've got nothing to lose.

We're the only car on the road, so I hit the gas. Might as well try to get to Ruth's as early as we can. Outside the windows, the desert flies by.

"If this is your way of apologizing," I say, "you're doing a pretty crappy job."

"Of course I'm sorry, I'm mortified. I thought . . ."

"Will you stop doing that? Finish your sentences."

"I thought that we were becoming friends," he mumbles.

"What are we? Ten? Who announces when they become friends?"

"You're different than I thought you would be," he says.

"How did you think I would be?"

"Just . . . different. Not as sharp, but not as sweet either."

"You sound like you're describing a cocktail, not a person."

"You didn't seem like someone I ever thought I'd be friends with."

I frown. "Well, that's insulting."

He laughs, really laughs, and it's both jarring and joyful. He sounds a little bit like a seagull, and I remember how he laughed the first night we met, with his whole mouth open, like the laugh was forcing his jaws apart to get out.

"What's so funny?" I ask, even though I'm starting to smile, because his laugh is so ridiculous and so infectious.

"Do *I* seem like someone *you'd* be friends with?"

"I never thought about it," I admit.

"Of course you didn't! Reiko, the possibility of us being friends was so far removed from your reality you never even thought about it."

"Well, we're friends now," I grumble.

He grins, showing all of his teeth. "I thought only ten-year-olds announced their friendships."

Now that Seth and I have acknowledged that we're friends, or something, the tension over him breaking the eagle evaporates. I'm still anxious about it, though, and worried that my mom is going to flip out.

It takes over two hours to drive to Newberry Springs. We go past casinos, a date farm, a buffalo ranch, and two ghost towns. Somewhere near Oro Grande, there is this huge outdoor art exhibition or junkyard, hard to tell which, called Elmer's Bottle Tree Ranch. It's like nothing I've ever seen before: hundreds of metal pipes with bottles of all shapes and colors hanging from them, like a bottle-tree forest. We slow down as we pass and watch the light dance off the glass. Interspersed among the bottle trees are wind chimes made of animal bones.

"Can you roll down the windows?" Seth is whispering, like we've come upon something holy, instead of a yard full of junk. I do as he asks. The tinkling sound of bottles clanking against one another and the old bones blowing in the wind come together in an eerie harmony.

I want to get out of the car to take a closer look. It's like something out of a twisted fairy tale. But I know we have to get to Ruth's house before it's too late. "We should come back one day," I say in a hushed voice, because I don't want to disturb the magic of whatever it is we're witnessing.

Seth glances at me. "Yeah," he says. "We should. So what else do you know about this Ruth Setmire lady?"

"Well, she was apparently best friends with my grandma Gloria," I say. "They grew up together or something. Ruth first got famous for making giant ceramic flowers the size of chairs. For a while, that was her thing. And then she made two thousand tiny elephants, each one with a different facial expression, and someone bought the whole collection for something ridiculous, like a few million dollars. I don't know what the hell they did with two thousand tiny elephants." I laugh a little to myself.

"What?" says Seth.

"I should probably just be glad my mom didn't buy them. That's the kind of thing she'd love. Two thousand tiny elephants all over our backyard."

"Maybe our moms have more in common than we think," Seth says with a wry grin.

I grin back. "Anyway, soon everyone wanted these tiny elephants. So Ruth became the tiny elephant lady. She stopped making them around ten years ago, stopped making anything, but you can still find her pieces in art galleries and in private collections. We even studied her in art history this year. Of course, nobody believed that I had a Ruth Setmire original in our house, because nobody has ever heard of her eagles, because she only made the two. That's why we've got to get this eagle. It's pretty irreplaceable, even without the emotional connection that my mom has to it."

"Do you have anything like that?" Seth asks.

"Like what?"

"Anything that matters that much to you?"

I think of the scrapbook. But I can't tell Seth about that.

"Nope," I say, keeping my voice steady.

"Yeah, me either," says Seth.

CHAPTER 16

THE SUN IS JUST SETTING, turning the sky a dusty pink, when we pull up to the gate of Ruth's property.

We ring the buzzer. And then again. And again.

Nothing.

"Maybe your brother was right," says Seth. "Maybe she died in there."

"We could scale that easily," I say, eyeing the wall around her property.

"Oh no. Hell no. We are not actually breaking in."

I'm considering taking a running leap at the wall to see how high I could get when the buzzer crackles to life. A female voice says, "I can see you. And I can see what you are planning. Get out of here before I call the cops."

I press the intercom on the buzzer as fast as I can. "Ruth Setmire?"

"I didn't ask you who I was. I know who I am. Not as senile as people seem to think I am. Now I said go away!"

"I thought you said she knew you," Seth says low in my ear.

"She knew my grandmother," I say. And then, louder into the

intercom, my words spilling out, "I'm Reiko Smith-Mori, Suzie Smith's daughter. Gloria Smith's granddaughter."

We wait for a moment. And then the gate swings open.

The house is ranch style, all one story, with a slate-gray roof and pale yellow walls. Seth is standing behind me on the front step, breathing heavily. It's making me anxious.

"You sound like you're having an asthma attack or something," I hiss. "Calm down."

"What do we do now?" he says. "This was a mistake, a big mistake."

I turn and glare at him. "You breaking the eagle was a mistake. What we're doing now is fixing that mistake." I turn back to the front door just in time to see it inching open.

An old woman wearing a cowboy hat is peering out at us. She has long white hair, almost to her waist, and her face is leathery and wrinkled. She's frowning.

I give her my most charming smile. "Thank you for letting us in."

She keeps frowning. "I haven't decided if I'm going to let you in. I wanted to get a look at you." She stares at me with bright blue eyes. They aren't that watery blue that some old people have—they are sharp, like pieces of broken blue glass. "You don't look a thing like Gloria."

"I look more like my dad's side of the family," I say.

The door has inched open the tiniest bit. "That boy isn't Gloria's grandson, is he?"

"No, ma'am. This is . . . this is my friend."

"Now I know who you are, or who you say you are, but I don't know why you are standing at my front door."

"I'd like to buy a piece of art from you—" I start, but Ruth interrupts me, waving her veiny hand out toward the desert. "Plenty of galleries in Palm Springs and Palm Desert have my pieces. I don't sell directly to buyers these days. Haven't for years."

"I'm looking for a very particular piece," I say. "One that won't be in any of the galleries."

Ruth purses her lips. "What piece?"

"You gave my grandma an eagle on her wedding day, and there is only one other one like it."

"You want my eagle?"

Seth clears his throat and steps up next to me. "It's my fault, ma'am. I . . . I broke the one you gave Reiko's grandma."

Ruth inhales like she's just stepped on a sharp pin. "You broke my eagle?"

Seth looks down. "I'm sorry," he says. "It was an accident."

"Well, I'd hope so! What kind of person would purposefully destroy art?"

We're getting off topic, and Ruth is getting agitated.

"The eagle means a lot to my mom," I say. "It's one of the only things she has of Grandma Gloria's."

I don't say that I know how meaningful it is to have something that belongs to someone you love. Someone who's gone.

Ruth shuts the turquoise door without a word, and I slump as I feel the weight of having to tell my mom about the broken eagle settle around my shoulders.

"Well, at least we tried." Seth's voice is quiet.

Then there's a click and the door swings wide open. Ruth is standing in front of us, still in her cowboy hat, and leaning on a walker. "I just had to undo the lock," she says. "Why don't the two of you come in and we can have a chat about my eagle."

"You live here all on your own?" Seth asks.

We're sitting in the living room. There are pieces of Ruth's work everywhere. The eagle, the one we've come for, is perched on a table in the corner. I try to keep from staring at it.

Ruth frowns at Seth's question. "I might be old, but I can look after myself," she says indignantly. Then she shrugs. "And a cleaner comes every other day, a nurse comes twice a week, and someone drops off meals for me every day. Better than living in an old folks' home. Now why don't you make yourself useful and get some chips and dip from the kitchen."

"Me?" asks Seth.

"Yes, you! Now scoot."

As Seth heads down the hall, Ruth calls out after him: "And don't break anything either!" She gives me a wicked grin. This is an especially impressive feat since she's missing several teeth. "Now," she says, settling into her leather chair, "let me tell you about your grandma Gloria."

We stay for longer than expected. I call home to check on Koji, to remind him to eat, and to let him know we'll be home late . . . but still with plenty of time to spare before Mom and Dad get home.

Ruth tells me about how she and Grandma Gloria used to go hiking in the mountains, looking for eagles. I lap it up. I didn't know that my grandmother loved desert adventures, too.

"Gloria loved eagles. That's why I made her one, to remind her that even if she couldn't see them, they were always up above in the sky, up in the mountains," Ruth explains.

"Like an angel?" Seth asks. The word *angel* is so incongruous and unexpected coming out of Seth's mouth, like spotting a polar bear in the desert, that I snort.

Ruth laughs her old-lady laugh and shakes her head. "No, not like an angel! Like an eagle. Eagles are real. Angels, who knows about those? I've lived a long time, and I've never seen an angel." She turns to me and takes my hand. "You've grown up more than a bit since I last saw you. Your mama should have brought you around more, especially after what happened to your family. I promised Gloria I would look out for your mama, but I don't think I've done a very good job of it."

I manage a smile, but I don't like her referencing what happened to Mika, especially in front of Seth. "I'll try to visit more. I didn't think . . . I didn't think you liked visitors."

"Well, I don't. But you aren't just any visitor. You're Gloria's granddaughter. So you can come see me any time." She nods at Seth. "And bring your boyfriend, too."

I feel heat climb up my chest and neck, into my cheeks. "Oh, Seth's just my friend. Not my boyfriend."

"He hasn't been able to take his eyes off you all evening!" Ruth says. "Don't think that just because I'm old, I don't see these things. There is nothing wrong with my eyesight."

Seth makes a choking sound and stares at his feet. "I wasn't . . . I wasn't staring at Reiko. I was staring at . . . the eagle."

Ruth cackles, tilting her head back so much that her cowboy hat falls off. "Of course. The reason you are here, after all. Tell me why I should give it to you." Her eyes are bright and narrow.

"Because . . . it reminds me of my grandmother?" I say.

"Lies!" Ruth shouts so loudly I jump. "I can abide many things but not a liar. Try again!"

"What is this, some kind of game show?" Seth mutters.

Ruth laughs again. "It sure is. And the prize is one bona fide Ruth Setmire eagle. Now the only one in existence. Thanks to you." She nods in Seth's direction and then turns back to me. "Try again. Let me know why you want this eagle."

"Because . . . I don't want to get in trouble?" I say.

"Warmer! Getting warmer!" Ruth yells. "You get one more chance!"

"Or else what? We don't get the eagle?" says Seth.

"Let the girl think." Ruth leans toward me. "I want honesty. I can always tell an honest answer. I can always read an honest heart."

"Because . . . I don't want to hurt my mom?" I say, waiting for Ruth to shout at me again, but instead she nods.

"Go on," she says, her frantic energy of moments ago simmering into something new, something different.

"Because I want her to be happy?"

"And . . ." Ruth prompts. She's staring at me so intently I feel like she's looking into my soul. Seth's watching me, too, and the combined intensity of their stares is too much, so I close my eyes.

"I don't want to disappoint her," I say. "I've disappointed her enough, and . . . and I can't add to it."

"Your grandmother was a people-pleaser, too, you know," says Ruth. "Sometimes you can get confused who you're doing the pleasing for. Don't worry so much what people think of you." She gives me a knowing look. "All that takes too much energy, if you ask me. Focus some of it on you, you hear me?"

"I've got plenty of energy," I say. "I've got everything."

"Everything but this eagle, right?" And then she makes this sound that is sort of a laugh and sort of a sigh. "All right. I'm convinced. And after all, I've got memories of your grandma Gloria, and it sounds like you've got nothing of hers. Nothing of hers that you can see, I mean. Because it is clear to me that you've got her spirit and her heart. *And* her urge to please all the time. She was very kind, your grandma. Yep, you're Gloria's granddaughter all right."

"So we can have it?" says Seth.

Ruth raises her eyebrows. "*She* can have it. On loan, that is. I'll make you a deal. I'll lend you this eagle, if you promise to come back in a year and tell me what you've learned about yourself. I've lived a long time—too long, some people might say—and I know how important it is to see yourself the way you really are. I don't think you've learned to do that yet, young lady."

I shake my head. "I . . . I don't know what you're talking about."

"Take the eagle and come back next year. If I think you've grown enough to earn the eagle, I'll let you keep it. Forever."

"But it isn't for me," I protest. "It's for my mom."

"Well, then this part will be for you. Now do we have an agreement?"

I nod, because I don't know what else to do. We seal the deal with glasses of apple juice for me and Seth, and brandy for Ruth.

On the way home, Seth sits in the middle seat in the back of the car, holding the eagle in his lap. Its wings spread out on either side of him. It just barely fits. We don't speak, partly because of how strange our interaction with Ruth was, and partly because we're both exhausted.

The roads are lit only by the stars, and as we roll along, every exit off the main road, every small side street, is calling my name, begging to be discovered and explored.

CHAPTER 17

WE GET THE SECOND EAGLE back in place, and my mother never notices it isn't the first eagle. Final exams come and go, and summer comes and stays. For the first few weeks after school lets out, I barely see my friends. I even ignore Dre. I don't want her, or anyone, to ask me questions. I don't want to think about the two parts of my life and how weird it is that I am spending so much time with Seth.

Seth and I venture out into the desert almost every night, looking for adventure. It makes me feel like I've found a part of me that I didn't know I was looking for.

We go back to the bottle-tree forest we saw on the drive to Ruth's. We spend hours wandering up and down the rusted rows of clanking, clinking junk. Because that is what it is, junk on display—but with a little bit of love and a little bit of light, it's transcended its origins to become something extraordinary.

A few nights later, we have one of those nights where we don't know where we're going but trust we'll know when we get there. I keep the windows rolled down as Seth and I drive into the dark, letting the wind taste my hair. The deeper into the desert we go, the darker it gets. We drive until there is nothing but stars and sand and mountains and us.

And still. We drive on.

Seth's made a playlist and the songs wash over me and fill the car, like we're swimming in music.

I listen to every lyric a little closer than I usually would. Wondering if he is trying to tell me something. Wondering if it is all in my head. Wondering if I want him to be telling me secret messages.

"Are we there yet?" he asks.

"Not yet," I say. Then I lean my head out of the window and howl into the night like a coyote.

"We could go to the coast," Seth says when I've stopped howling, but I ignore him and turn the music up louder.

I don't like the coast. It's too close to the ocean.

So we always drive inland.

"One day," Seth says, "we should drive all the way to Yosemite or something. Climb El Capitan. See the redwoods. See something else, *anything* else, other than desert. We could at least go up the tram one day."

Something about the idea that one day we'd drive so far together, combined with this idea of future plans, makes me skittish. I like being in the moment with Seth. No future and, most of all, no past. Just now.

"We see mountains," I point out.

"Desert mountains," he grumbles. "Desert everything."

We drive on in silence for a few minutes and then he takes a deep breath. Like he's preparing himself for something.

"Think we'll still do stuff like this together when school starts?" he asks.

I pretend I don't hear him. I don't like thinking about Seth at school. About what my friends, my real friends, would say, if they saw me cavorting with Seth Rogers. "Let's get out here," I say, suddenly wanting to be beneath the wide sky. I pull over and clamber out of my side of the car.

Seth shines his flashlight toward me. "You look like Wendy Darling meets Indiana Jones," he says.

I'm wearing hiking boots and a pale blue nightgown.

"I'll take it," I say.

We wander in the dark, careful not to step on rocks or bump into a cactus, until we get to the base of a low mountain and spy a trail grinning at us in the moonlight.

"Ta-da," I say, pointing up at it. "Told you we see mountains. Let's go to the top."

"It's pretty dark," Seth says. He's moved closer to me, and if I wanted to, I could reach out and grab his hand.

But I don't.

"We'll be fine. Just use your flashlight."

We climb up up up. And then we sit and wait for the sun to rise. It feels like it is rising below us, not above, like we're summoning the sun from the earth.

I let my head drop onto Seth's shoulder, just for a minute.

Only because I'm tired.

When we get back in my Jeep, we're both covered in a fine film of dust and sweat. As I pull my hair out of its ponytail, I catch Seth watching me intently. Usually I'd ignore it or pretend I hadn't seen, but this time I meet his gaze.

"What?" I ask.

"What what?" he says, a slow smile spreading over his face.

"What are you looking at me for?"

"I was looking at the sky."

Maybe he was. Maybe he wasn't. Sometimes, especially when I'm tired, especially when night blurs into day and when dream blurs into reality, I can't tell what I'm imagining and what is real.

"Don't you think it's weird," I say, looking up at the pale sliver of a moon, "that the moon goes to sleep when we wake up? Do you think the moon misses what happens in the day?"

"For someone who is so good at science, you sure have a lot of weird ideas about the moon," he says. "It's just a chunk of rock in space."

I bristle, offended on behalf of the moon.

It's more than that, and I know it.

As we're heading back into town, we pass a dusty liquor store on the side of the road and Seth asks me to slow down.

"Need a coffee or soda or something?" I ask, even though I know he wants me to buy him cigarettes. I don't approve of his smoking, but once we started spending time together, he somehow wrangled me into helping him buy cigarettes. It's probably because he told me that he only does it to feel close to his dad. He's never met him, but he was a smoker. And that is pretty much all Seth knows about him, so Seth smokes, too, because it is the one thing he can have in common with him.

The thing is, Seth has no way of knowing what brand his dad smoked. His mom can't remember. So every week he smokes a different brand of cigarettes. He figures, eventually, he'll hit on the brand his dad smoked, and then, at least for a week, they would have smoked the same one.

We never try to buy them from anywhere in Palm Springs—we don't want to risk getting spotted by someone we know—so instead we stock up at random gas stations and run-down grocery stores when we go driving at night.

"Will you buy me cigarettes?" he asks, just as I expected.

I pretend I don't hear him.

"Come on, please. The guy won't say no to you," he wheedles. He always uses this argument. "Nobody says no to you."

It's true, but hearing it makes me uncomfortable. It's a power I want, but one I'm also a little afraid of, if I'm honest. I know I'm not supposed to notice people watching me, not the individual looks and not the culmination, and I'm definitely not supposed to like it. But, somehow, worrying about getting *too much attention* and trying to get *more attention* is all mixed up in my brain.

Like one time we had this substitute teacher last year—a young guy, in his twenties, and he wasn't even that cute—but I saw how he looked at me, just a half second longer than he looked at anyone else, and I kind of loved it. It made me feel strangely powerful. But it scared the hell out of me, too.

Like *what*? This guy, this teacher, this *man*, likes to look at me? What am I supposed to do with this kind of information? Am I supposed to ignore it? Pretend I haven't noticed? Sit in the back with my head down? Nobody tells you what to do. All they say is: Be careful. *Be careful.* Like I'm fine china and I should be bubble-wrapped all the time.

After what happened to Mika, I don't want to be careful. I want to live. I need to live. Enough for the both of us. I owe it to her. But then, sometimes, I just want to stay home and be with her and never leave. Sometimes I feel like I'm two people, like I'm split between my fear of living and my fear of *not* living.

"If my mom ever catches me buying cigarettes . . ." I say.

"Your dad is from Japan! Isn't smoking, like, the number-one pastime in Japan?"

"Funny." I'm not amused.

"I'm right, though, aren't I? Smoking and sushi? Key parts of your culture."

"Seth . . ." If he hears the warning in my voice, he ignores it.

"Just try to buy a pack from the guy behind the counter. Give him one of your Reiko smiles. He won't even check your ID. Come on."

"I think this is the reason you became my friend," I grumble. "Because you knew I would enable your ridiculous cigarette addiction."

"It isn't a cigarette *addiction*. It's an *experiment*."

"If it isn't an addiction, why don't you stop?"

"Reiko, do I hassle you? Do I lecture you about any of your bad habits?"

"I don't have bad habits." At least, none that he knows about. Unless hanging out with him counts as one of my bad habits.

"You do realize that you don't look cool smoking, right?" I say later, when I've bought him the cigarettes, because of course I bought them. Just like nobody can say no to me, recently I haven't been able to say no to Seth.

"I don't know, Reiko, maybe this is who I'm meant to be," he says. His feet are on my dashboard, one arm is out the window, and he's blowing smoke out of the side of his mouth. "Debonair. Mysterious. Maybe you're rubbing off on me."

"I don't smoke," I say. "So if that was true, you wouldn't be smoking. And I don't think I've ever been debonair in my life."

"Sometimes, when I'm in this car with you, it's like a taste of a different life. A better life. You know?"

His words make my skin feel too tight.

"This is just my life," I say. "So, no, I don't know. I do know, though," I go on, reaching over and plucking the cigarette out of his hand, "that I don't like it when you smoke in my car. Save your filthy habit for your own time." I toss the still-lit cigarette out the window.

"Fire hazard," Seth says. "It's hot out there."

"You're the damn fire hazard," I say. But still, I glance out of the window to make sure that the cigarette butt hasn't sparked and started a fire that will burn the whole desert down.

"Are you saying I'm hot?" Seth asks.

I snort. "You're ridiculous."

"Ridiculously hot, according to you. Fire-hazard hot."

I laugh despite myself. "That's it. That's the last time I'm ever buying you cigarettes."

"That's what you said the last time," he says, with a grin that makes me dizzy.

It must be the heat.

It must be my lack of sleep.

It must be the sun.

It definitely isn't Seth.

It can't be.

CHAPTER 18

I HAVEN'T SEEN DRE VERY much this summer, and tomorrow she's going to Guadalajara with her family for two weeks, so I've invited her over for dinner. My dad is making tempura tonight, and it's her favorite. We've got some time before we eat, so we go up to my room to hang out. When we do, she flops down on my bed.

"So . . ." she says, not looking at me.

"So . . . ?" I say.

"So what the hell, Reiko? What is with the silent treatment? I haven't seen you all summer!"

"I wasn't giving you the silent treatment," I say, pulling at a loose thread on my bedspread. "I just needed to be by myself."

Dre sighs so heavily I'm expecting the walls of my room to blow down.

"Don't be mad," I say.

"I'm not mad, even though I should be. Pretty shitty when you just go off radar like that." She pokes me in the stomach. "I get worried. That's all. You know?"

That's worse than her being mad.

"You've got nothing to worry about," I assure her.

"Reiko. Stop lying to me, stop lying to yourself. You are always giving me something to worry about. Disappearing for days, going off in the desert by yourself—"

"I'm not always by myself."

"Really?" Dre sits up and stares hard at me. "Who are you with, then?"

I know what she's insinuating. She's asking me if I see Mika. If I'm going out into the desert with Mika.

I pull away from her. "It isn't what you think." Which is sort of the truth and sort of a lie.

"Well then, what is it?"

"I'm just stressed about applying to college," I blurt. And as I do, I realize that I mean it. "What if I don't get into UCLA?"

Dre rubs my back. "Of course you'll get in. You're Reiko Smith-Mori. You have practically perfect grades. Hell, you're a practically perfect person."

I don't know if her words make me feel better or worse, but I manage a smile. "Thanks, Dre. And . . . sorry for going MIA."

"That's okay, babe. You can owe me."

At dinner, Koji bickers with Dre like she's his sister, too. He always has. It's not the same as having two real big sisters, but it is the next best thing.

"So, Reiko," says my mom, passing me my plate, "Koji said you

101

had a boy over. I was wondering how his trunks ended up wet in the laundry."

Shit. I glare at Koji. So much for sibling solidarity. Seth and I have used the pool a few times when my parents have been out. I figured Koji wouldn't bother to mention it to our parents because he usually isn't interested in what I'm doing. But I guess I was wrong.

"What?" he says. "I didn't know it was a secret."

"Ohh, a *secret* boy," Dre singsongs. "And what boy would that be?" Her tone is light, but I can tell she's annoyed.

"My question exactly." My mom winks at Dre.

"I must admit, I'm curious as well," says my dad.

"It isn't a big deal," I tell them. "Dre, how long are you in Mexico again?"

"Uh-uh. We can talk about my holiday plans after. First, you can tell me who Koji is talking about." The edge in her voice is getting sharper.

"Yeah!" Koji chimes in.

"Or Koji can tell us?" Dre goes on, grinning wickedly.

I kick her under the table.

"I would, but I forgot his name," says Koji with his mouth full of shrimp tempura.

"It isn't important," I say. What I mean is, he isn't important— or at least I can't admit that he is. Not out loud. Not yet.

"Seth!" Koji exclaims, suddenly remembering.

Double shit. I bite the inside of my cheek in frustration.

"Seth Rogers?" Dre says incredulously. "The guy from the ice-cream shop?"

"Unless Reiko knows another Seth," says Koji. "Do you?"

"No," I say with a scowl.

"Oh! The boy with the physics notes. I remember now," Mom says. She turns to Dre. "What do you know about this Seth Rogers?"

"Not much, actually. He's kind of a lone wolf at school." Dre gives me a confused glance.

"That doesn't sound like Reiko's type," Dad says. "She usually goes for the big-man-on-campus type."

"I do not," I say.

"Well, Ryan Morris definitely fit that description," Dad says.

"What do you think, Koji?" Mom asks. "You're the one who has met this mystery man."

"This Seth guy seemed nicer than Ryan was. Nicer than the guy before Ryan, too. What was his name?"

"Julian," Dre supplies.

"Julian was plenty nice to you," I say to Koji. "And so was Ryan."

Koji shrugs. "Julian was a creep. He treated me like some dumb kid."

Julian and I dated at the end of my freshman year, when he was a senior. My parents were not exactly thrilled about it, and it didn't last long. I don't even think I was that into Julian; I was just into the fact that a senior was into me. Now that I'm about to be a senior, I can't imagine any of my guy friends dating a freshman. I mean, I can imagine it, but it would be creepy. No wonder all the senior girls used to glare at me.

"And what was wrong with Ryan?" I take a piece of sweet-potato tempura off Koji's plate. Ryan and I got together in sophomore year, and then his dad got some big job opportunity in New York, so his family moved out there in the middle of the year. We weren't ever that serious. We made out a lot in the back of my car, in the back of his car, pretty much anywhere we could. We didn't have all that much in common, but it didn't really matter. What mattered was I was into him, he was into me, and we had the same friends. My mom used to say that when I was older, when I was in college, I'd meet guys I had more in common with. She said that the guys I dated now were just fillers.

I can't figure out if Seth is a filler or something else. Not that we're dating. Or ever will. Which is why I don't want to have this conversation.

Dre finally notices my discomfort and takes pity on me. "So, Ken," she says to my dad, "what are you working on these days?"

As Dad launches into a long explanation about his most recent project, Dre winks at me and I scowl back.

I know this conversation isn't over.

"I don't get it," Dre says later. We are back in my room, and she is French-braiding my hair, swearing as the strands refuse to stay in place. "What the hell do you guys do?"

I shrug, keeping my eyes down. I'm not going to tell her that we roam the desert looking for its secrets or go searching for hidden streams to dip our toes in, the water a sharp relief from the ever-present heat, or make up stories about the family of cacti we found, or dance wildly when the sun is high, just to see our shadows jump.

"We just talk," I say.

"If you say so." Her tone is skeptical.

I don't know how to explain me and Seth. How do I say that in the past few weeks, he's become something to me? Become *someone*.

I just don't know what.

"He's, like, a really good friend," I say eventually, my voice overly casual.

Andrea isn't buying it. "Reiko, *I'm* your best friend. I should know who your 'really good friends' are."

I throw a pillow at her. "You don't know everything about me."

Her face goes serious. "That's what worries me, Rei."

"Dre, you don't have anything to worry about. Honestly. And it isn't as weird as it sounds. But I don't know how Libby and everyone would react. So maybe don't mention it?"

"Since when do friends keep other 'friends' secret?" she says, brow raised.

"Come on, Dre. Please?" Dre is reacting way better than I thought she would, but then again, she's Dre. She'd be on my side, no matter what.

"I have to admit, it does sound a little weird," she says. "I mean, would he say you two are really good friends?"

"Yeah, probably." Or he would if he thought it would make me happy. He likes to make me happy. I like having someone who cares so much about making me happy.

That makes me happy.

After Dre goes home and I've showered and gotten ready for bed, I find Mika hiding in my closet.

"Mika! What are you doing in there?"

"Hiding from you."

"Well, I've found you."

And then, completely unexpectedly, she bursts into tears.

"Mika!" I say, dropping to the floor and wrapping my arms around her. "What's wrong?"

She looks at me with reproach. "You're all doing everything without me!"

I've never seen her like this. She's trembling with frustration.

"Mika, Mika, everything is okay," I say, patting her back. Then I take a deep breath. "Do you want me to stop going out at night? Do you want me to tell Koji to stop playing music?"

She shakes her head. "No, I don't want that. I just . . . I want to do it, too."

"I know," I say. "I want that, too." I keep rubbing her back as her tears subside. "Hey, let's go up on the roof and watch the stars."

CHAPTER 19

SETH AND I HANG OUT so much now that half the time I
don't even text or call before I show up at his place. The night after
my talk with Dre is no different. When I knock at his front door, his
mom calls out that the door is open, so I let myself in. She is sitting
at the only table in the whole place, sifting through a junk haul.

I tug on the diamond pendant around my neck. It's the kind
Lucille would celebrate finding, and the kind that I probably
wouldn't even notice if I lost. I know all the stuff I have can't make
me happy, but it's still nice to have it. Part of me wants to take my
necklace off, though, and leave it hidden in the trailer for her to
find. But another part of me knows that would be a tasteless, tacky
gesture. The kind of thing my mom would call gauche.

"Hi, Lucille," I say, going over to look at what she's got. "Find
any treasure?"

"Not yet." She looks up at me and grins. "But the night is young,"
she adds with a wink. "Seth's in his room—you can go on in."

Seth's room is tiny, more of a glorified closet. I've only been in it
once or twice before, but I know that the door doesn't open all the

way, because the room is too small. I open it carefully to avoid knocking the foot of the bed and then slip in through the small space. Seth's sleeping, curled up on his side, his mouth open a little bit. I can hear him breathing.

"Seth?" I say, quietly at first. Then, more loudly: "Seth!"

Still nothing. I gently, so gently, reach down and tap his shoulder, and he jolts awake.

"Reiko? What are you doing here?" He blinks up at me, like I'm not real.

"I'm here on a secret mission," I say. Then I perch on the edge of the bed and touch him on the leg. "I'm here to see you, obviously."

I swear he starts to glow from the inside out.

We drive for hours, passing our usual favorite spots. Nothing feels right tonight. Nothing gives me that little fissure of excitement I get when we find something magical, when we discover somewhere that feels like it is only for us. We turn down roads we've never been down and up through canyons, and when the wind starts to pick up, really pick up, we're miles and miles and miles away from home.

I pull over, not because it feels like there might be something there, but because the way my car is teeter-tottering on the road is making me anxious.

"Crazy storm," I say, and Seth nods, but I can tell he's not really listening.

"It's my birthday next week," he tell me, looking down. "On the Fourth of July, actually."

"Oh," I say, because I'm not sure I want us to do birthdays together. Celebrating time passing is not something I want to happen with Seth. I like that we are outside of time. Separate from the rest of the world.

"I was hoping . . ." He starts to gnaw on a nail, or what is left of one. He chews his nails down till they are raw and red and I can't stand to look at them.

"Stop biting your nails," I say, sharper than I mean to, because he's so clearly nervous about something and it is putting me on edge.

". . . we could spend it together. Do dinner or something?"

"Just us?"

"You say that like we never do anything just us. We do everything just us."

Now I wish he'd go back to biting his nails because he's staring at me with a fierce intensity that makes me feel like squirming.

He plows on. "I've got something planned."

Alarm bells start to chime in my head. Not just an average dinner. Something *planned*. And suddenly I'm scared of what we're heading toward, scared of what *he* thinks we're heading toward.

"But don't you want to spend your birthday with . . . your friends?" I ask, buying time.

Your other *friends* is what I mean. *The friends you hang out with at school*. Although, maybe he doesn't have any. Like Dre said, he's kind of a lone wolf.

"Are we not friends?"

I take a deep breath. "That's not what I said. I'm just . . . surprised you'd want to spend your birthday with me. With just me."

I shouldn't be surprised, but I am.

The wind is creaking all around us, and I feel like it is asking me to come out and play. The car is getting smaller and smaller, and if I don't get out soon, it will keep shrinking until it crushes me.

"Let's get out," I say, turning off the engine and unlocking the door. I have to push hard to open it against the wind, and then the wind changes its mind and flings it wide open. Sand swirls into the car.

"Come on!" I jump out into the desert, not caring that the sand is stinging my eyes, not caring that we don't know where we are.

There is so much sand in the air that it looks like the actual air is glowing a pale gold. I reach down to pick up a handful and throw it in the air, adding to the sand celebration, because that is what this is.

"What is this place?" Seth is right next to me, but he has to yell to be heard because of the wind. "Where are we?"

"We're on an adventure!" I say, dashing out into the dark, through the swirling gold.

I'm wearing a long, billowing skirt, and as I spin around, it picks up the wind. Soon I don't know if I'm spinning the skirt or if the skirt is spinning me.

"Rei! Come back!" Seth's words whip around me, but I don't stop. I keep running. I keep spinning. I want to put distance between me and whatever is happening with us. I don't want complicated. I want for us to go on being out in the desert in the dark with no thought as to what might happen. No pressure. No promises.

"Come catch me!" I call back, but my voice gets lost in the wind.

"Reiko, I think this is a sandstorm! We have to get back to the car!"

Why would I want to get back to the car when I'm flying? I love how the wind feels on my face, in my hair. I love how I feel like I could lift up into the sky and fly away away away.

"Let's dance!" I scream back at Seth, and he reaches out for me, but the wind is on my side and it pushes me just out of his reach.

"Reiko! I'm serious! We need to get back to the car!"

"I need to dance! Dance dance dance!"

I raise my hands up to the sky and keep spinning. I'm spinning so much that I can't tell if the stars are above me or all around me. I think I might rise up into the night sky and never come back down.

The wind is whistling a melody that only I can hear and it is glorious. "The stars are singing!" I yell.

I close my eyes tight tight tight against the sand, against the wind, against the sky, close them tight against Seth's birthday wishes, and I wonder if when I open them, the wind will have scooped me up and dropped me off in Oz.

When the wind stops to take a breath, I open my eyes and start to laugh. I'm coated in a fine layer of sand. I can feel it in my hair and in the corners of my mouth and in between my fingers.

"Reiko! Get back here!" Seth is shouting.

I go toward his voice, because where else am I going to go? What else am I going to do? I'm not in Oz. I'm still here. He's still here.

I pick up my long skirt and run back toward my car. Seth is still standing next to it; he hasn't moved, but he's wearing the same sand coat I am.

He's not laughing.

"What was that?" he asks as we clamber back inside and I turn on the car. We're getting dust and sand all over the seats, but I don't care. "Why did you take off like that?"

"I wanted to go on an adventure." I start driving back the way we came. "Isn't that the reason we go on the drives?"

"Running headlong into a sandstorm isn't exactly an . . . adventure," says Seth, and it sounds like he is chiding me. Then he lowers his voice. "It felt like you were running away from me."

No, not from him, but from the inevitable thing we are tipping toward. I want to fight time; I want us howling in the wind, covered in sand, dancing with the stars. But I know that Seth wants more from me than desert escapes. He wants for us to exist in real time, not just out here.

We drive back to his trailer in silence, and I cut the lights just as we pull up next to it so we don't wake his mom.

"Well, good night," I say.

Seth doesn't get out. Instead, he reaches down into his backpack. "I got you something." He hands me a small white box. I eye it like it's a snake.

"What for?" I ask.

"Why are you so suspicious?"

Because I'm worried that accepting the present will be accepting something else.

"It's just a little thing. A belated birthday present for you." His voice catches on the word *birthday*. "Your birthday was right before we met at Joshua Tree. May ninth."

He's right and it makes me uneasy because what else does he secretly know about me? What other facts is he hoarding, waiting for the right moment to unveil them?

"A pretty belated gift then, huh?" I say, smiling, like I always do to mask my unease. I take the box, tilting it slowly to the side, and hear something clink.

"Careful," he says, watching me with wide, wide eyes.

I open the lid warily, like there really might be a snake inside.

There isn't.

Instead there is a crescent moon charm, a silver one, hung on a silver chain so fine it looks like it might disintegrate.

"Oh!" I say, because it is so unexpected, so beautiful, so delicate, like when a hummingbird flutters close to you.

"Do you like it?"

"It's beautiful," I say, because it's the truth. "But, Seth . . ." We both know he can't afford something like this.

"My mom found it," he says quickly. "Well, she found the moon and the chain, but I put them together."

The fact that he made it from something his mom scavenged in the desert only makes it worth more to me.

"Are you sure your mom doesn't want to sell it?"

His lips close in a tight frown, and I immediately regret what I've said.

"If you don't want it, just say so."

"Of course I want it." I take it out of the box. "Help me put it on?"

When his hands brush my hair away from the back of my neck, they're trembling. He swears under his breath as he fiddles with the clasp. I sit still, so still that I'm not even breathing.

"There," he says, sounding proud.

The moon hangs from my neck, glinting and shimmering in the dark. I don't ask him if he remembers what I said about getting me the moon.

I know he does.

Seth swallows, and the sound is loud in the quiet car. "So . . . next week? The Fourth?"

"Sure," I say, keeping my voice steady as I can. Because I know we are hurtling toward something I can no longer stop.

His smile lights up the night.

CHAPTER 20

I WAKE UP ON THE Fourth of July feeling apprehensive. Celebrating Seth's birthday with him feels like we're cementing our friendship, our relationship, our whatever-this-is-ship, in the real world.

And I don't like it.

I can't shake the feeling that as much as I want to keep us existing either in the moonlit-desert-night world or a sun-scorched-delirious daydream, he wants the opposite. He wants to pull whatever we are into reality.

But I text him *happy birthday*, because I'm not a monster. He says thanks, then asks me to *prepare a feast* for tonight. I'm not too surprised. His mom never cooks and Seth doesn't even know how to make pasta, whereas my parents—and by default, me—are seriously into food. My dad taught me how to cut sashimi properly when I was eleven. I know how to put together a perfectly composed cheese platter. I can break down a whole chicken, and stuff it, too. I even know how to use the kitchen blowtorch to make crème brûlée.

I grab a picnic basket (and when I say picnic basket, I mean *picnic basket*—we've got these designer Red Riding Hood ones, which are also super modern and double as coolers). I fill it with stuff from the fridge: a block of cheese, some crackers, a bottle of apple juice, avocados, chips, some leftover duck breast, carrots, hummus, and chocolate-covered cherries.

I list everything out in a text, ending with: *Satisfactory?*

He replies: *Perfect.*

Then Dre's face pops up on my phone. I answer, and before I can even say hello, she's shouting down the line. "Rei-Rei! I'm baaaaack! Did you miss me? I missed you!"

"Hey! How was Mexico? How is your family?" I say. I don't tell her that I've been so busy going on adventures with Seth I have barely noticed she's been gone. It took me a minute to even remember where she's been.

"It was amazing but, oh my God, my cousin, the one who was getting married? Well, turns out that my aunt Carmen—you know Aunt Carmen, she came out for my quinceañera—anyway, she knows the mother of the guy that my cousin is marrying, and apparently they had some issues way back when, and then my aunt Carla got involved . . ."

I zone out as Dre launches into a long, complicated story about her extended family, only snapping back to attention when she says, ". . . anyway, it was crazy. I love my family, but I am so ready for no drama! And I'm so glad we got back in time for the party tonight."

"What party?"

x

116

"*What party?* Even I know about the party tonight, and I've been in Guadalajara for the past two weeks! Down at the old track. It's gonna be sweet. Tori's boyfriend is even going to hook us up with drinks." Tori is nineteen, but her boyfriend is twenty-one.

"Oh yeah," I say, like I'd just forgotten, not that I hadn't known about it. I press my hand on my chest to calm the anxiety starting to snake its way up my throat. *Why didn't you know about the party, Reiko?* it hisses in my head. *The world has carried on while you've been out with Seth Rogers in the desert. Who do you want to be, Reiko? A weirdo who hangs out with Seth Rogers or someone who gets invited to the biggest party of the summer?*

"What time is everything getting started tonight?" I ask, trying to keep my voice steady.

"Probably around nine. I'll come over to your place first to get ready?"

I pause. I want to go to the party, but I've promised Seth I'll spend his birthday with him. Maybe there's a way to do both. "Oh, um, actually, I've got . . . a family dinner tonight. So I'll meet you there later?"

I can practically hear Dre's eyebrows go up. "A family dinner on the Fourth of July?"

"Yeah, um, my dad is really into it, remember?" It's plausible. As proud as my dad is of his Japanese heritage, he also loves to embrace being American.

"What time should I come over? We can hang with your fam and then sneak off for the real party. Your parents will be cool with that, right?"

"Actually, I think . . . this is just family."

"Oh. All right! I'll see what the other girls are up to. I guess I'll get ready with them and see you at the track?"

I'm annoyed, mostly at Seth. And I know that is irrational and unfair because it's me who's just lied to Dre and bailed on her, but I'm still jealous of whatever she is going to do without me. School is starting soon and I don't want everyone to get used to doing stuff without me. I wonder how late Seth wants us to hang out. Maybe we can wrap up his birthday dinner early.

"I can't wait to see you," Dre says. I can tell she thinks something is off but can't figure it out.

When I hang up, I see I have another text from Seth: *Pick me up at 7?*

What about 6?

It's got to be 7.

Why?

You'll see. It's a surprise.

I feel a twinge of guilt that I don't have a surprise for Seth, considering it is his birthday. He shouldn't be planning the surprise. The least I can do is go along with it.

And maybe bake him a cake.

On second thought, it's too hot to bake. I'll just buy one.

CHAPTER 21

"CAN YOU GUESS WHERE WE'RE going?" Seth is practically bouncing in the front seat. I'm driving, but he's directing. We're heading out of Palm Springs, up toward Cabazon. I can only think of one thing in this direction: Morongo, the hotel and casino where his mom works.

"Morongo?" I guess. "Are we going to meet up with your mom for dinner?" I can't decide if that would be better or worse than doing something just the two of us.

Seth snorts. "No, we're not going to Morongo, and we're not meeting my mom. And you brought dinner." He reaches back and pats the picnic basket that is sitting in the back seat. He hasn't seen the cake. All the grocery-store bakery had were Fourth-of-July-themed cakes, so it is decorated like an American flag. At least I convinced them to pipe *Happy Birthday, Seth* across it in frosting.

"You really don't know where we're going?" he says.

I shake my head.

"I've got the keys to the dinosaurs," he says, right as they come into view.

When I was little, I thought the dinosaurs were real. I remember the first time I saw them, how they rose up out of the landscape, life-size. I named them Betty and BoBo. BoBo was the longneck and Betty was the T. rex. I found out later that the artist who created them had originally named them Dinny and Mr. Rex. They were how I marked time—on our way back from the LAX Airport, I knew that we were almost home when we passed the dinosaurs.

The desert is full of all kinds of weird stuff and weird people. People go a little funny after being in the sun all the time. Being in the heat. The Cabazon Dinosaurs are just one other strange thing out here. Enormous dinosaur sculptures, out in the middle of the desert. They look like they are just part of the landscape. Like they've always been here.

Inside the belly of the longneck one is a museum. It isn't a dinosaur museum, or even a desert museum. No, inside these man-made desert dinosaurs is a *creationist* museum, run by a pastor. This drives my father nuts. For him, a sculpture of a dinosaur with a creationist museum in it goes against everything he stands for.

And now Seth is saying he has the keys to get inside.

"How did you get them?" I ask as we park between Betty and BoBo.

"My mom found them when she was out scavenging around here. And I remembered how much you liked them as a kid, but you never got to go inside."

"So . . . you want to spend your seventeenth birthday in a creationist museum in the belly of a dinosaur?" I say as I get the picnic basket out of the back seat.

Seth grins again, a brighter, bolder grin than before. "We're not going into the museum," he says. "We're going to the top of the T. rex."

It's dark inside the T. rex. Dark and empty and hot. I'm not scared of the dark, and nothing is darker than desert dark, but I don't like being in here. I feel trapped.

"Just head up the stairs," says Seth, switching on a flashlight. The insides of the T. rex, the walls, are painted blood red. The staircase is steep and goes up so far I can't see where it ends.

"Seth, what if we get caught?" I say as I start to climb the metal steps, holding on to the railing with sweaty fingers. The stupid fancy picnic basket is hanging from the crook of my arm, and I'm worried it's going to knock me off balance.

"We won't get caught. They don't even have a security system. There's nothing in here. The actual museum and gift shop are where everything is kept." He's climbing up below me, and it makes me wish I was wearing shorts instead of a short dress. The dress isn't that fancy, just a blue halter neck, but it feels completely out of place in here. It isn't meant for this; it is meant for the party tonight.

It feels like the two parts of me are on a collision course: the part that wants to be with Seth and the Reiko that needs to be at that party. I really don't want to miss it. People will wonder where I am.

By the time we reach the top of the T. rex, where its head is, the sun has gone down and the sky is turning inky. There's a small viewing platform up here, and the gaping mouth of the T. rex is the window. The teeth block the view a bit, but the mountains and the desert are still an impressive sight, even in the darkening night.

"Wow," I say. "This is pretty cool."

"I told you," Seth says. "And it is going to get cooler in just a few minutes." He gets an old beach towel out from his backpack and spreads it on the floor. "Thanks for bringing dinner."

Now that I realize this is *it*, this is the birthday event, a picnic in the mouth of a T. rex, I start to think I should have done more to make it all a bit more special because however much I want to deny it, or pretend it isn't happening, Seth and I are friends, and I do care about him. I wish I hadn't just raided our fridge for leftovers, and I should have got an actual birthday cake instead of a Fourth of July one.

"I should have brought steak sandwiches or something," I say, as I start to unpack the picnic basket. "Something more carnivore-appropriate." The jumble of food that I thought looked good this morning now looks random and unappetizing. I get out paper plates and pour apple juice into plastic cups. "Cheers," I say, passing Seth one. "And happy birthday!" My excitement sounds forced. It *is* forced.

We eat in silence for a few minutes, staring out of the mouth of the dinosaur. This doesn't feel like one of our usual adventures. There's more behind it somehow, like Seth has pinned all his hopes on it.

I can see why Seth thought this would be fun and cool and interesting, though. I mean not many people can say they have had a picnic in a dinosaur head, and maybe if it wasn't his birthday, if we were just up here having fun, I would be enjoying it more. But it *is* his birthday. And that changes everything.

Seth peers into the picnic basket. "What's that?" he asks, pointing at the cake box that is looking slightly smushed.

"It's a birthday cake! And"—I rummage around in the basket until I find the birthday card—"this is for you."

"You got me a cake? And a card?" I wait for him to make a crack about the fact that it is an American flag cake, or say something sarcastic about the smashed state it is in. "Thank you," he says. So sincerely I have to look away.

"I don't have candles," I say, taking the cake out of the box. I am officially the worst friend ever. "But, umm . . ." I take a deep breath and quickly sing "Happy Birthday."

"Can I make a birthday wish without any candles?"

"Hey, I don't make the rules," I say, and he closes his eyes tight and blows all over the candle-less cake. "Happy birthday," I say again when he opens his eyes.

"This is one of the best birthdays I've had in a long time."

This? This is one of his best birthdays? A smushed cake with no candles and fridge leftovers? And just . . . me? There's a weight pressing down on me now. His expectation, his hope, it is getting heavier by the second and I'm trapped in here with it.

Seth keeps looking out the mouth of the dinosaur and back to his watch like he's waiting for something and just as I realize what his big plan is, why he wanted us to come up here—

The fireworks go off. Of course, fireworks for the Fourth of July. I was so stressed out about this whole birthday evening that I forgot about the fireworks. The sky is an explosion of red, white, and blue. We scoot forward, leaving the cake behind us, and peer between the teeth at the sparks dancing in the air.

"I thought we'd have a good view from up here," Seth says, looking at me with so much *hope* it makes me feel a bit sick. Like when you walk through the perfume section of a department store and there is just so much perfume in the air that it is in your nose and on your skin and in your hair and in your mouth and you can't get away from it.

Seth's hope is like that. It is all around me and it is making me dizzy, making me want to get out of here.

My phone pings. It's a tipsy text from Dre. She's already started drinking.

Reikooooooo! where r u? Tonitds is gorging to be the brest xoxoxoxoxo

And then: *hahahahha the best!*

And then a picture of her cleavage. *the best brests hahahaha*

She's being an idiot, but it makes me smile.

"You're missing the fireworks," says Seth. "Who is it?"

"Just Dre," I say. "She got home from Mexico yesterday." Then: "She's out tonight." I deliberately keep my voice casual. "I might . . . I might meet her later."

"Later?"

"Yeah, there's this party . . ." My voice trails off.

"But . . . aren't we hanging out?"

"We *are* hanging out . . ." I know what he's saying, but I play dumb because it's easier.

"I thought . . ." He looks out at the fireworks, still blasting into the night. "I thought we were going to hang out, like, all night. Maybe go on a drive or something."

"I haven't seen any of my other friends all summer, Seth. I've only seen you. Is it so bad that I want to see my friends?" My tone is snippier than I mean it to be.

"Is it so bad that I want to spend my birthday with you?"

"Stop telling me it's your birthday! I know it's your birthday! That's why we're up here! Dre is already at the party, okay? Everyone is already there, and I'm not because I'm spending time with you on your birthday!"

My words echo in the dinosaur skull. It all feels too much and it's hot and close in this dinosaur head and everything is pressing in on me. I don't like how nasty I'm being, but it's like all my frustration with him and this night and my anxiety about missing the party have joined forces inside my head and are making me be this ugly person I don't want to be.

Seth starts to pack up the picnic basket. "Well, I don't want you to miss it because of me."

I feel terrible. "Don't be like this, Seth." I reach out to him, but he jerks his arm away. I can tell he's trying not to cry.

"It's my *birthday*, Reiko," he says, his voice cracking, like he's going through puberty all over again. I can't look at him, not the way his chin is wobbling, because it's my fault and I just want to get out of here.

"I brought you a cake! And a card! What more do you want?"

The words are out before I can stop them. The weight of them nearly knocks us both over. I wish I could take them back, because I didn't mean them, not really. I just don't want to be dealing with this right now.

He takes a deep breath, inhaling my question.

"What I want," he says, and his pupils are huge. I feel like they are going to keep expanding and expanding until I'm staring into two black holes, until I'm falling into them, and I'll never be able to get out. "What I want is for you to want to spend time with me on my birthday."

"And I did! I spent time with you on your birthday!" My voice is high, too high. I sound like a cartoon character. My dress suddenly feels too tight—it is squeezing all the air out of me. This isn't how it's meant to be with us. I'm lost and I don't like it. Because I know what he means and I wish I didn't.

"Let's just go," I say, desperate to escape this situation.

Then I run down the stairs, so fast that my shoe slips off and I have to go back for it, like I'm some sort of twisted Cinderella—only instead of running from a party, I'm running to one.

The whole drive back to Seth's place, I keep expecting him to say something to make it better.

He doesn't.

"Have fun at your party," he says.

He leaves what remains of his birthday cake, and his card, behind.

I tell myself I don't care. I tell myself that he's overreacting. I tell myself that he's asking too much of me. And I ignore the feeling inside that is whispering that maybe, just maybe, it might be my fault, too.

CHAPTER 22

WHEN I GET TO THE old racetrack, all I can see are shadows. I can't tell who is who, and the closer I get, the more I realize I don't recognize anyone. It makes me feel like I really have been in a different world this summer. I can't find Dre or Tori or anyone I know from school. I don't even see Peter or Michael or Zach, or any of the guys from the football team. Libby's in Hawaii, so I know she won't be here, but Megan and the others would never miss a big party like this.

It's been years since the track has been used as an actual racetrack. Sometimes people come out here and race on bikes, but mostly it's abandoned. It's far from any houses, far from anything. It's the perfect place for a party.

But I'm just not in a party mood after the whole thing with Seth. Partying the hardest, laughing the loudest, and living the most used to be the best way to forget about Mika. But recently, being out in the desert with Seth, driving or exploring, has been an even better balm.

Still. I don't want everyone to think I'm some weirdo who just disappears into the desert by herself.

"Reiko Smith-Mori, where the hell have you been all summer?" Zach Garcia has materialized next to me. He looks good. But then again, he always looks good.

"Around," I say. I take a step closer to him, smelling his cologne. Could Zach Garcia make me forget, make me feel alive the way being with Seth Rogers does?

"Rei, did you hear me?"

I blink up at Zach.

"Sorry," I say, putting on my prettiest smile and batting my lashes. The face I put on at parties. "What was that?"

"I asked if you've seen Dre? She's been looking for you all night."

"I just got here. I haven't found her, and she's not answering any of my texts."

"Well"—Zach gives me a slow smile, the smile that has been breaking hearts since the third grade—"let's get you a drink and then we can find Dre."

"Reiiiii!" Dre comes at me like a comet. "I've missed you so much!" she slurs, her beer sloshing out of her cup and down my dress. "What took you so long? You are slow late." She laughs a great big hiccuping laugh. "Didja hear that? *Slow late!* Because you are late? And slow?"

"Yeah, yeah, she heard you." Dre's sister, Tori, takes the red cup out of Dre's hands. "Dre, I think you've had too much to drink."

"Have not!" Dre says indignantly. "And Reiko just got here!"

"Well then, Reiko probably needs a drink, not you." Tori holds the cup to me.

"I'm good," I say. "I'm driving."

"You are better than good," Dre declares. "You are *great*!" She gives me a wet kiss on the cheek. You'd think she'd been gone for months, not two weeks.

"This is my best friend!" she shouts at anyone and everyone who passes us. "This is my best friend!" Then she hugs me again. "I'm so glad you're here!"

"Me too!" I say, hugging her back.

And I am.

Mostly.

Mika climbs into bed with me the next morning and snuggles up next to me. I stroke her hair. Then she looks at me and frowns. "Reiko, what's wrong?"

She can always tell when something is wrong.

"I don't think I'm being a very good friend to Seth."

"Why?" She sounds genuinely curious. "You're always with him. You spend even more time with him than with me."

"That's not true."

"Yes, it is," she says in her matter-of-fact way. She doesn't sound upset, though.

I take a deep breath. "Yesterday was his birthday and . . ." I pause. "I kind of ditched him." It feels good to admit it out loud.

"Oh," she says, tilting her head to the side. "Well . . . can't you just say sorry?"

I give her a smile. She's wise, for fourteen.

"Anyway," she goes on, "Seth could never stay mad at you."

She kind of has a point. And that gives me comfort. I'm in control of how Seth and I are together, and if I don't want anything to change between us, then it won't.

CHAPTER 23

SETH WON'T LOOK AT ME when I get to his place. He lets me in and then goes to sit on the couch and stare at the wall as intently as if he were watching TV. I sit next to him, close, real close. So close that I can hear his breathing.

"I'm sorry," I say, and I don't realize how sorry I am until the words are out.

Seth's whole face changes, as though he was wearing his anger like a mask and now that I've said sorry, he can take it off.

"Go to the summer fair with me," he says. This isn't what I'm expecting him to say at all.

"Please? It'll be fun," he adds. "I really want to go to the fair with you, Reiko." He's looking at me now, eyes wide and hopeful.

"Okay," I say. It feels like I'm saying yes to more than the fair, especially after what happened yesterday, but I convince myself that it's all fine, because I don't want to hurt him again.

"What about Wednesday? I'll have my mom's car. I can drive us."

"Okay," I say again.

And when he beams at me, his smile does what it always does: It makes me smile, too.

When Seth picks me up for the fair, I can't get over how strange it feels. It feels like a *date*. Even more than the dinosaur picnic did. Maybe it's because Seth has dressed up a bit. He's wearing a collared shirt. I've never seen him in a collared shirt. I didn't even know he owned one.

And he's done something with his hair. He's put . . . gel in it. Or something.

Or maybe it's because he's driving. Seth never drives. It feels weird to be in the passenger seat. I'm used to being the driver.

Or maybe it's because he's so *happy*. Nervous happy. Happy nervous. He's whistling tunelessly and keeps looking over at me and grinning his wide, crooked grin.

His happiness is spilling out of him. It is sparkly and bright and *beautiful*. I bury my face in it, breathing it in, feeling it spread throughout me, too, until I'm grinning back at him, and we're just beaming like a pair of maniacs.

And then.

And then his hand is reaching over and taking mine, and he's squeezing it and it is like my heart is in my hand because I swear it isn't my hand he's squeezing but my heart. Gently, so it doesn't hurt, but it scares me all the same.

I don't want Seth to be able to do anything to my heart.

And I feel like an idiot, because I knew this was coming and I didn't stop it.

* * *

We get to the fair just as the sun is dipping down behind the mountains. The sky is the same color as the cotton candy Seth insists on buying me.

"I don't even like cotton candy," I protest, but he doesn't hear me, or doesn't care, and he buys the biggest size he can. I try not to wince as a bead of sweat drips down the hand of the man swirling the pink clouds on the white cone and disappears into the fluff.

Seth holds the candy out to me like a bouquet. The sugar-sweet smell mixes with the smells of the buttered popcorn and hot dogs and the sweat of all the people here. It makes me feel panicky. Makes me feel trapped.

"Aren't you going to have any cotton candy?" Seth asks.

I don't want to disappoint him, so I take a fistful. It starts to disintegrate in my hands, the fluff giving way to sugar grit. I put the whole piece in my mouth, and it is so sticky-sweet it makes me feel like I'm going to throw up. It isn't disintegrating fast enough, so I start chewing chewing chewing until it is all gone.

But even then it isn't really gone. My tongue is sugar-coated woolly.

"Do you want anything else?" Seth asks, like I was the one who wanted the cotton candy in the first place. "Popcorn? Hot dog? Ice cream?"

What I want is to be out in the desert, where all I can smell is the sky and the stars and the sand. Or even in my backyard or my own car. I want to be anywhere but at the fair on what feels like a date with Seth because I feel out of control. I don't know what is going to happen, and I don't like it.

I take a deep breath, inhaling all the tastes of the fair again, and force down the panic, force my heart to calm, force my mouth to smile, force my body to lean toward him, nudging his shoulder with my own.

"Maybe you could get me some water?" I say.

And if he's disappointed that I don't want him to get me something from every stand at the fairground, he doesn't show it.

"So . . . want to go on the bumper cars?" he says, in the same hopeful voice he's been using all evening.

"You really want to do this whole . . . fair thing, don't you?"

He gives me a funny look. "That's why we're here, isn't it?"

His words make me relax. That is why we're here. To do fair things.

I'm being self-centered and reading into things that aren't there. You know when someone holds out an ink blot and says what do you see? And sometimes you are supposed to see two people kissing or a unicorn or something. And sometimes it is just an ink blot. This whole day I've been seeing something that isn't there: seeing a unicorn when it is just a big old ink blot.

"Let's go on the bumper cars," I say.

It's actually pretty fun. There isn't anyone else in the pavilion, so we bump into each other over and over again, and I don't know why it's so funny but it is. I'm hunched over my little steering wheel, in my little car, laughing so hard I can barely catch my breath.

When the ride is over, we stumble out, our legs cramped and unsteady. I link my arm through Seth's for balance, and it feels normal.

"What do you want to do now?" he asks.

I grin back at him "Whatever you want," I say, and I mean it. I can make up for ditching him on his birthday by making this day his day.

"What about"—he pauses like he's thinking, but I can tell he already knows what he's going to say—"the Ferris wheel?"

"If that's what you want."

"It is. It really is." His smile is so wide it makes my own cheeks hurt just looking at him.

CHAPTER 24

WE GO UP UP UP, our bright yellow chair creaking in the desert wind. The people below us shrink to dolls, and then smaller still. It's peaceful, being so high up. We're quiet, and it's nice. Silence with Seth is nice. I feel like I can be quiet with him in a way that I can't be with anyone else except for Mika.

"Rei?" Seth shatters the silence, and something about the way he has just said my name makes me tense.

"Yeah?"

"I have to tell you something."

My heart tries to jump out of my chest. I wish I were wearing sunglasses. I'm worried Seth will see the panic in my eyes.

"You probably know what I'm going to say." Seth sounds equal parts resigned and hopeful.

Oh no, please don't say what I think you are going to say, please let everything stay how it is, please don't—

"I'm really into you. Like *really* into you." He pauses, and my mouth goes dry. "I can't just be your friend anymore. Or your night-driving buddy. Or whatever the hell we are."

The Ferris wheel dips, and my heart goes with it. Our chair is swinging high above the ground, and there is nowhere for me to go. I look down and contemplate jumping off. I think I could survive the fall.

"Rei?"

Seth moves closer to me, and the movement makes our chair swing even more wildly.

"Stop!" I don't know if I mean *stop moving* or *stop talking* or both.

"Rei?" he says again, and his voice is so soft and so small that it blows away, taking my name with it. I watch it flutter to the ground and hope nobody steps on it.

The Ferris wheel grinds to a halt as someone else gets on.

"You look like you are going to throw up." Seth's disappointment smells like rotting flowers.

"I'm just . . . I'm just processing," I manage. "Give me a second."

I concentrate on breathing, on taking in one breath after another. I don't know why this has come as such a shock. I knew, on some level—of course I did—and I did nothing to stop it. Even after the disaster at the dinosaurs, I still agreed to come to the fair, and I stayed, even when it felt like a date. It's like I was tugging at a thread in a sweater, but instead of pulling out one loose thread, I pulled too hard and the whole thing unraveled, and what was once a sweater is now a big tangled mess.

"You don't have to say anything," he says, and that stench of rotting flowers is so strong I have to hold my breath.

The Ferris wheel starts to move again, the ground coming closer and closer, and we are going to get off. I'll be able to handle this all so much better once my feet are on the ground, and then—

"One more time, kids?" The ride operator winks at us like he's giving us a present, and before I can say *NO*, we're going up again.

"I'm sorry, I shouldn't have told you," Seth says, turning away from me.

"Don't be sorry," I tell the back of his head, focusing on a mole at the nape of his neck. I'm grateful he's not looking at me. It is much easier to have this conversation with a mole than with his face. I don't want to hurt him. "Just give me some time."

He turns back toward me. "Really?"

"Really," I say.

And then as I think about it, really think about it, something strange starts to tick through me.

I can't imagine my life right now without Seth.

CHAPTER 25

WHEN WE GET BACK TO my house, Koji is in the living room, watching some guy on a guitar on the TV and trying to mimic what he's doing.

"Hey," he calls, without looking at us as we walk in.

"Are Mom and Dad home?" I ask.

"Nah, they're at some dinner."

"Cool."

And then I pause. Maybe we should just go sit in the living room with Koji. Maybe we should play a round of Monopoly or Settlers of Catan with him. Hell, maybe we should even watch this guitar tutorial with him.

I feel like what Seth and I do now is going to set us on one course or another, and then Seth is slyly taking my hand, tugging me toward the stairs and pointing up toward my room. If I want to stop this, I know this is the moment, but there is a small part of me—no, not small, a pretty significant part of me—that is curious, that wonders where this path will go.

The stairs feel endless, like we're trying to go up a downward escalator. Seth is breathing heavily. I wonder again if I should stop this, but I don't, and then we're in my room.

"So," Seth says, leaning against my desk.

"So," I say.

I swallow. I care about Seth, I do. But do I feel like *that* about him?

Only one way to find out, really.

I lean toward him, and he must know what I'm thinking because his eyes brighten and smolder in rapid succession, and he leans toward me, too, and then his mouth is on mine. He is all tongue, so much tongue that it feels like there is no room for my own tongue in my mouth, so by default it has to go in his mouth and as soon as it does, he moans, really moans, so loudly that I'm worried Koji will hear. And he's tightening his grip on me and he's hard and pressed up against me.

I pull away sharply. He's staring at me like he wants to *devour* me. And something shifts inside me. Because knowing that he wants me this badly does something to me. I feel like some sort of femme fatale. Like I've got all the power. And that's both intoxicating and strangely comforting. It reminds me that I'm in control.

"Was that your first kiss?" I demand, even though I know the answer.

He grins a little sheepishly and sits down on the edge of my bed. "That bad, huh?"

"Let's try again," I say, kicking my bedroom door shut, just in case Koji wanders upstairs or my parents get home early.

I tug my hair loose from the bun on top of my head so it falls around my shoulders. Then I take a slow, deliberate step toward Seth. When he makes a move like he's going to stand up, I put my hand on his chest. "Stay there," I command, and he nods.

I sit next to him, and this time, I lead on the kiss. I put his hands where I want them. I kiss him the way I like to be kissed.

This time, it's better.

When we finally pause to catch our breath, my lips are swollen from so much kissing. I've had better kisses, but we're already miles away from that first sloppy mouth smash. He flops back on my bed, looking as smug and satisfied as I've ever seen him. It's a completely unfamiliar expression, and it changes his face. I don't like it. It makes me feel like I've been making out with a stranger. It makes me wonder what I've started, what I've woken up in him by doing this. It makes me think that maybe I should have stopped it.

"I can't wait to tell everyone," he says.

"What?" I scramble up from the bed. "You can't tell *anyone*." I thought that was obvious.

"What do you mean, I can't tell anyone?"

"Seth, this is between us. Don't . . . ruin it by telling other people."

He sits up, frowning. "You mean, don't embarrass you."

I tug on my hair. "That's not what I said."

"No, but it is what you meant."

"I just need a little time, okay? To get used to all this."

"To what? To me?"

"To . . . this."

"Okay, Reiko. Whatever you want. Just like usual."

The doorbell rings. "Can you get that?" I shout down to Koji. He doesn't respond. The doorbell rings again. I look out the window. Libby's car is parked in the driveway.

Shit. Shit. Shit. What is she doing here?

She sees me and waves. "Baaaaabe! I've missed you! We just got back from Hawaii!" She turns toward the front door. "Oh, hiii, Koji! I don't have any presents for you, but how about a kiss?"

Koji mumbles something unintelligible back. He's had a crush on Libby for the past three years, and she knows it. She teases him mercilessly.

Please don't tell her Seth's here, please don't tell her Seth's here, I silently message Koji, desperately hoping that this is the moment we get a telepathic sibling connection. Although, knowing Koji, he won't be able to form a full sentence around Libby anyway.

Seth is still sitting on the bed, staring wide-eyed at me. I smooth my shirt down and pull my hair back up into a bun. The front door slams and Libby's giggle floats up the stairs. She'll be up here any minute. "Be right down!" I call out, hoping to stall her.

"What should I do?" Seth says quietly, but not quietly enough.

I flinch. "Just . . . can't you hide or something? In the closet maybe?"

"What? You're not serious, are you?"

"Just be quiet and stay up here! Don't you dare come down."

Hurt shoots across his face, like a beetle scuttling across a mountain trail, leaving tracks even after it has disappeared.

When we first get settled on the couch, Koji looks at me, confused, but when he says, "Where's—" I interrupt before he can say Seth's name.

"Dre's out with her sister," I say. "Shopping."

Koji frowns but keeps his mouth shut.

"Why do you want to know where Dre is?" Libby says, swatting Koji on the arm. "I thought I was your favorite!"

This is enough to distract Koji, and he doesn't ask anything else about Seth.

Libby tells us all about her trip to Hawaii, the hikes she went on, the dolphins she swam with, all the amazing seafood she had. "Oh my God, Rei, the sushi. You'd die. So much better than anything we have here. It is, like . . . real sushi? You know?"

"Sounds really . . . real," I say, distracted. How could I have left Seth up in my room like that? I feel sick.

Libby is still talking. "But you know what Hawaii didn't have? Decent Mexican food! We went to this one place and it was all wrong. I'm dying for a real taco. Want to go to Cactus Tacos?"

I do actually. I want to get in Libby's little silver car and go for tacos and forget about Seth. I want to make plans for the rest of the summer and talk about the parties we want to throw in the fall and gossip about who has hooked up with who . . .

Oh God. Seth and I fall into that category. Thinking about people talking about me and Seth hooking up makes me really dizzy. What am I doing? It was one thing when it was us out in the desert, us up on the Ferris wheel, even us up in my room, but if it gets out . . . I shake my head, banishing the thought. That won't happen.

"Let's go," I say, standing up. I need to get out of here before Libby goes up to my room or Seth comes downstairs.

My brother's eyebrows wrinkle together. It's the same face he's made since he was a baby whenever he's perplexed. I know he's going to mention Seth again, so when Libby looks down at her phone, I mouth "Please" to him. He shrugs, but his eyebrows stay furrowed.

And I leave. I don't go upstairs. I don't say goodbye to Seth. I walk out of the door and get in Libby's car, and we drive away.

I get out my phone and send a single text.

I'm sorry.

He doesn't reply.

CHAPTER 26

LIBBY AND I GO GET tacos, but I'm distracted the whole time. And I know she can tell something is off, but she doesn't know what.

"Sorry I'm a little out of it," I say as we drive back to my house. "I've got a headache."

"No worries," she trills.

As we pull up in front of my driveway, I get a text from Koji.

That was really weird. Seth left btw. Didn't say anything to me, just left.

"Who is it?" Libby asks.

"Just Koji. Wants to know if I'm bringing him back food."

"Aw, we should have!"

"It's fine. I'll order him something," I say. "See you on Monday?"

"Bye, babe!" She blows me a kiss, and I do the same.

After I get out of the car, I wait for Libby to drive away, and then I get straight into my car and drive to Seth's.

* * *

The moon is high as I pull up in front of Seth's place. The days are so long in the summer; I can't believe this is the same day that we went to the fair, the same day he made his big confession, the same day we kissed. It all seems so long ago, and it was only a few hours. I wish I could go back and start this day again. I don't know what I would do differently, but I'd do it better.

The curtain in Seth's bedroom window flickers. He knows I'm here. I wait for him to come outside. He doesn't.

I get out of the car and go up to the window and knock on it. The curtain flickers again but doesn't open. "Seth!" I call. I know he can hear me.

"Reiko, is that you?" Seth's mom has opened the door. I didn't realize she was home. "What are you doing hollering at Seth's window? Why didn't you ring the doorbell like a normal person?"

I smile at her. "How are you?" I ask, ignoring her question. I can't exactly say, *I was worried he wouldn't come to the door because he's mad at me.*

I guess the possibility of me having an awkward encounter with his mom overrules Seth's anger because he shoots out of his room and out of the front door so fast he nearly knocks us both over.

"We're going on a drive," he calls out over his shoulder as he jogs to my car.

"Of course you are," says his mom. "That's all you two ever do. Go on drives and waste gas and waste time." Her indulgent smile belies her words.

"Nice to see you," I say.

I get back in my car and unlock the door for Seth, who gets in without a word. I start to drive into the deepening dark, not knowing where we're going. I just drive. And drive. Neither of us says a word.

Finally, after the silence gets so thick I'm worried I'll choke on it, I say something.

"I really am sorry."

"About what?"

I frown. "About . . . leaving you."

"Is that it?"

"What do you mean?"

"You aren't sorry you told me to hide in the closet? You aren't sorry you left me up in your room for such a long time?"

I take a deep breath. "I'm sorry for that, too. I'm sorry about all of it. Okay? This . . . it is just a lot. I need a little bit of time. To get used to everything."

"To get used to me?" The strain in his voice makes it unfamiliar.

"No." I glance over at him. He's turned away from me and is staring out the window. "No, not you. Just . . . to us, I guess. I don't know. It's stupid. I'm sorry, okay? I'll make it up to you." I don't know how, though.

I turn down a road we've been down before, wondering if this is going to be one of those nights where we don't find anything magical.

"Hey, stop the car," Seth says. "I think I see something." And for a second, his voice sounds normal, the way it used to.

I stop the car, and we get out. Seth leads, and I follow.

At first all I see are cacti, but then as we go closer, I gasp. The cacti are all covered in hundreds of white and yellow blossoms. They look like stars fell from the sky and got caught on the cacti needles. The cacti are dripping in stars.

"Night flowers," I breathe. I reach out, carefully so I don't prick myself, and stroke one of the petals. It's like we're in an enchanted garden. "My mom's told me about these. I don't know if these are the right kind, but some night flowers are paired. If you pluck one, another one on the cactus will die."

"That's bleak," says Seth. He's inspecting one of the blossoms.

"Or romantic."

"We could try it," he suggests.

"Plucking one?" The idea horrifies me. "No way."

"Why not? It's just a flower," says Seth, and with precision he pulls one of the blossoms off the cactus. "Ow. I got pricked."

"Serves you right." I turn away from him and back to the flowers. "You should have left it alone."

The smell of the flowers is intoxicating and heady. I feel like if I inhale too deeply, I'll fall under a spell. I could spend all night here, but I can tell Seth is antsy. He's usually just as excited as I am about our desert discoveries, but maybe he's distracted by everything that has been happening between us.

"Can we go now?" he asks after a while.

"Sure," I say, blowing kisses to the flowers as we leave.

* * *

Back in the car, I can't stop talking. "Those flowers! They were incredible! I didn't even think they were real. It was like . . . magic."

"They weren't magical," Seth scoffs. "Just because something is hidden doesn't make it magical."

"Sometimes it does," I say, still thinking about the night flowers winking in the moonlight. Like stars you could smell.

"Is that what makes me special?" he says. "What makes us *special*?"

"What?" I slide my eyes away from the road and over to him, and the car skids, sending billowing clouds of sand and dust up around the wheels and in front of the windshield.

"Jesus! Watch it, Reiko!" Seth cries out.

I pull over properly. "Sorry," I say, breathing heavily. "I . . . I thought I saw something in the road."

"Are you sure you weren't just startled by what I said?"

I turn to look at him. "Don't be ridiculous."

He ignores me. "So, am I just going to be a secret? Is *this* going to be a secret?"

"I don't even know what 'this' is!" I say, resting my head on the steering wheel. "Seth, maybe, maybe we should . . ."

"Should what?" His voice sounds like it is coming from far away.

"I don't know. Maybe just go back to how things were?"

He laughs and it is a mirthless sound, nothing like the barking joy that I'm used to. "Go back to what? To me hoping that one day you'd see me as more than a friend?"

"But . . . you *are* my friend," I say.

A car roars past us, the headlights illuminating Seth's face. He looks pained. I hate seeing how hurt he is. I hate knowing I'm the one who is hurting him.

"I don't think I can be just your friend anymore, Reiko," he says. "I don't think I can go back." His voice shrinks to a whisper. "I thought, maybe, you wanted this, too?"

"I don't know what I want." And I think that's the first honest thing I've said to him in days.

"Can we at least try? Just give me a chance. Give us a chance."

Another car flies by, and I turn my face away so Seth can't see my expression as I try to think about what will change. I can imagine it in the summer. I don't think it'll be that different, but when we go back to school, back to real life . . . I wonder where Seth will fit in with my friends, where he will fit in with my life.

I still have a few weeks to figure that out. At the moment all I know is that I can't lose him.

I turn toward him and take his hand. "Okay," I say. "We can try whatever this is. But for now, we keep it between us, okay?"

Seth squeezes my hand. "What about when we go back to school?"

I squeeze back. "We'll figure something out." Because I'm sure we will. I just don't know what.

CHAPTER 27

I SEE SETH ALMOST EVERY day the following week. We make out in my car and in my room and even against the big boulders next to his trailer. He's still a sloppy kisser, and a lot of the time when his tongue is in my mouth, my brain goes haywire because it's *Seth Rogers* and we're kissing and it doesn't make sense. But other times, when we're out exploring, I'm happier than I've been in a very long while. I think if he had it his way, we'd just kiss all the time, though. But even with all the kissing, it doesn't start to sink in how much we are really becoming an actual *couple* until he asks if I want to go to the movies.

"Why don't we just watch a movie at my place?" I say, because people from our school might be at the movie theater, and I'm still not ready to share whatever it is that is happening between us.

"There's this new horror movie out," he says. "It looks really good."

"I don't like horror movies. You know that. And I especially don't like them on the big screen."

"But I really want to see this one, and I want to see it in the theater."

"Then go with someone else," I say, rolling down my window. We're on our way back from a hike, and I'm sweaty and hot and all I want is to take a shower and maybe a nap.

"Who?"

"I don't know," I admit.

"Reiko, I want to go with you. Come on. We always do what you want to do."

"That's because what I want to do is what you want to do."

He laughs, and it isn't a kind laugh and it isn't a cruel laugh. It is somewhere right in-between. "No, that's just what you think."

"What?"

He shrugs. "I mean, I like going out in the desert and stuff, too, and I like being with you, but it's all really your thing."

"But . . . but don't you feel the magic? Like the night flowers?"

"Reiko . . . you know magic isn't real, right? We just find random shit. It's cool, but it's not magical."

Random shit. I bite my lip and grip the steering wheel with both hands.

"Anyway, can we go to the movie tonight?" he persists. "Please? And then tomorrow we can do whatever you want."

"Fine," I say, and he grins. "But not in Palm Springs. We can go to the theater in Cathedral City. And not tonight; we can go tomorrow."

His grin slips off, but he nods. "Whatever you want, Reiko. Like usual."

We hold hands the whole movie, and I spend 95 percent of it with my eyes shut and face buried in Seth's shoulder. I can't block out the sounds, though, and the sounds are the worst part. All the stabbing and groaning and screaming.

"So, what did you think?" Seth asks as we walk back to my car.

"It was awful."

"How do you know? You had your eyes closed the whole time. It was excellent. You missed out."

"I'm choosing the next movie." I think about the kind of movies I like. The foreign films I watch with my parents, and the cheesy romances that Dre and I watch together, and the big sweeping period films like *Titanic* that I watch with my mom.

I tell Seth this, but he doesn't seem to hear me. "You choose everything all the time," he says.

"You chose dinner and the movie tonight."

"Hey, there's a first time for everything, right?"

I don't like how he's being, but I can't put my finger on why it is bothering me so much.

"Let's go on a drive," I say when we're in the car. I think that will help make me feel better about everything. Feel better about him.

"All right," he says. Then he pokes me in the side. "If that's what *you* want."

I don't answer. I just drive.

We drive for about an hour, but we don't find anything special. I can't shake the feeling that the reason we can't find anything is because of what Seth said yesterday. That it was all just "random shit" and nothing special, nothing magical. Seth doesn't even seem bothered that we haven't found anything tonight. He's whistling to himself, and his hand is on my thigh. I'm about to ask him why he never told me that he thought it was all a bit silly when he looks out the window and grins.

"Hey! This looks like a good spot," he says.

And I'm so relieved that I pull over without a word. I'm about to get out of the car to see what we've found, and I hope it is something *amazing*, something he won't be able to dismiss as "random shit," when he grabs my face and kisses me. Hard.

I pull back. "I thought you said this was a good spot?"

"It is," he says, leaning back toward me. "For this."

So we keep kissing.

And kissing.

And his hand is creeping up under my shirt, and it isn't that I'm a prude, but I'm just getting a little bored.

I push his hand away.

"Don't you think kissing gets . . . a little boring after a while?" I ask. I wonder how we can have so much chemistry out in the desert and so little between our lips.

"You read my mind," he says, reaching for the top button of his jeans.

"Oh whoa, that is not what I meant," I say, laughing a bit. But it isn't a full laugh. It's a wisp of one.

"Wait, so you meant you think kissing me is boring?"

"I mean, it is fine for a bit—"

"*Fine?* Kissing me is just *fine?*"

"Why are you getting so worked up?"

"Because my girlfriend doesn't like kissing me."

"Who said I'm your girlfriend?" I say, starting to feel trapped in my car. "Why can't we just . . . *be?*"

"Well, if you aren't my girlfriend, what are you?"

"I thought we were taking some time to get used to this. To figure it out. We don't need to label everything."

"Right, because labeling it would mean you would have to tell people about it. Don't pretend you aren't embarrassed to be dating me. I know you are."

"That isn't it," I say. "Why are you being so pushy?"

"You only like me when I'm compliant and happy to just do your bidding. You never think about what I want."

"What are you talking about?"

"You're selfish and spoiled, and usually you can get away with it, because you're beautiful and charming."

"If you think this conversation is going to help convince me to be your girlfriend . . ."

"That's what I mean!" he says, throwing his hands up in the air. "I shouldn't have to convince you. Do you like me or not?"

"I do," I say. "Of course I do. But, maybe, we should take a couple of days apart. Just to get a little space to figure this all out."

Seth sighs and lifts his shoulders up around his ears. He looks like he's trying to make himself disappear. "Sure, Reiko. Whatever you want. Like always."

We drive back to his place in silence.

"So I'll see you in a few days?" I say.

"Sounds like a plan," he says, and his voice is scratchy.

We don't kiss good night.

CHAPTER 28

WHEN I MEET UP WITH Dre and Libby for coffee the next day, I'm sharper than I usually am. Stuff with Seth is making me jittery. I don't like that he called me spoiled. How can a person who has lost so much be spoiled? But still, his comment cut closer than I'd like, and so did his claim that I only like him because we do what I want to do. Like he's some sort of subject, bowing to my every wish. It isn't like that. *We* aren't like that. I just need a little space to figure out my feelings.

Dre and Libby can tell something is up. They keep exchanging meaningful looks that they think I can't see. So I'm not that surprised when Andrea waltzes into my room a few days later and says the bouncer at Morongo—the one her sister knows—is working this Friday, and it is the perfect chance for us to go clubbing before summer ends.

"We gotta live it up, right?" she says.

"Right," I say.

And it is just the thing to get my mind off Seth and how . . . weird things have gotten between us recently.

I sneak a look at my mom's calendar and see that she and my dad will be at a benefit dinner on Friday. Perfect. The girls and I can pregame at my place before we go out.

And for just one night, I'll pretend that whatever is happening between me and Seth isn't happening, and I'll just go out with my girls.

I'll pretend that everything is the way it used to be. Before I met Seth.

Friday night is surprisingly cool for late August in Palm Springs. Tori, Dre, and Libby come over just after five. Tori's friends are meeting us at the club. She's here to help us get ready—to help us look twenty-one instead of seventeen.

"Come on, Rei," says Tori, looking me up and down appraisingly. "Let's glam you up a bit. No one is gonna believe you are twenty-one with that baby face."

"I don't have a baby face," I protest, but Tori is already brandishing eyeliner at me. "Close your eyes, baby doll," she says.

After she's done, the liner is so thick it looks like she put it on with a crayon. I smudge it a bit when she isn't looking, trying to make it a little more smoky, a little more me. We're sitting on the floor in front of my mirrored closet door, and Andrea and Libby are watching from the bed, makeup scattered all around them.

"Lipstick," says Tori, and Dre obediently tosses her a bright red lip liner and matching lipstick. "Open," Tori says to me, as if she's performing surgery and not just putting on my lipstick. "Purse . . . Now rub."

"Damn, you look hot," says Libby. She's hopped off the bed and is crouched down next to us to watch Tori do her magic. "Tori, do me next?"

"You babies need me for everything." Tori leans back to admire her handiwork. *"Tori, get me into the club! Tori, do my makeup! Tori, Tori, Tori."*

"You love it," says Dre, and Tori doesn't deny it. She's the ultimate big sister. She's what I would want if I still had a big sister.

Tori's expression changes from one of critical inspection to soft concern. "You all right, Rei-Rei?"

"I'm good," I say. Then I push my thoughts away and grin as wide as I can, like a jack-o'-lantern. "Who wants a drink?"

A drink turns into two, then three, and I lose track at four. And I'm relieved because when I'm drunk, I don't think about Mika, I don't think about Seth. I just live right in this moment. We jump on my bed, singing at the top of our lungs, and I could stay here all night. I'd have as much fun, if not more, in my house . . . but the girls want to go out, and they expect me to as well. I'm Reiko the party girl. Plus, my parents will be home soon.

"Koj!" I call from the top of the stairs. "Tell Mom and Dad that I'm sleeping at Dre's!"

"'Kay!" he calls back. It is only when we are tromping across the living room behind him—*tromping* is the only word for four drunk girls in high heels on a hardwood floor—that he looks up from his video game.

"Whoa," he says, eyebrows raised. "You look, um . . ."

"I look what?"

"A little . . . um . . . exposed."

Libby cackles. "That's the point, little brother. How do I look?" She leans forward suggestively, pouting.

Koji turns bright red.

"Libbs, knock it off," I say, but I'm laughing. It's funny. It is all so funny. Us, drunk in my house. Libby, hitting on Koji. Although I'm not sure I actually like Libby hitting on my little brother.

"Where are you really going?" Koji asks.

"You won't tell?"

Koji rolls his eyes. "Come on, Rei."

"Yeah, come on, Rei. Have a little faith in little brother." Libby is still batting her lashes and shimmying in his direction.

Koji is studiously not looking at her, and I love him all the more for it.

"We're going to Morongo to see DJ Falcon," Libby says. "Tori, can't we sneak Koji in, too?"

"Seriously?" says Koji, eyes wide. "That would be so sick!"

"No way, sweet pea," Tori scoffs, rolling her eyes at me. "One thing to get you girls in, a whole other thing to get an actual child into a nightclub."

"I'm almost fifteen!" Koji exclaims.

I laugh and hiccup. "Koj, you just turned fourteen."

"Exactly," says Tori. "An actual child."

"Next summer," I say to my brother. "Promise."

Libby twirls around in her heels. "I'm ready to dance, bitches!"

"Don't tell Mom," I say to Koji, and if he hears the slur in my voice, he ignores it.

"I won't," he says testily before turning back to his video game. And then quieter, not looking at us: "Be careful."

I totter over to him and lean down and give him a hug. "I love you," I declare, and he shrugs me off. "Ahem. I said I love you." It's important to me that he knows this. I don't think I tell him enough. And I need to know he loves me, too, that I'm being a good sister, even if I'll never be the kind of sister Mika was.

"Yeah, yeah, love you, too," he says, eyes still on the screen. "Have fun."

My phone rings. The car is here. Or maybe it has been here awhile and the driver is calling back because we are taking too long? I can't remember.

As we head down the driveway, I look up at my bedroom. The lights are off, but I can see a shadow in the window. Mika. Watching us leave. I feel a sharp pang, like stepping on a pin. I should be staying at home with her and Koji. I shouldn't leave them.

But Libby and Dre are pulling on me, dragging me toward them, giggling and glittering, and I follow their light into the car. Into the dark.

CHAPTER 29

MORONGO HAS STYLED ITSELF LIKE a miniature Las Vegas casino and club. Or at least that is what Tori always says. I've never been to Vegas.

Tori gives the burly bouncer a big hug, and then he looks at our faces, looks at our bodies, shrugs, puts a stamp on our wrists, and steps aside, like he does every time we come.

It's loud inside. Loud and crowded. For a minute, I feel like the walls are closing in on me, like the people are going to trample me, like I won't be able to breathe . . .

"Isn't this awesome?" Dre shouts in my ear. "Let's get a drink and dance!"

A fog machine and a strobe light go off at the same time, and it is like the whole crowd has never seen something so amazing because everyone starts yelling and jumping and dancing together. Dre grabs my hand and pulls me into the middle of it. As long as I've got Dre, I'll be okay. She'll keep me afloat.

* * *

I'm sweaty. So sweaty. Dre and I are standing at the bar. Libby is in the crowd with Tori and her friends. Someone taps my shoulder and I jump, sure that it is the bouncer kicking me out.

But it isn't the bouncer. It's a guy who looks like Chris Hemsworth. Blond, tan, a little rugged.

He leans toward me. "Hey, can I buy you and your friend a drink?"

I catch Dre's eyes over his shoulder.

"Your call," she mouths.

What's the point of going to a real club if we're going to play it safe? We came out to party, after all.

"Sure," I say. "That would be great."

"What are you having?"

I can't think of the name of a single drink. I want to be cool and sophisticated.

"Sex on the Beach!" I say. Dre giggles, and I'm suddenly very grateful it is so dark in the club because I'm sure I'm turning red.

The guy just nods and orders the drinks. I can't imagine any guy at my school not making a big deal about the name of the drink.

"He's super hot, but I think he's older than us," Dre whisper-shouts in my ear as the guy pays.

"Of course he's older than us," I whisper-shout back. "Isn't that why we came here? To get drinks from older guys?"

"I thought we came to dance."

"We can dance in my room. What's the point of going clubbing if we aren't going to talk to people?"

"You're right," says Dre. "And he is really hot. And totally into you."

"You think?"

"Totally. And I don't want to third-wheel."

Before I can tell her she isn't third-wheeling, the guy passes us our drinks. "So," he says. I notice he's talking to me, not to Dre.

"I'm Reiko," I say. "And this is Andrea."

"I'm Charlie. I've been watching you all night."

I don't know if I should be flattered or creeped out, but I think I'm a little bit of both.

"You two are the prettiest things in here," he says. And now I know I should be flattered.

Dre winks at me and downs her drink in one gulp. "I've got to find my sister," she says. "But thanks for the drink!" For a second, I want to chase after her. But I remind myself that I'm here to have a good time. To distract myself.

"What about you, Keko? Are you going to disappear?" Charlie smiles at me.

"It's Reiko," I say, but I don't know if he hears me.

"Want to dance?" He is looking at me like I really am the prettiest girl in here. No, more than pretty, like I'm *desirable*.

"Sure," I say, and I lead him out onto the dance floor.

I know I'm a good dancer. I feel confident and sexy, and I love how his eyes drink me up as I move in front of him.

Then he's pulling me closer.

"You're trouble," he shouts, his hand moving down my back, over my hips, down my butt. "I can tell. But I like a bit of trouble."

And I don't want him to know that I'm in high school. I don't want him to know that I'm scared. So I keep dancing. And when he puts his hands back on me and leans toward me, I know what he wants. But I'm more curious than anything else, and the lights are flashing and the music is loud, and it seems like the most natural thing in the world to kiss this man I've just met, so I do.

It goes on for too long, but I don't know how to get him off of me. I don't want to cause a scene. Also there is that feeling of being so wanted—a little bit like what I get from Seth—so I keep kissing him, and his stubble is rubbing against my face and he's making this kind of groan in the back of his throat that I can hear over the music and we're still kissing and I'm not really into it anymore, and I know with a sudden clarity that it is wrong wrong wrong and we shouldn't be doing it. I don't even really want to be kissing him. I want to be kissing *Seth*, and I rear my head back and pull away from him.

"What's wrong?" he asks, looking dazed.

"I've got to find my friends!" I say, wishing Dre had never left me. Wishing this guy had stayed as the hot guy who bought us drinks. Not the stranger I made out with on the dance floor.

His eyes harden and his face changes. "You goddamn tease," he says, and his hand grabs my arm like a vise. "I know what you and your friends are like. Think that guys should just buy you a drink for the hell of it."

I yank my arm out of his grasp and push my way through the crowd, heart pounding. *Where is Dre where is Dre where is Dre where is Dre?* I finally find her puking in the bathroom.

"Dre, I have to go home," I tell her when she's finished.

She looks up at me with bleary eyes. "Libby saw you making out with that guy." She gives me a thumbs-up. "I knew he was into you."

"I don't know if I was into him," I say.

"Then why were you kissing him?" she asks, words slurring.

"I don't know," I say, feeling miserable.

"You coulda come with me when I left. I just didn't want to be a cockblock," she says, and then vomits again.

I find Tori and Libby on the dance floor. "Dre's drunk!" I shout.

Libby shimmies up to me. "So am I! So are you!"

"No! She's sick! We have to go!" I keep looking over my shoulder for Charlie.

We finally leave. As we walk out, I think I hear someone shout my name, but when I look back over my shoulder, all I see are strangers.

CHAPTER 30

I WAKE UP IN DRE'S bed with a pounding headache, a sick stomach, and a guilty heart.

Then Seth calls and asks if I can come over.

"I don't know," I say, shutting my eyes against the light that is blaring through Dre's windows. "I don't feel very well." It isn't a lie.

"Yeah, I bet," he says, and something in his tone—dismissive, mocking, rude—makes my eyes fly open.

"Excuse me?" I say. My stomach is churning, and I know I'm going to be sick.

"Just come over," he says, then hangs up.

Dre rolls over next to me. "Who is calling you so early?" she groans. "Please tell me it is someone who is going to bring us pizza. I need pizza. Or tacos. Or maybe pizza and tacos."

"Will you two shut up?" Libby moans from the floor. She's still in her dress from last night and is wearing one high heel. At least I managed to put on a pair of Dre's pajamas.

"I've gotta go," I say, getting up out of Dre's bed.

"To get me pizza?" Dre says hopefully.

"I've just . . . gotta go," I say. "Can I borrow something?" There is no way I am going over to Seth's in what I wore to the club last night. I don't ever want to wear this dress again. I want to forget about this dress and forget about the night and pretend it never happened.

Dre gestures at her closet. "Mi casa, su casa," she says. "Or I guess, mi armario, su armario."

I shower first, and by the time I go back into Dre's room, she and Libby are snoring again.

I have a text from Seth: *Are you coming over or what?*

I don't like the feeling that he is summoning me.

I don't like the realization that maybe I've been taking Seth's affection for granted, like something I could never lose.

Most of all, I don't like the feeling that I've done something very, very wrong.

The whole drive over to Seth's house, I wonder if I should tell him about the kiss. He doesn't need to know, surely. It was a stupid mistake. Everyone makes mistakes.

When Seth opens the door, I lean in to kiss him, suddenly desperately needing to kiss him, as if kissing him will cancel out kissing that guy in the club last night. But he pulls away from me, and instead of letting me in, he steps around me, shutting the door behind him.

His blue eyes are steely, and he's looking at me in a way he's never, ever looked at me before. Like I'm something dirty that he's stepped in, something he wants to get away from.

"My mom saw you at Morongo last night," he says, and my lungs must have shrunk because all of a sudden I can't breathe. I tell myself to calm down. So she saw me. That doesn't mean she saw me kiss a guy on the dance floor.

"But that you didn't see her," he adds.

"Oh," I say. Like it is no big deal. "Is she here?"

He shakes his head. "No. But even if she was, I don't think she'd want to see you. I don't even know if *I* want to see you. But . . . I want to at least hear it from you. The truth."

I swallow. I feel like I might pass out.

"I don't know what you mean," I say, because maybe Lucille didn't see the kiss. Maybe she is mad at me because she saw me stumbling out of the club, drunk.

"So I really have to ask, huh?"

I put my hand on the door frame because I'm about to fall over.

"Did you kiss someone at the club?" Seth says. His voice is a dead thing.

"Seth," I say, and my heart contracts. Because I do care about him—our nights in the desert, our exploring—and I don't want to lose him.

"Did you kiss him?" he asks again.

"Seth." I make my voice as light as I can, and I press myself against him, and whisper in his ear, "I was out with the girls."

He is a statue.

"Did you kiss him?"

I wonder if I could lie and say his mom confused me with someone else, some other Asian girl. It was dark in the club, after all.

But my hesitation is answer enough. I push my shoulders back, trying for defiance.

"I was drunk," I say. "I was just dancing."

"With your lips?"

"Okay," I say, and I close my eyes. "I think I might have kissed a guy last night. But like I said, I was drunk."

"You were drunk." The robot voice is back. "Are you trying to say he took advantage of you?"

There is a sliver of hope in the question, and for a moment, I consider telling him that I had blacked out. That I didn't remember kissing that guy until Dre told me about it this morning.

But that thought goes up in flames as I realize what he's asking me. What he's hoping. He's hoping, actually *hoping*, that I was taken advantage of. That, to him, is preferable to me *choosing* to kiss someone.

Who hopes that someone they care about has been taken advantage of?

I stare at Seth, suddenly feeling like he's a stranger. "*I* kissed him," I say, with emphasis. "I was drunk, but I knew what I was doing." Because I did. I wanted it. At first.

My words detonate, and after the explosion I'm surprised we're still standing, staring at each other.

"All right, then," says Seth. Which is what I was hoping he would say, but . . . something is off. Something is wrong.

"All right?" I ask.

He shrugs, eyes slightly unfocused, not looking at me, looking over my shoulder.

"So, we're okay?" But what I mean is, *Do you forgive me?* My voice is at a pitch it's never been with Seth. Never been with anyone. Because I suddenly realize just how big of a mistake I've made. That technically, I cheated on him. Because even if I hadn't said I was his girlfriend, and even if we hadn't told anyone we were together, in his head, we were. And in my head, too.

"That's not what I said."

I shake my head, as if I could shake this whole conversation away, this whole situation, and start again.

"Seth," I say, leaning into him again, and when he stiffens and *pulls away from me . . .* something twists inside of me, and I start to wonder why I told him the truth. I feel like the ground has shifted beneath my feet, and I feel scared again, out of control, like I did with that guy last night.

"Seth," I say again. I want to tell him that I stopped kissing the guy because of him, because I realized I like him, Seth. *I finally realized it.* But I can't say that because it doesn't sound right and I know it won't make it better.

I reach for him again, and this time when he pulls back, it's like he's snatched a life ring out of my hands and left me stranded and drowning, and I can't think about drowning—I won't think about drowning—because Seth takes me away from all that, from the memories of Mika. I'm in control when I'm with him. I'm safe in the desert, far away from the ocean. But something is wrong wrong wrong. This isn't how this conversation was meant to go . . . It should have never happened, and I need to fix it . . . I'll fix it . . .

I press my lips to his, but his mouth is hard and unyielding. It is like kissing stone.

"Come on, Seth," I say, pleading now. "It was just a kiss."

"I think you should go home."

"You can't . . . you can't . . . be mad at me?"

His laugh is harsh. "Apparently, I can be."

I feel the heat rising to my cheeks.

"That isn't what I meant." Even though that is exactly what I meant. "What I meant was—"

His gaze sharpens. "I know *exactly* what you meant, Reiko." He folds his arms across his chest. "I guess I should have expected something like this. But I didn't want to, you know? I wanted you to be perfect."

"Nobody's perfect, Seth."

"I know that now," he says with a sneer.

"Jesus, Seth! It was a kiss. A kiss! Give me a break!" I know I was wrong to do it, but still, it was just a kiss. A stupid kiss that I wish I could take back.

"What? Am I supposed to be grateful you didn't sleep with him? Just a kiss? Was it *boring* like it is with me?"

"Please, Seth . . ."

He backs up again, farther, and I want to go toward him, but a chasm has opened up between us and I'm scared that if I take one step closer, I'll fall into it and fall and fall until I disappear.

"You did this, Reiko. You did this, remember? You told me *you* kissed him."

I bite my lip to keep it from trembling:

the guy's hands on my hips

pulling me into him

the flutter of excitement turning into panic

and the feeling I got when he looked at me

like I was the prettiest thing he'd ever seen

and I let it happen.

I kissed him back. Because I was curious to take a bite out of what is always being offered to me. Because I'd tasted it with Seth—the feeling of being desired more than anything else—and I wanted more. The music was loud and my head was buzzing and I looked sexy and I felt sexy and I wanted to *be* sexy.

But it wasn't sexy.

Because the guy didn't even know my name.

And Seth looks at me like I'm Reiko, like a better Reiko than I'll ever be. He sees a Reiko I want to be.

And I thought I could bury what happened at the club forever and pretend it never happened.

But I can't. I can't ever forget it now. Seth won't ever let me forget it now.

"I *was* drunk," I offer limply. "And he . . . he approached me . . ."

"And you what?" Seth's eyes are burning. "Told him to go to hell? Because that is what you should have done."

Should.

What is the use of a word like *should*? It clings to you and drags you down. *Should should should.* I should have held tighter to Mika. I should never have let her go. But you can't ever go back to fix something. So *should* shouldn't even matter.

"I was stupid, okay? People are stupid. People make mistakes. Even me, Seth. Even I make mistakes." And I want to cry because the biggest mistake I ever made was five years ago, on a beach, with my sister.

"Reiko, were you even going to tell me? If my mom hadn't seen you?"

I hesitate, only for a second, but it is too long.

And then we stand, staring at each other across this chasm I've created. I keep looking in his eyes, but they look like a stranger's eyes—as unfamiliar as the guy's from last night, and I wonder if Seth does really know me. If I really know him.

He runs his hand through his hair and takes a step back.

"I need some time," he says. "To process everything." And then he gives me a mean little smile, and it is like someone has slashed a knife across his face. "You should be all right with that, right? I gave *you* time, didn't I?"

"Sure," I say, hugging my body and taking a step away from him. "Whatever you need."

What you need is me. Please need me.

CHAPTER 31

I KNOW MIKA WON'T UNDERSTAND what has happened, or why I'm so upset.

So I go back to Dre's.

Luckily, Libby has left and it is just her. "You okay?" she asks. "You left super fast this morning and seemed upset."

"I think I like Seth Rogers," I say without preamble. "And . . . we've sort of been seeing each other. In secret. And his mom saw me kiss that guy at the club and now he knows and now he hates me and I've screwed everything up."

Dre is watching me closely, eyes narrowed and focused as I stumble over the words, trying to explain. She holds up her hand, silencing my wobbling confession. "Rei," she says, frowning, "why are you so upset?"

"What do you mean?" I sputter. "Haven't you been listening?"

"I just don't get it. Like, are you actually into him?"

"Yes!"

"Then why was it some big secret? You could have told us."

When she says it like that, so simply, I don't know why I wanted to keep it a secret. Just that I did. But now that Seth is slipping through my fingers, I want to tell people about us because I've realized that it is the only way I can hold on to him. Because that's what he wants: to be in my life. My real life. Not just my midnight-moonlit life.

"I don't know," I say, my voice quiet. "I should have told you. I'm sorry."

"It isn't about me," says Dre, scooting closer to me and rubbing my back. "I don't think I'm the one you should be saying sorry to."

"I've already said sorry to Seth. I don't think he's forgiven me. I'm not sure he's going to."

Dre blows air out of the side of her mouth. "Whoever thought that Seth Rogers would be forgiving *you* for anything? You spend too much time in the sun." She sits back and scrutinizes me some more. "All right, if this is what you want, you know I've got your back. I mean, weirder things have happened. But, Rei, it doesn't seem like it is making you very happy. You are all jumpy and nervous. And you were weird even before we went to Morongo."

"I was weird because I didn't like keeping it a secret," I say. Which is mostly the truth.

Dre shrugs. "My mom always says sunlight is the best disinfectant. Being honest about this is going to make it better." She shakes her head again. "I should have known. You should have told me."

"Dre, what am I going to do?"

"Hon, what do you *want* to do?"

I pull my knees up to my chest and rock back and forth. "I just want to fix it, because this is something I can fix."

Dre reaches out and holds my hand. She knows this isn't just about Seth anymore. "Of course you can," she says.

CHAPTER 32

I'VE BEEN SITTING OUTSIDE SETH'S trailer for the past hour. He's ignoring my calls. *Seth* is ignoring *my* calls.

Seth is ignoring *me*.

A light goes on inside and then the door to his trailer opens and a figure stands silhouetted in the doorway. It's dark and ominous, and almost unrecognizable as Seth. I'm momentarily scared to walk toward him, this stranger, but after a minute, I get out of the car and go toward him.

"What do you want, Reiko?" he says, and his voice is weary. Like he's tired. Tired of *me*.

"I wanted to see you. I want to make it up to you. Kissing that guy . . . I shouldn't have done that."

I'm close enough now that I can see the effect that my words have on him. He closes his eyes and his jaw tightens.

"Come on," I say, making my voice low and husky and reaching for his hand. Whatever happens tonight will shape how things are going to be with us from now on, and I need to take control. I need to be the one to decide how things are going to be.

He lets me take his hand, and when I pull, he follows.

"I can't say no to you," he says, and there is no warmth in the statement. Just tired resignation. But still, hearing him say it calms my galloping heart.

"Come on," I whisper again, and we disappear into the darkness.

Kissing him is easier than it has been before. I would have to gear myself up for it before, tell myself that yes, I did want to kiss him. But now that he might not want it, might not want *me* . . . I want it more, because I want him to want me. I want him back the way it was.

I press my lips against his, my mouth hungry and searching, and I run my hands up under his shirt. I can feel his body reacting against mine, and the thrill that goes through me is something primal. He's right. He can't say no to me.

Kissing Seth is how I'll keep him.

That, and one other thing.

"We can tell people," I whisper against his jaw.

"Tell them what?"

"Tell them that we're together."

"Are we?"

I push myself off of him. "Isn't that what you want?"

"I thought it was."

Was. Past tense. My head feels too heavy for my body. Like it is going to topple to the ground and pull me with it. And it'll be too heavy for me ever to get back up again.

"We'll really be together," I manage. My eyes search his, but it is too dark to see what is reflected there.

"I thought we already were together," he says, closing his eyes, closing himself. "Didn't you say that it didn't matter if other people knew? That we knew we were together and that was enough? And that other people would ruin it?" His voice is trembling.

"Please," I say, and this makes him open his eyes.

"Okay," he says, and everything feels upside down. I think I just asked Seth out, but I'm not sure, and I think this is what I want, but what I really want is Seth not to stare at me like I'm a monster. I want him to want me again, the way he always has, the way I've come to need him to. I can't lose that.

I can't lose him.

I've lost too much already.

CHAPTER 33

"GUESS WHAT?" I SAY.

Mom is putting on her makeup. She's going to another dinner party with my dad tonight. Sometimes I wonder if my mom feels like she has to live as much as she can, too. If all the galas and luncheons and functions do for her what the desert does for me.

Makes her feel alive.

"What, sweetie?" she asks.

"You know that guy Seth Rogers who I've been hanging out with? We're kind of dating now."

Mom pulls back from the mirror and turns to look at me. She's only finished her makeup on one eye so she looks uneven. "Really? That seems . . . a bit sudden. We haven't even met him. I wish we knew him a bit more. He didn't sound like your type from what your brother said." I know that she's saying more than that. That he doesn't seem like the type she'd want for me.

I have that dizzying sense of being on a seesaw—of trying to make everyone in my life happy, of trying to balance what is increasingly starting to feel like two lives.

Of wanting everyone to think that I'm perfect.

"Well, I guess he is," I say, tugging on a hangnail.

"Don't do that. We can go get our nails done this weekend. Is it serious?"

"What?"

"You and Seth? Is it serious? I mean, are you exclusive?"

I hesitate, not sure how to answer.

I want to tell her that I kissed a boy—no, that I kissed a *man* in a club, a strange man—and at first I liked knowing that he wanted me, that it made me feel powerful, but then when his grasp got tight, and I felt his tongue in my mouth and his stubble against my face, and he had his hands on my ass and was pulling me into him, I knew that I didn't have any power, at all. And that mistake has turned everything topsy-turvy with Seth.

"I guess we're exclusive," I say, shrugging.

"Have you told your friends?"

I scowl. "I mean, I haven't announced it or anything." There is absolutely no way I am putting this on social media.

"Dating seems so complicated now," my mom muses.

"It's fine. We're fine," I say. What I mean is, *I'm fine.* Ever since Mika died, my mom is always wondering if I'm fine.

My mom locks eyes with me in the mirror. "I never said you weren't." Then she smiles. "Well, we'll have to have him over for dinner sometime soon."

If I thought telling my mom was hard, telling Libby is practically impossible. At first, she thinks I'm joking and laughs so hard she snorts. Then, when she realizes I'm not laughing, and neither is Dre, she gets upset that Dre knew first and we have to deal with that, and then once I've mollified her enough, she turns to me with wide eyes.

"Seriously?"

"Seriously," I say, my eyes daring her to say something else.

She flops back on my bed. "He's kind of cute," she goes on slowly. "I guess. In, like, a lanky, weird kind of way."

"I think he's cute," I say, surprised by how defensive I feel.

"And that is what matters," says Dre with authority.

"Oh my God, what are you going to do at school?" Libby asks. "Are you guys going to be like . . . making out all over the place?"

"No way," I say, a bit horrified by the idea. "We're just going to be . . . normal."

"So not talk to each other at all? Because that is what you usually do at school."

I bite the inside of my cheek. "It'll be fine."

"I wonder what everyone is going to say," Libby says quietly, more to herself.

I stiffen, but before I can say anything, Dre puts her hand on my arm.

"Who gives a shit? It's Reiko. Our best friend. We don't care what everyone says."

"Obviously," says Libby, like she wasn't just wondering what people would say.

"If we act like it is normal, it is," Dre goes on.

Libby snorts again.

"Libby!"

"If you say so," she says. Then she rolls over and nudges me with her foot. "So is Seth a good kisser or what?"

CHAPTER 34

SCHOOL STARTS NEXT WEEK, SO I only have a few days left to try to make things better between me and Seth. School is going to be tricky enough without things being weird with us. If I'm going to be confident about him, I need to be confident about us.

I need to make some kind of grand gesture. He loves a grand gesture.

I've got a surprise for you, I text. *Be ready in an hour?*

It's like the dinosaur picnic all over again, but this time, I'm the one with the surprise. When I told Dre and Libby about the dinosaur picnic, they melted.

"Oh my god, that is the cutest thing EVER!" Libby cooed.

"And you ditched him to go to a party at the track?" Dre asked, eyes askance.

"You were the one who said it was going to be the party of the summer!" I protested.

"That was before I knew you were out on, like, the most romantic and creative date of all time," she said.

"Plus, it couldn't be the party of the summer without me," said Libby. "Please." She rolled over on my bed. "Who knew Seth Rogers was so romantic?"

Me! I wanted to scream, *I knew it!* I knew it and I still screwed up.

So now I'm making it better.

Seth texts me back. *K* is all I get, but I'll take it.

We've got all day. All day to go on an adventure. All day to make things better. He's quiet in the car, but the closer we get to our destination, the more his eyes light up.

"Are we going . . . up the tram?"

I grin at him. "I remember you saying that you wanted to but never had."

He grins back at me, and then it is like he remembers that he's supposed to be mad at me, because he shuts it off. The ghost of his grin lingers, though, and he still looks happy, even though he's not smiling anymore.

"Good memory," he says.

"I know what you like," I say. Because I do. I know him.

I know him.

I buy the tram tickets for both of us. The tram starts in the valley and ascends two and a half miles up the mountain. Apparently, it's the largest rotating aerial tram in the world. At least, that's what the signs tell us.

"The largest rotating aerial tram *in the world*!" I say, nudging him. "Come on, that's pretty impressive."

He shrugs. "I guess."

I nudge him again, keeping my arm close to his body. "I know you think it's cool."

His grin, the one he's playing hide-and-seek with, comes out again. "All right," he says. "It's pretty cool."

And it really is. It's like being inside a slowly spinning snow globe. As we climb, the world changes before our eyes. Cacti turn into evergreen trees, and the yellow sand of the desert gives way to a stony mountain face dotted with dirt trails and patches of green grass.

"We're going through five biomes," Seth says in my ear. Even if he's mad at me, he can't not share facts. "We started in the Sonoran Desert, the low, hot desert, and we'll pass through the Upper Sonoran, and then open woodlands, Canadian, Hudsonian, and end in the Alpine. All in twelve minutes. All on the same mountain."

"We're going through Canada?" I say, widening my eyes.

Seth snorts. "Don't play dumb, Reiko. It doesn't suit you."

"I was just kidding. You know how into natural history my dad is. Of course I know what the five biomes are. And that this mountain has all of them."

It *is* amazing, though, a bit like watching a nature documentary, when time is sped up and shows the different seasons, but it's all happening in real time, right below us.

"Rei! Look!" Seth has his nose pressed to the glass. "Quick!"

I look up just in time to see a hawk soar past, its wings spread wide. It is so close, I can even see the brown-and-white pattern on its tail feathers.

"It's beautiful," I breathe. It is the freest thing I've ever seen.

When we get to the top, we're surrounded by firs and evergreens, and the desert below looks like another planet. Seth tilts his head back to take it all in. I think he's remembering how he used to feel about me and why we make such a good team.

We wander along one of the trails, farther and farther away from the mountain tram station, farther and farther away from the people who came up in the tram with us, farther and farther away from the desert. We stop when we get to a small clearing coated in pine needles.

"Wanna play pine cone baseball?" I haven't played in years, not since I was little and my dad used to take Mika and Koji and me up here.

"What the hell is pine cone baseball?"

I pick up a large stick. "This," I say, "is our bat. And these"—I gesture to the pine cones all around us—"are our baseballs."

Seth looks skeptical.

"Oh, come on. What? Are you worried I'll beat you?"

In response, Seth picks up a pine cone and lobs it at me. I hit it so hard it explodes, raining pine cone bits all over Seth.

"I'd say that's a home run," I say, running a small victory lap around the clearing. "You're up!" I toss him the stick I used as a bat.

He catches it and then stands awkwardly next to a tree, the stick hoisted over his shoulder.

"Heeey, batta batta batta. Swing, batta batta batta," I sing out, pretending to throw the pine cone.

"Come on, throw it!" Seth shouts.

"What kind of stance is that?"

"Just throw the ball! I mean the pine cone!"

I throw and he swings wildly, so wildly he nearly knocks himself off balance and misses.

I laugh. "Strike one!"

I throw again, and again he swings and misses.

"A swing and a miss!" I call out like a sports announcer. "One more strike, and you're out!"

"Who taught you to throw like that?"

"I used to play catch with my dad for hours."

"Maybe that's why I'm so bad at sports. No dad to play catch with."

"This can't be your shtick forever, you know."

"What?"

"The whole I-don't-have-a-dad thing. Lots of people don't have dads."

"Spoken by someone who has no idea what it is like not to have a dad."

"Seth, you know I'm just trying to be helpful."

"Well, you're doing a crappy job at it," he says. Then he sighs. "Just throw the damn pine cone."

This time, I throw the pine cone straight at him.

He makes contact, and it sails up through the trees into the sky and disappears.

We both wait a minute for it to come back down. To land on our heads.

It doesn't.

After I lose count of how many pine cones we've lost and exploded, and we're both getting sweaty and hungry and tired, Seth pushes a stray hair behind my ear. His hand brushes my cheek, and it sends unexpected sparks through me.

"I worry that you're going to hurt me." Seth's voice is so quiet I almost don't hear him. He doesn't say *again*, but he doesn't have to.

"I won't hurt you," I say, and the silent *again* floats in between us.

"People never know what they'll do," he says.

CHAPTER 35

THE NIGHT BEFORE SCHOOL STARTS, Mika comes into my room. She puts her head on my shoulder. "I never got a senior year," she says, and I feel a chill dance up my neck.

"I know," I say. "So I've got to make sure mine is perfect, for both of us."

"Do you think you'll be homecoming queen? Like Mom was?"

"I hope so."

"You will be. I know it. You have to be. For me and for Mom."

"Okay, then," I say, with more confidence than I feel.

"It doesn't seem like you've been getting ready for senior year. It seems like you've just been with Seth." She wrinkles her nose in distaste.

The funny thing is that Seth isn't taking up as much of my time now as he was at the start of summer. Since what happened at Morongo, we haven't been hanging out as much. But he is taking up quite a bit of my thoughts. When I'm not with him, I'm thinking about him, and wondering if he is thinking about me. I've never felt like this about any guy. Never worried about them this much.

"I don't see what is so great about Seth," Mika grumbles. "He isn't even very handsome."

I raise my eyebrows. "What do you know about boys being handsome?"

Her face drops. "Nothing," she whispers. Then she turns away from me. "I shouldn't be here." Mika never talks about where she should or shouldn't be. I don't want her to be anywhere but here. I don't want her to disappear.

"Of course you should," I say. "Where else would you be?"

"I should be in college."

The chill spreads all over my body. And I'm reminded again again *again* how much life she'll never get to live.

"I should be playing music in college. Maybe have a boyfriend. But Koji is playing music now. And you have a boyfriend. And I have nothing."

It's then that I notice the water around my bed. It rises quickly until it is lapping at the blankets and starting to soak my pillow. It's coming higher and higher—

. . . *water, so much water . . . Mika reaching for me . . . water slapping me in the face . . . choking . . . water so much water . . .*

I wake up with a gasp.

I'm sweat-drenched, but my room is dry. There is no water anywhere.

And Mika isn't there either.

I look at my phone. It's two a.m. I wish it wasn't the night before the first day of school. I wish I was out in the desert with Seth. I wish I hadn't screwed things up with him, the one person who makes me feel like I'm just living in the moment—or at least he used to.

I wish I could go back in time and fix everything.

Bigger things than what happened with Seth.

But I can't.

After a minute's hesitation, I call him.

"Hello? Reiko? Are you all right? It's two in the morning!"

"Hey," I say, suddenly feeling shy and awkward. We've never really talked on the phone before. Nobody I know does, except me and Dre.

"Why are you calling?"

"I just wanted to talk to you."

"Reiko, we have to be up in, like, five hours. What do you want?"

His curt tone cuts through me.

"I'm sorry," I say. "I just couldn't sleep. I had a bad dream." That's the closest to the truth I can get.

"So since you couldn't sleep, you wanted to make sure I couldn't sleep either?"

"Well, no. It's just that . . ."

"What?"

"I wanted to tell you that obviously we'll hang out at school," I say, my words tumbling out faster than I mean them to.

"I mean, I'd hope so. We're dating now, right? Like, actually dating?"

There's so much venom in his voice that I hold the phone away from my ear, like it might hurt me.

This isn't the Seth I'm used to.

"Can you stay on the phone with me?" I ask.

"Look, Reiko, I've got to sleep. You do, too. I'll see you in the morning."

"Come to the back parking lot," I say, desperate to keep him on the line a bit longer. To win him over. "I'll introduce you to everyone."

He laughs a little. "Reiko, I know who all your friends are."

"You know what I mean."

"Yeah," he says, and his voice is warmer now. "That'll be cool."

"See you tomorrow," I say.

"Good night, Reiko."

I click off and turn over.

But I can't turn off the hurt buzzing inside me.

FALL

CHAPTER 36

"GUESS WHAT I DID?" LIBBY is bouncing like a rubber ball, her cheerleading skirt swishing around her hips.

We've been back at school for three weeks. After the first week, my group of friends went from seeing Seth as a bit of a novelty, like he's a goat I insisted on bringing to school, to seeing him as a real person. A person who is becoming part of our group. Libby is especially flirty nowadays, tugging on his long hair, draping herself over him in a way that would be totally unacceptable if he was anyone else, but since he's *Seth Rogers*, the new toy, it's fine.

He's goofing around with Zach, Peter, and Michael at the moment, in the parking lot where we all hang out. It's a funny thing because the boys who ignored him or picked on him for years and years are now hanging out with him. Ever since I said he was with *me*, he became one of *us*, almost like he always was.

When I see him with my friends, I wonder if someone is going to tell him about Mika. But that would be a weird thing to just bring up. And they must all assume he already knows. Because that would be the type of thing a girl would tell her boyfriend.

I just never did.

I wonder if he knows. If he's always known.

I wonder if that changes anything or doesn't matter at all.

I shake my head, shaking the thoughts away.

"I nominated Seth for homecoming court. Isn't that inspired?" Libby goes on.

"*My* Seth?" I choke out.

"*Your* Seth?" Libby's laugh tinkles like cut glass.

Dre is watching me carefully.

Help me, I tell her silently.

"Who else's Seth would he be?" Dre says, voice low.

"Oh, I'm just teasing; of course he's your Seth. Come on, Reiko! God. I thought you'd be pleased." Libby rolls her eyes. "Anyway, I nominated him! Him, Zach, Peter, Michael . . ."

I wonder if I should have nominated Seth. Since I'm his girl-friend, after all. But I feel weird about it. I don't know why. It's just that homecoming is my thing, like my friends were mine and Seth was mine. And now everything seems to be bleeding together, almost without me, and I'm not sure how I feel about it. I remember what Libby used to say about Seth. And now she's acting like he's some sort of catch. Seth has changed around Libby, too.

"I thought you said Libby was an idiot," I reminded him a couple of weeks ago after he called her cool.

"She's all right," he'd replied, shrugging and watching her walk away, hips swaying.

"Well, I nominated Reiko," says Dre now, still hovering close to me.

I grin at her. "I nominated you, too."

"Hope one of you bitches nominated me," Libby says.

"I did," Megan says.

"Aw, babe!" Libby coos, linking her arm through Megan's and staring pointedly at me and Dre. This has been happening more and more recently. We've never hung out with Megan that much outside of school, but in school it always used to feel like we were a four. Now it feels decidedly like a two and two. Me and Dre. Libby and Megan. Of course, we all still hang out, but . . . something is different.

And I don't like it.

Dre and I are walking back to my car after school when she stops and nudges me. "Oh my God, is that Nick Forrester?"

Nick was a senior when we were freshmen, and he was the undisputed best-looking guy in the whole school. Even when I was dating Julian, and they were friends, I would get totally tongue-tied and awkward around Nick.

And now he's walking toward us—no, not just walking, swaggering. He's grinning, too.

"Reiko Smith-Mori, right?" He doesn't say anything to Dre.

"Nice memory," I say.

He looks into my car. "This your car?"

I hold up the keys.

"Cool," he says. "I like a girl in a Jeep."

I snort. "Whatever the hell that means."

Nick hasn't aged well. He's got a beer belly that he didn't have in high school.

He shrugs and finally looks over at Dre. "I don't know if I remember you. What's your name again?"

"Andrea Torres. My older sister is Tori?"

"Oh *yeahhh*. I remember now. Didn't she throw that sick party after prom? The one that the cops busted?"

"Yep. And that's why my mom won't ever let me throw a party," says Dre.

"Man, we had some wild times here." His eyes crawl down me. "Weren't you there? With Julian?"

"Yep," I say.

"A shame he got to you before I could," he says.

"Excuse me?"

"It's a compliment," he says. "Come on."

"Whatever," I say, swallowing my anger. "What are you doing back anyway?"

"It's my mom's birthday."

"I mean back *here*, at school. In the parking lot."

He shrugs. "Thought I'd come back and see how it was holding up. See some of the guys on the team."

He misses it, I realize, with sudden clarity. He misses being king of high school. These were his glory days. I never, ever want to be like that. Like him.

"How is it in Arizona?" I ask.

"Yeah, it's all right. Why? You thinking of going there? If you want to come check out the campus, you could always stay at my place. I've got a sweet apartment."

The invitation is heavy with the other, unspoken invitation.

I flash him a smile full of teeth. "Maybe," I say. What I mean is *never*.

"I heard you're dating that Seth Rogers kid. I remember him. Real weird guy."

I stiffen. Why would Nick Forrester care who I was dating?

"Standards slipping?" he says with a sloppy grin.

"What the hell is that supposed to mean?" I say.

Dre is bristling next to me.

"You just always came off as real picky about guys. Even as a freshman. You don't meet many freshmen who are picky about what seniors they hook up with."

That's it. I don't need to put up with this crap. "What the hell?" I say. "You think you can just strut up to me and start insulting me? You don't even go here anymore."

Nick holds up his hands. "Whoa, whoa. Calm down. All I've done is compliment you. Jesus."

"Well, it didn't sound like a compliment," I say, unlocking my car. "And if you'll excuse us, we've got to get going."

"Yeah, you jackass," says Dre.

"I don't even remember you," Nick says.

"And I don't even care," Dre retorts as we get in the car. "What an ass," she says. "You okay?"

"Yeah, I'm fine."

In my rearview mirror, I see Nick go up to Seth, and they do that guy fist-bump thing, and Nick points at my car and laughs, and I can only imagine what he's saying, and I expect Seth to—I don't know—walk away at least, but instead he laughs, too.

I hope Dre didn't see.

CHAPTER 37

THE NEXT DAY, ZACH GARCIA asks Dre to homecoming by surprising her at soccer practice with the school marching band playing "I Wanna Dance with Somebody" by Whitney Houston and a huge poster asking her to go with him. So far it tops the way anyone has been asked to the dance this year. And it doesn't even mean that Zach is into Dre or anything. He just wanted to ask his date in the best way because he's competitive like that.

Because at my school, it isn't enough for someone just to ask someone to homecoming or prom. Oh no, it has to be done in a special way. It gets increasingly creative every year. Nobody wants to do something that has already been done. And if you don't ask someone in a clever way, it looks like you haven't made an effort. How you're asked can be just as big of a deal as who you're going with or what you're wearing. People go out of their way to do over-the-top dance "proposals," even if they aren't in a relationship. It is just a thing people do at our school.

Seth hasn't asked me yet. And the dance is in just two weeks. Of course we're going together, but I wish he'd hurry up and ask me.

In a way that is even better than using a marching band.

Although, ever since I saw Nick Forrester—former quarterback star and homecoming king—trying to hang on to his high school glory days, part of me doesn't care about any of this. I don't want being on homecoming court, or even being queen, to be my crowning life achievement.

But I still want it. Even though I know it is stupid. But I don't just want it for me. I want it for my mom.

I want it for Mika.

It's the week before homecoming, and Seth still hasn't asked me. And then they announce who is on homecoming court. Two of the court will be chosen as the king and queen. I'm on it. So is Libby. Dre's not. She shrugs, like she doesn't care, but I know she's stung.

And Seth's on it.

I don't believe it. For one horrible, nasty moment, I wonder if it is a joke.

What does that say about me? That I think my boyfriend getting voted popular is a joke.

Even worse:

I didn't vote for him.

I didn't want him to make court.

I'm scared that he's becoming someone else, someone I don't know, someone I don't like.

Someone who's not mine.

* * *

Finally, I ask Seth to the dance myself.

"So we're going to homecoming together, right?"

We're in my car on our way to get ice cream. It's the first time we've hung out just the two of us in weeks.

"Of course we are," he says without looking at me.

"When were you going to ask me?" I ask, trying to keep my voice casual.

"Ask you? I didn't think I had to."

"But . . . people always ask. Even if they're boyfriend and girlfriend."

"And we're definitely boyfriend and girlfriend?" he says, eyes sliding sideways at me.

My stomach does a somersault. "What? Of course we are!"

He shrugs. "Cool. I guess I never really know with you."

"What is that supposed to mean, Seth?"

"You know what it means, Reiko." I don't like how he says my name these days. "I guess I should be surprised you didn't hook up with Nick Forrester when he was in town, since you seem to have a thing for older guys these days."

I'm shocked. "Seth, that isn't fair!"

"Might not be fair, but it's true."

"Why are you being like this? We never hang out anymore, we barely talk. It's like we aren't even in a relationship."

"You just said we were." He lights a cigarette.

"Don't smoke in my car," I say.

"I think you can find it in your heart to forgive me just this once," he says, blowing a smoke ring.

CHAPTER 38

IT'S FRIDAY AND THE NIGHT of the homecoming game.
My mom does my makeup and lets me wear one of her shimmering
gold designer gowns from her days as a model. Tonight is when
they crown the king and queen, and I need something glamorous.
Something fit for a queen.

When I'm dressed, Mom tells me how beautiful I am, and I
know we're both thinking about Mika.

I have to be crowned queen tonight. It's like Mika said: It's not
just for me, it's for Mom, and for her, too.

I spend the first half of the homecoming game with the rest of the
girls on the court waiting for halftime, when we'll all be presented
and the king and queen will be crowned. We all smile and compliment each other, but there's a tension between us, especially
between me and Libby.

Libby and I have always been competitive in a way that Dre and
I haven't. It used to be fun, like a way to push ourselves. Recently,
it's had more of an edge to it, and I can't help remembering the

shady stuff Libby's done over the years. Not just hooking up with Dre's date at the dance but also copying homework and just being kind of bitchy. Fleetingly, I wonder why I hang out with her. But I remind myself she's Libby Carter and I'm Reiko Smith-Mori and, together with Andrea and Zach and everyone else, we make up the crew, and of course we hang out together.

The wind blows, ruffling my curls and sending goose bumps dancing down my shoulders. I shudder in my gold dress. The stadium lights are so bright and harsh. I hear the buzzer go off, signifying the end of the quarter, and I know it is almost time for the presentations.

We're playing a football team from some high school in the Central Valley, and their side of the stadium is almost empty. No one wants to go to a rival team's homecoming game. But our side, the home side, is spilling over with people. Everyone is wearing the school colors, blue and gold, and cheering.

Koji is somewhere out there in the crowd with my mom. My dad is already waiting on the field with the other parents of the court, getting ready to escort us down the red carpet during the halftime show.

Before I left the house, Mika kissed me on the cheek and told me I looked beautiful. "You'll win," she said, eyes wide. "You have to. You are too beautiful not to. How could anybody beat you?"

I don't feel beautiful right now. I feel cold and alone. I wish Mika were here.

Then someone calls my name, and it's time to get in the cars. There are five of them—vintage convertibles that will drive slowly around the football field so that everyone in the stadium can see the court. We go in pairs with the boys in the front, and the girls on top of the trunk of the car, skirts spread wide, smiling and waving, like real princesses.

Seth and I are in the same car. "So adorable!" the other girls squealed when we saw the running order. And at first I thought so, too. I thought it would make me relax. But . . .

He barely glances at me, even when one of the girls says, "Doesn't she look beautiful?" He just nods like a wooden soldier as he slides into the front seat.

I wonder if being beautiful is enough.

I wonder if I'm enough.

The car rumbles to life, and we start to make our way slowly around the stadium. I wave and put on my brightest smile.

Seth stares stonily ahead until we are in front of our friends. Then he does smile and wave. But he looks awkward. I can tell he's nervous. And I want to comfort him, so I lean forward and put my hand on his shoulder, trying to reassure him.

He shrugs me off, still waving, still smiling awkwardly, and I jerk back up like I've been burned.

I turn my smile up even brighter. So bright that every single person in the stadium can see it. So bright that I'm surprised they aren't shielding their eyes. Seth's not going to ruin this for me. This moment is bigger than him.

I will shine.

* * *

As we slow to a crawl, I hear Maria Chavez introducing court. We're the fourth car in the five-car procession, so our white convertible idles as she introduces Megan and Peter, Zach and Libby, Kelly and Tony—the people in the first three cars. And then it is our turn.

The cheering rings in my ears. We pull in slowly, in front of the red carpet leading to the stage. The carpet is lined with cheerleaders, football players, and all the kids on student council, who have planned everything.

My dad steps forward, beaming, and holds his hand out to help me off the back of the car. Seth has already gotten out of the front seat and is standing next to his mom, waiting to walk down the red carpet with her. I stand next to them as everyone else goes down the red carpet with their parent. Zach is with both of his moms, and the crowd roars their approval.

I keep my eyes on Seth. I wonder if anyone else can see the twitch in his jaw, and I realize he's nervous because of how much he wants this. And that surprises me. When did Seth start caring about homecoming? Maybe it's more than my luck that he wants to rub off on him. Maybe it's my life. The thought scares me.

Then it's our turn and my dad takes my arm, and we walk together, in perfect time. We wave like real royalty. He's grinning from ear to ear, his smile even brighter than mine.

"This is so exciting," Dad murmurs in my ear. "I'm so proud of you."

For what? For being beautiful? For being popular? For being alive? For being me? I hate that I have these thoughts going through my head right now. I hate that I'm getting anxious when I should be celebrating. But Seth's behavior has thrown me.

"And this year's homecoming king and queen are . . ." Maria Chavez shouts, "ZACH GARCIA AND REIKO SMITH-MORI!"

A confetti cannon goes off, showering us all in hundreds of tiny, brightly colored stars.

I smile, but I'm more relieved than happy.

I had to win this.

I had to prove that I'm the best.

That I'm the Reiko everyone expects me to be.

The Reiko I need to be.

As everyone starts clapping and shouting and whistling, Zach and I step forward. He's still in his football uniform, still sweaty from the game. He takes my hand, and I can feel Seth's eyes on me, and I'm surprised his stare doesn't go all the way through me.

Libby and Kelly and Megan are there, too, all clapping and smiling, but their eyes are sharp as well. I'm surprised by just how sharp Libby's eyes are.

Zach leans down and kisses my cheek. "Too bad we aren't going to the dance together tomorrow night, huh?" he whispers in my ear, and I smile back at him.

Then we raise our conjoined hands up high before taking a bow, like we've done something worth bowing for. Then we walk back down the red carpet, and it feels like the ceremony has lasted forever, but it must have been less than ten minutes since I got out of the little white convertible.

And I keep smiling.

CHAPTER 39

DRE IS JUMPING AROUND, SQUEALING. She's so happy for me, happier for me than I am. The only person happier than her is my mom. She runs toward me and holds me so close that I can feel her heart beating like a tiny bird in her chest.

"My beautiful girl," she says into my hair, and then my dad is hugging me again and Koji is giving me high fives.

"Congratulations," Koji says, winking at me, and I wonder if he knows how silly I think this all is, but also how much I wanted it.

Sometimes I feel fractured, like I'm two Reikos. And I suppose I am in some ways, because I have to make up for being one when there should have been two.

Winning homecoming queen is just one small thing—one star in a universe of darkness—but I'll keep going, doing whatever it takes, till I light up the night the way that Mika would have.

Seth hasn't said congratulations yet. He's standing with Megan and Libby, and he's laughing, and I remember Libby making fun of his laugh—how he opens his whole mouth really wide and kind of barks while he rocks back and forth—but she's laughing with him now and leaning against him, and it makes me go hot and cold inside.

"Babe." Dre is nudging me. "You all right?"

"I'm fine," I say, keeping my eyes on Seth, Megan, and Libby. "I'm great." I drag my eyes away and turn toward Dre.

She glances quickly over my shoulder at the trio, and then she hugs me tight, a Dre hug, the kind that simultaneously makes me feel invincible and like crying in her arms.

"You're okay," she whispers in my ear like an incantation. "You're okay."

And because Dre says I am, I am.

Seth's probably embarrassed that he lost. That's why he hasn't come up to me. It's fine. I understand.

This is what I tell myself as I make my way through the crowd toward where he and Megan and Libby are standing. Seriously. What is Libby's deal?

She's being nice to your boyfriend, a small voice chirps in the back of my mind. *She's being a good friend. Stop being so paranoid and weird.*

You aren't being paranoid, says another voice. A snarkier one. *Libby is the one who tried to hook up with Ryan Morris when you guys were still together, before he moved to New York. Libby is the one who Seth smiles at—the way he used to smile at you.*

I shake my head, silencing both voices. I'm being silly.

I go up to them, smiling, smiling like I couldn't stop if I wanted to.

"Hey!" I say.

"Oh, look, the queen is gracing us with her presence," Libby drawls, and I bite back a bitchy reply.

"We need a picture!" I say instead, pulling the girls toward me, away from Seth.

He's watching me warily, like I'm a coyote he's stumbled across out in the desert.

I thrust my phone at him. "Here! You can take it," I say, making sure our fingers brush.

"Kissy faces!"

"Smiles!"

"Hugs!"

We take turns shouting out commands for our photos and then break away.

"I knew you were going to win," says Megan, but she's smiling. Genuinely smiling. Like she's happy for me. But not as happy as Dre is for me. And not as happy as if *she* had won.

"Of course you won. You win everything." Libby isn't smiling. "You must be proud of your girlfriend," she says to Seth, bumping his hip with her own.

He grins back at her. It is the grin I think of as his Reiko Grin and here he is giving it to Libby. He used to always tell me how dumb he thought she was. How promiscuous. I was always defending her. And here he is, smiling at her like she is *special*. Like she is his person.

I step forward and grab Seth's hand. It's sweaty. He looks up at me and the smile slips off his face, replaced by the look I've started to dread.

"You're right," he says, nodding toward Libby. "Reiko does win everything."

"I don't," I blurt, but Dre is here now and she's laughing, and I wish I could wear her laugh like perfume, because it is making me feel so much better.

"Oh, Rei, we all knew you were going to win!" she says, and the warmth in her words wraps around me.

"It's stupid," I say, not making eye contact with any of them.

Seth raises his eyebrows. "I don't think you think it's stupid," he says. Then, louder: "But I think it's stupid."

Libby and Megan laugh. And it makes me want to take my crown off and stomp on it.

Our team wins the game. Everything is exactly how it should be: I won, Zach won, our team won, but something still feels off. Nobody is partying tonight. The dance is tomorrow, and nobody wants puffy eyes or dark circles. But even if we aren't partying, we still need to celebrate. "In-N-Out Burger!" someone cries out, and everyone agrees, because it'll be fun and festive and all-American and isn't that what homecoming is all about?

I'm still in my gold dress because I didn't bring a change of clothes. I wrap my arms around myself as I wait for Seth. He's talking to Libby and a few of the other girls.

"Rei!" It's Zach Garcia. "Do you need a ride?"

I shake my head. "I'm all right. I've got my car. Seth and I will meet you guys there." My parents have already left with Koji.

Seth looks up at his name but then turns away from me. For a minute, I think he's going to leave with Libby, until he smiles and shrugs and starts walking toward my car in the parking lot, leaving me to scamper after him.

We get into my car in silence. It isn't like the silences I'm used to with Seth. The good, comfortable kind. It's heavy. A silence that doesn't want to be broken.

I put the key in the ignition and start to drive toward In-N-Out. My phone is beeping like crazy with people texting me congratulations and telling me to meet them.

"I'm tired," Seth says abruptly as I change lanes.

"It's not even eleven," I say.

"Look, I'm not really up for In-N-Out. Can you take me home?"

I thought I didn't like the silence, but I miss it now. His words are worse. I ignore him and drive on toward In-N-Out.

"Reiko? Did you hear me?"

"Come on," I say. "I haven't had dinner. I want a burger." I don't really, but I like the idea of sweeping into the restaurant in my gold dress. Like the old Reiko would. It feels empty now. Seth is ruining this moment for me. It's making me realize that winning homecoming queen hasn't changed anything. Mika's still gone. No matter what I do, I can't ever make up for her not being here.

"No. I don't want to go," he says, his voice so sharp I'm surprised I'm not bleeding.

"Do you . . . want to go somewhere else?" Maybe he is feeling uncomfortable with my group of friends. Maybe he wants it to be just us. "We could go out in the desert. Like we used to."

"If I don't even want to go to In-N-Out, why would I want to go out in the desert?" he says.

"Okaaaay," I say. "It was just an idea."

"Reiko, I've already told you, I just want to go home. Please take me home."

When we get to his house, he doesn't even kiss me on the cheek. "Good night, I'll see you tomorrow. Thank you for the ride." Like this was just a friendly carpool.

"Good night," I say, but he's already slammed the car door, leaving me alone.

I drive back to In-N-Out so fast I'm surprised I'm not pulled over. Before I go inside, I look at myself in the mirror and repeat my mantra: *I'm Reiko Smith-Mori. Everything is good, nothing is wrong.* I glide inside just as my friends are sitting down at a booth to eat and, ignoring the whispers and the glances, I order two burgers, a chocolate shake, and French fries all for myself.

CHAPTER 40

IN THE MORNING, I CALL Seth to confirm the logistics for the day. I act like nothing is wrong—not like last night he hadn't wanted anything to do with me, and not like I have realized that being homecoming queen is a hollow victory. It might have made my mom smile last night, but my plastic crown can't fill the holes inside of me.

Seth's got his mom's car tonight, and even though I'd rather be in the driver's seat, I'm going to let him drive because I know how rare it is for him to get to use the car.

"Everyone is getting to my house at five for pictures and then on to Morton's for dinner at seven and we'll get to the dance by nine," I say.

"I saw the schedule you emailed out," he says, and I don't miss the smirk in his voice.

"You know how I like a plan." I try to keep my voice, and the moment, light.

"Reiko the planner," he says, and the scorn slides through the phone like oil.

I shake my head, like I can shake it off. "I've got to go. I'm late for my nail appointment. I'll see you tonight."

I hang up before he can say anything else, taking what little control I have left, like a horse rider gathering the reins close. It is all an illusion, though. Sure, you might be holding the reins tight, but at the end of the day, that horse can throw you any damn time it wants.

I spend the day driving from one appointment to the next. It all seems a bit silly, but I still want to be beautiful. I *have* to be beautiful. Nails, hair, makeup. I'm just pulling on my black dress for the dance (it's much shorter and tighter than the dress I wore last night) when my friends arrive at my house. I hear my dad greeting them at the door. My mom isn't here. She's gone to take pictures of Koji. It's his first homecoming and he's going with a girl named Maggie. His friends are taking pictures at her house.

Mika wanders into my room, smacking on bubble gum.

"Help me zip this?" I say, turning so she can tug up the zipper.

"It's stuck," she says. "I can't get it up."

I take a deep breath. "Try again."

"Still stuck. It isn't you, it's the zipper."

"I'll get someone else to do it." I step away from her. "What are you doing tonight?" I ask.

She shrugs. "I'm just going to read. Maybe watch a movie if Dad wants to." I've seen her sitting next to Dad when he watches a movie, laughing when he laughs.

He never sees her, though.

"I wish I was going to homecoming instead." Her eyes are wistful. "I never got to go."

"I wish you were going, too."

"It's okay," she says, even though it's not okay and it never will be. "You just have to have an extra good time for me, all right?"

I squeeze her hand. "I can do that." And I will. For Mika, I'll do anything. I'll have more fun than anyone has ever had at a dance.

Even if my boyfriend is being an ass.

"Reiko! Your friends are here!" Dad shouts from downstairs.

"I'll be down in a second!" I yell back. I go to the top of our banister and spy Dre. "Dre! Come here!"

Dre zips up my dress no problem, and while she does, Mika disappears.

"Let's go, babe," Dre says. "Everyone is waiting for us downstairs to take pictures."

Dad has laid out platters of snacks and jugs of water. "Must keep hydrated!" he says, and some of the guys laugh, but it isn't at my dad—it's because we're going back to Peter's after the dance and everyone will be drinking there. And we won't be drinking water. Seth is standing with Michael, and he's so stiff. He looks nervous. It must be because this is his first time going to a dance. I try to hold his hand, but he pulls away and goes to talk to Peter.

I want to remind him that Peter was the guy who made Seth's life a living hell in middle school. But here they are, in my house, in my entryway, talking and fist-bumping, and you'd never guess that one boy used to make the other one cry.

I wonder how Seth can be so forgiving of Peter, but not of me.

"This must be Seth," Dad says. "Nice to meet you, young man." He knows all the other guys, has known them for years.

"Nice to meet you, too, Mr. Smith-Mori," Seth says.

"Please, call me Ken." My dad's tone is polite, but his eyes are sharp. I can tell he's assessing Seth, trying to see what it is about this boy that has me so interested. I don't even know if I could tell him that. I don't even know if I know that.

"Girls pic!" Libby shrieks, and Dre, Megan, and I dutifully go and line up on the stairs, one hand on the railing, and smile.

"Get one of me and Rei," Dre says, pulling me to the side.

Dad grins at us and snaps away. His favorite camera is swung around his neck, and he looks at the viewing screen every few minutes to see what pictures he's taken. "You all look beautiful!" Then he looks up at me. "Reiko, I haven't gotten any pictures of you and Seth. What about out by the pool? The lighting is so nice now."

We break away from the group and follow my dad outside. My heart feels like it's on a yo-yo, up and down and up and down and up and down.

"Reiko, you stand here, and, Seth, like this, arm around her waist. Ah! Perfect! Smile at me!"

I can always smile on command, so I do. I wonder what Seth is doing with his face.

"Now, look at each other, ah, yes, this is excellent!"

The camera clicks and clicks and then my dad coughs. "Seth, try . . . try to . . . loosen up a bit? Your face looks a little stiff.

Here, how about you take a few pictures of me and my beautiful Reiko?"

Seth steps away from me and takes the camera from my dad.

Dad loops an arm through mine and beams. "This is how you smile when you are next to a beautiful girl, Seth. Like this!"

"You guys look great," Seth says from behind the camera. And he sounds sincere. It is the first time he's complimented me in a long time.

"Now you two again," Dad says. "Just a few more. Reiko, I know you will be happy to have these. I wish I had more pictures from when I was in high school."

I don't know if Seth manages to smile or not in those last few photos. If he doesn't, my dad doesn't say anything.

"Okay, everybody! One last group shot!" Dre is shouting over her shoulder as she comes outside, the rest of our group snaking behind her like a conga line.

We squeeze together, girls in the front, dates behind us, and all I can think about is the fact that somehow Seth is managing to not touch me at all.

CHAPTER 41

THE DANCE ITSELF IS IN a big ballroom in a conference center that's been dolled up as much as we have. Security guards pat everyone down as we go in. Peter gets stopped, and our vice principal personally smells his breath. We're not that dumb, though. Our school has a zero-tolerance policy on alcohol, which means one strike and you're out. It isn't worth the risk. We can drink later at Peter's house.

As soon as we get inside, we line up to take our professional pictures, because even though we've just spent over an hour taking pictures at my house, we still need the professional ones. Couple pictures, group pictures. Dre and Zach do a joke pose, and it's hilarious, and I wish that Seth and I could take a jokey photo, too, but instead, we stand in the standard "prom pose" with him behind me, arms around my waist. I try to snuggle up to him, but it's like he's a mannequin.

After that we follow the pulsing, pumping sound of the music to the huge hall where the DJ is. It's dark in here, and the flashing colored lights turn us red and blue and green and back again.

I don't know why we bothered getting so dolled up. Maybe this is why we spend so much time on pictures.

Being in the middle of so many bumping, grinding, shaking, shoving, sweating people sends me back to Morongo. I reach out for Dre, needing a friend, but she's dancing with Zach, really dancing with him, like she's in a music video or something, and so instead, I spin away and luckily Megan is right behind me so we start dancing together, shimmying and shaking and throwing our hair over our shoulders and dipping and dropping and I've got a smile plastered on my face and I'm laughing really hard, like I'm having

so

much

fun.

I keep looking for Seth, and I can't find him, so I keep dancing with Megan until Peter starts dancing with her and then it is just me.

Dancing by myself.

I do what I always do when I'm anxious. When I'm scared. I take all that anxiety, and I light it on fire inside of me. I turn it into fuel.

After a while, I go up to Dre and Zach and start dancing with them, and Dre doesn't mind, because it's just Zach and we've all known each other for years. It isn't like they're together or anything just because she's his date tonight. The three of us are dancing, and Zach has his hand up and he's shouting, "Rei-Dre sandwich! Rei-Dre sandwich!" and Dre and I are giggling.

We're not trying to look sexy anymore; we're just jumping around and shaking our asses and yelling the lyrics of the song. Dre's hair is plastered to her scalp and her eyeliner is smudged and I can feel my armpits getting damp, but it doesn't matter because we are having

so

much

fun.

But then Dre's face changes and she leans toward me, and it is like it is in slow motion and she has to shout to be heard and she says, "Do you see Seth and Libby?"

And I turn, slowly, like the way they do in horror movies, and right behind us are Seth and Libby. Dancing.

No, Seth's not dancing. Libby is dancing on him. And he's looking at her in a way that I didn't think he could look at anyone other than me, and where the hell is her date? I can't even remember who she came with. All I can think about is the expression on Seth's face, and it's like I've just swallowed a bad piece of fish. I think I'm going to be sick.

I can't stop staring at them in the flashing lights. They go red and blue and green and back again. And every time Seth's face is lit up, he's still looking at Libby the way he used to look at me, and I wonder if it was never about me for him. If I just happened to be in the right place at the right time. If Libby had turned up that night at his house asking to borrow his notes, or Dre, or any pretty, popular girl, would he have fallen for them instead?

"Reiko!" Dre is tugging at my arm. "Come on! Let's get some air."

"I don't need air," I say, yanking my arm away from her.

Dre and Zach have stopped dancing, and their stillness makes them look like little islands in the middle of a sea of movement.

My little islands.

I swim to them.

To safety. And they pick me up and we keep dancing.

Finally, Libby disappears to somewhere else on the dance floor. I slide up to Seth. I know my hair is dance-tangled and my false lashes are crooked and I'm sweaty, but it shouldn't matter because it's Seth and it's me.

"Hey!" I take his hands and mock swing dance. "Where have you been all night?" Like I haven't seen him and Libby.

He gamely spins me around. But he won't make eye contact with me.

"Where have *you* been?" he tosses back.

And that taste of bad fish comes back because I realize he isn't pretending. He doesn't know where I've been all night and he doesn't care.

"I've been dancing!" I say, forcing a smile and twirling in front of him. Then I lean in. My lips brush his earlobe, his cheek, and his jaw. "Remember when we danced in the desert? With the stars?" I want to bring him back to me.

He pulls away. "I never danced. It was just you dancing, and all I ever did was chase you." His voice is quiet, but his stare is loud.

And I'm crumbling. Was that what it was? How could we have both been so wrong about what was happening between us?

The song ends and the DJ announces that this is the last one, and it's something cheesy, the kind of song that makes everyone throw their arms around each other's shoulders and sway back and forth, and I get swept up in it. Seth is on one side of me, his arm heavy on my shoulders, and Dre is on my other side. Zach is next to her. Dre looks so happy—everyone looks so happy—and we are young and this is our last homecoming, so I try to be happy, too. I don't want to miss this moment—I know I won't get it again—so I smile smile smile and I sing along with everyone until the song ends and the lights come on.

CHAPTER 42

EVERYONE IS GOING BACK TO Peter's house. We filter out into the night, our hair tangled, dresses sweat-stained, makeup smeared, ties loosened, heels off.

"See you at Peter's!" Dre calls out, looping her arm through Zach's.

"See ya," I yell back as I get into Seth's mom's car.

I know Libby will be at Peter's, too, and I'm dreading it. It's easy enough to ignore, or at least pretend to ignore, your boyfriend dancing with someone else in the dark. It's harder to ignore it when it is happening right next to you.

I don't realize that my breaths are coming in and out in and out in and out faster and shallower than normal until Seth turns to me.

"Reiko, are you all right?" he says, and there is real tenderness in his voice. Real tenderness that I haven't heard in weeks. Tenderness that I was starting to think I'd imagined.

"Yeah, I'm fine," I lie. "Tonight was fun, yeah?"

He nods. "Yeah, it was." He's drumming his fingers on the steering wheel.

"Do you know how to get to Peter's?" I ask.

"I don't know if I'm up for going to Peter's place," he says, just as I realize that we're driving back in the direction of my house.

"Oh," I say. "I thought you two were getting along fine."

Seth lets out a sharp bark of a laugh. "That's not why I don't want to go to Peter's."

"Do you . . . do you want to go somewhere else? We could hang out? You could come over. My parents won't mind." What I mean is that my parents will be asleep.

He gives me a tight smile, one that is so different from his big goofy grin that always makes me smile in return.

"I don't think so, Reiko," he says, and there is so much gentleness in his tone that it slips into something else. Into pity.

And then I know.

"Pull over, Seth," I say, and he does what I ask. Like he always used to. "What . . . what's going on? With us? I thought . . ." I swallow hard. "I thought you wanted us to be together? That's what you said up on the Ferris wheel."

"That was before," he says. He's looking away from me, just like he did up on the Ferris wheel when he told me how he felt about me.

"Before?"

"Before you kissed that guy at Morongo."

"I don't think that's what you mean," I say. "Or at least, that's not all of it."

"Oh?"

"No." My voice is starting to crack, but I don't have any control over it, just like I don't have any control over the words that are pouring out of me. "You mean that it was before you had friends. Before you had girls interested in you. No use for me now, right?"

The back of his neck goes red, and it makes me want to throw up. I didn't want to believe it was true.

"You were the one who wanted us to be together!" I say.

"Well, now I don't."

I start to cry.

I'm not just crying. I'm sobbing because I knew this was coming, and I should have done something to stop it. Because now Seth gets to be the one who dumped me. And that's not fair. Seth Rogers shouldn't dump me, and I wonder when everything got so mixed up between us. When did we switch places? When did I lose control of him, of us?

Outside the window, high above us, the crescent moon is crying, too. I'm sure of it.

"Please stop crying," he says, but he won't look at me. He's still turned away.

"You don't mean it," I say, even though I know he does.

"I'm sorry, Reiko."

He doesn't sound very sorry.

And in that moment, anger, white and hot, shoves my sadness away. I want to hit him. Because I never wanted this in the first place. I wanted the desert and adventure and fun. Not this pain inside of me, like something is clawing its way out.

"Why?" I say.

"Why what?"

"Why any of it?" Why couldn't things have stayed the same? Why'd he have to ruin what we had by pushing us into this? I was fine without him, and then he was in my life, and now I can't remember what my life was like before him. And I don't know how to go back. And now he's even destroyed homecoming for me, which was something I've worked toward for years, because it was something I thought I wanted. Something I thought would fix me.

He turns to me then.

"People never know what they'll do," he says, echoing his words from the day we went up the tram. "All I know is that I don't want to be with you."

CHAPTER 43

HE DRIVES ME HOME AFTER that, and when we get to my house, he kisses me on the cheek.

"I'm sorry," he says.

And now I'm standing in my dining room, staring at a reflection of myself in a mirror on the wall, trying to recognize who it is, because surely this crumpled, sad, keening animal of a person can't be me.

I don't look like that. I know what I look like.

And if I didn't, there are forty, maybe fifty, pictures of me staring up from the dining-room table. Pictures from tonight. My dad must have already printed them. As a surprise.

I keep looking at the girl in the mirror and the girl in the pictures, and I can't comprehend how they are the same person. How they are both me.

In the pictures, I'm glossy and glamorous and gorgeous. But still not good enough for Seth.

Not good enough.

I pick up one of the pictures with shaking hands. It's of the two of us, from just hours before. I'm leaning on him, looking up at him, smiling, like my dad directed. But Seth doesn't look happy at all. His jaw is stiff and he's clenching a fist. How did I not see it? Except I did. It was just easier to brush it aside.

There's only one picture in which Seth looks happy and relaxed. It's the one where he's talking to Libby.

I rip up the picture, sobbing as I do. Then I tear off the necklace he gave me and throw it in the trash.

The stairwell lights flicker on.

"Reiko? What are you doing home? I thought you were sleeping at a friend's house?" Dad is yawning and rubbing his eyes. Then he sees the state of me. "Reiko! What's wrong?" He immediately envelops me in a hug, holding me close like I'm a little girl again. He hasn't held me like this in years.

I keep crying.

"Reiko, Reiko, are you all right? Are you hurt? Do we need to call someone?"

I take a deep, shuddering breath. "I'm all right. I'm not hurt." Not physically. And I know that's what he means.

My father sags with relief at my words. "What, what is it then?" He guides me to the couch and passes me a blanket that my obaachan knitted for me when I was little. "I'll make us some tea, but first you have to tell me what's wrong."

"Seth . . ."

Dad tenses. "Seth what?" And for the first time I can remember, I see anger cloud my gentle father's eyes.

It makes me realize that getting dumped is not the worst thing that can happen to a girl on the night of the homecoming dance.

"Seth broke up with me," I say. "He . . . dumped me." And now that I've said it out loud, it makes it both real and . . . silly. Here I am, bawling my eyes out, because of that.

I know that girls can have a lot more to cry about.

Dad lifts up my chin so I'm looking at him. "Reiko," he says, "Seth is a shit."

It is so unexpected that I start to giggle. Dad never swears. "You only met him tonight," I say, in between hiccuping giggle sobs.

"I did! But clearly, he is a shit. You"—Dad gives me another hug—"you are better than him, Reiko. You know this. I know this. He knows this. Everyone knows this." Then he frowns. "Like I said. He's a shit."

"Thanks," I say. Both my giggles and tears are starting to subside.

"I'll make us some tea." And he starts to go into the kitchen. He pauses next to the table, where all the pictures are, and his face falls. "Oh no! Reiko, I'm so sorry. I thought this was a good thing to do. I thought it would make you happy." He sounds almost more upset about the pictures than about Seth dumping me.

"I know, Daddy," I say. "Thank you for printing them."

"Do you want me to get rid of them?"

I shake my head and wipe my dripping nose on the back of my hand. "No. They are nice to have."

"Are you sure?"

I nod. "I'm sure."

* * *

We drink tea together in silence, my dad alternating between making comforting sounds while patting my back and cursing Seth in Japanese.

"Do you want me to get Mom?" he asks.

"I'm okay," I say, even though I'm clearly not. "I think I'll just go to bed."

"It's just been such a long time since I've seen you cry . . . like this."

I don't like thinking about the last time I cried this hard. The last time I cried at all.

"I don't want to upset Mom," I say.

"Oh, Reiko, she won't be upset," Dad says, petting my hair. "She'll want to make you feel better."

And while I know that is true, I also know that if she sees that I'm upset she'll assume that it's about something much worse than just stupid Seth Rogers breaking my heart. She'll assume this is about Mika. She'll assume that I've fallen back into the place where I can't stop crying, where I can't speak to anyone. I don't want her to think I've relapsed in my grief, and guilt, or that, like grief, this is something that can be "cured" by going to rehab. The last therapist we saw, after my breakdown about Mika, told my parents to let me heal in my own way, and if that meant not talking out loud about Mika, that was fine. That was two years ago. And I haven't cried since then.

I take a deep shuddering breath. "I'm okay," I say again. "I'll be okay."

"Of course you will," my dad says, squeezing my shoulder. "You are a Smith-Mori! We're always okay."

That's a lie, but I know what he means. That even if we aren't okay, we say we are and carry on.

The next day my mom comes into my room and opens up the blinds on my windows, and light blares in. I scrunch my eyes shut and burrow into my pillow, away from the loud, loud light.

"Reiko, sweetie. Dad told me what happened." Mom's voice is both gentle and firm, the kind of voice she uses when she goes horseback riding. "You need to get up. It's almost two in the afternoon."

I hear the curtains swish, and then there is somehow, impossibly, even more light in my room.

A small body crawls under the covers and curls up next to me. Mika.

"You heard Mom," she whispers in my ear. "Get up. It'll make her sad if you don't." She knows this is the thing that will get me going. I fling my covers off in a sudden movement, startling both Mom and Mika.

"Okay," I say, and my voice is all fugged up from my stuffy nose, and I know my eyes are puffy. "Let me just shower first."

"Are you . . . are you okay?" my mom says. "Dad said you were very upset last night, and I don't blame you—"

"I'm fine. It's fine." My throat is starting to clog, and my eyes are starting to leak, and I won't let it happen. I'm stronger than that. I won't let anyone see me weak.

Especially not over a stupid boy like Seth Rogers.

"I thought we could go to Las Cas for lunch," Mom says, sitting at the foot of my bed. "You and me?"

I glance at Mika, feeling guilty, as always, that she can't come.

"Go," she says. "Las Cas makes everything better." She smiles at me. "I want you to feel better, Reiko."

So I go, but only for Mika and my mom.

Las Casuelas smells incredible. It's my family's favorite restaurant; we've been coming here for years. Mom used to come with her parents when she was little—apparently, they knew the original owners.

The restaurant makes me think of Mika, but it doesn't hurt the way so many things that remind me of Mika do. Maybe that's because all my memories of her here are so happy. Mika, ordering more than all of us and out-eating everyone. Mika, making friends with the bartender and convincing him to give her unlimited virgin margaritas. Mika, determined to try everything on the menu and almost making her way through it.

Mom and I slide into a wooden booth and look at the menus, even though we both know what we want.

"So," Mom says, voice overly cheerful. "Your regular? I remember how it used to always make you feel better."

"You know that enchiladas don't fix everything. I don't know why you're pretending they do," I say with a half smile as the waiter walks up. But I still order what I always have. One cheese enchilada, one chicken, and a ground-beef taco.

"They might not fix everything, but they help. Reiko, sweetie, tell me what happened."

I close my eyes and pinch the top of my nose. I can feel a headache building. But it isn't a normal headache. This one is coming up from my heart, snaking up my throat and all the way through to right behind my eyes.

"I want to be here for you," Mom says.

Since I won't talk about Mika, Mom never feels like she's been able to be there for me, so I know she's jumping at the chance to help with something. To finally fix me. She doesn't understand how her grief is so different from mine. How I'm still drowning in it years later, and the only way for me to stay afloat is to not talk about it, not think about it.

"Thanks, Mom," I say, and I mean it.

I tell her a condensed version of what happened last night.

"He's not worth a single tear," Mom says with authority as the waiter puts our steaming plates of food in front of us. "You're so much better than him. It was obvious even from before the night of the homecoming game."

I smile, but I'm wondering, *If I'm better than him, then why did he dump me?*

Another thought occurs to me: *If I'm better than him, then surely I can get him back.*

It's just a matter of time.

I can fix this.

CHAPTER 44

ON MONDAY, DRE STICKS TO my side like an over-protective bodyguard, practically biting anyone who looks at me funny. Anyone who looks at me at all.

I don't expect to see Seth much—surely he'll go back to wherever he used to hang out before this all happened. So when I see him in the parking lot, with *my* group of friends, it's like a punch in the stomach. And when I walk up to him, expecting him to at least say hello, and all he does is give me this confident little head nod that is so completely out of character, it sends me staggering back, because where did this confidence come from, who *is* he? And I'm so aware of people watching us that all I can do is my own version of the stupid head nod back. Then I turn away from him first. But I hear Libby's laugh and his laugh, and I want to run away, but instead I slip my arm through the person's next to me (it's Zach Garcia), like *he* was the reason I came over to this part of the parking lot.

For the rest of the week, I can't get the sound of Libby and Seth's laughter out of my head.

The week drags on. I can't tell if people are watching me more now or less, and I don't know which would be better. Dre offers to sleep over for the whole weekend, to be with me, and I love her for it, but I don't want her.

I want Seth.

"I'll be all right," I lie. "I'll call you if I need you."

Anyway, I don't need her because I've got Mika, and Mika listens as I plot how to make everything right again.

October turns into November, and I still haven't made any progress with Seth. If anything, it seems like he's making progress of a different kind. Everyone seems to be into him now. He wears his new confidence like a cape. He's even started dressing differently. It infuriates me, because I was the one who saw him when he was invisible to everyone else. I *gave* him that confidence. Now that he has it, he doesn't need me anymore, and he can just cast me aside.

"Why do you care so much?" Dre asks. "It isn't like you ever really liked him, right?"

But I did, I did, *I did*, and I didn't know it because I was confused by what love was. I know now, though. Seth is the only one to really know me, the real Reiko. And apparently, he didn't like what he saw. But I can change that. I can be everything he wants. I can be his wildest dream come true. Like, I know he's into the schoolgirl look. It creeped me out before, but I can definitely pull that off. I order a pleated skirt online, and pair it with a collared shirt. I even braid my hair. I look hot.

I start to think that maybe I took it too far when Dre says, "Reiko. Why are you dressed like Britney Spears circa 'Baby One More Time'?"

Shit. I was hoping it wasn't *that* obvious.

"Reiko," she goes on, "does this have anything to do with—"

"I don't know what you're talking about." I hold my head up high, the way my mom taught me.

Zach Garcia whistles appreciatively as I walk by. "Lookin' cute, Rei-Rei."

"Just cute?"

"Maybe more than cute."

I wink. Like I care what Zach Garcia thinks.

"Laying it on a little thick, don't you think?" Dre says. "Who exactly are you trying to impress here?"

I know Seth notices me because how can he *not* notice me? Everyone is noticing me. But just like the week after Seth dumped me, I can't tell if it is a good noticing or a bad noticing, but I decide it doesn't matter. I don't care. Everything is good, nothing is wrong. The principal clucks in disapproval when I walk by, but technically I'm not violating the dress code, so I just smile at her.

"You look ridiculous," Dre says at lunch. "Like seriously ridiculous."

"I don't know," says Megan, tilting her head to assess my outfit. "I think she pulls it off."

Dre rolls her eyes. "Of course she pulls it off. Reiko pulls everything off, but it is still ridiculous."

"I bet Krissy Tran wears something similar tomorrow," Megan says, grinning wickedly. "And then her whole little crew will, too."

"It is kind of adorable how Krissy styles herself like a mini Reiko," Dre admits, reaching over to grab a Dorito out of my bag. "She's been doing it for years now."

"Reiko, Reiko, Reiko, what the hell are you wearing?" Libby has sauntered up behind us and is smirking at me.

I tug at my skirt but keep my head tall.

"I mean, this doesn't have anything to do with a certain someone, does it?" says Libby, leaning in.

I can't believe we used to be friends. Or even pretended to be friends. Dre and I should have dropped her after the winter formal fiasco last year.

I toss my hair over my shoulder. "Libby, will you chill out? A photographer friend of my mom's is doing a photo shoot this afternoon and I said I'd help out. I liked the outfit so decided to wear it all day. But thanks for your concern." I smile with my mouth shut.

"Oh," she says.

"Really?" Megan asks, mouth askance.

"Yes, really," I snap. "I didn't want to make a big deal about it, but, since Libby wouldn't shut up about my outfit, I didn't really have a choice."

As we walk away, Dre lowers her voice. "That's bullshit, right?"

I give her a wide grin. "Totally. But you know you're going to have to take some pictures of me in this now, right? Something I can post online to make it look like I really had a photo shoot?"

Dre sighs and shakes her head. "Nobody can accuse you of not being thorough."

"Why are we walking this way?" Dre asks after lunch as we make our way across campus.

"Don't hate me," I whisper, and then I start laughing like she's said something really, really funny. Seth is walking toward us.

"Are you kidding me?" she whispers back, but she puts on her biggest, brightest smile and laughs with me.

I don't know what I'd do without Dre.

I see Seth pause for a minute and look at me, once, twice, and then he kind of shakes his head and keeps walking.

Once Seth is past us, I stop laughing and so does Dre.

"Not cool, Reiko," she says lightly.

"I know," I say. But I'd do it again and we both know it. "Remember Chris?" I ask, nudging her with my shoulder. Dre had a huge crush on this guy who was a year older than us and worked at a hardware store, and we used to go to that store every other week and look at paint samples, giggling every time we passed Chris at the register. Whenever Dre wanted to go to that hardware store, I'd go with her.

"Yeah, but, Reiko, that was different," Dre says in a strained voice. "You know I'm here for you, always, but . . . you can't keep this whole thing up forever. Whatever this is."

She's right.

I need a new plan.

CHAPTER 45

I NEED TO CHANGE MY schedule.

I already know what Dre will say. That it isn't healthy. That the more I see him, the more upset I'll be.

She doesn't know that the more he sees me, the better. It just means more opportunities to prove that he made a mistake. I really am the Reiko he thought I was. Even though I fell off that first pedestal, I survived, and now I'm climbing up to one that is even higher. If he thought I sparkled before, just wait till he sees me shine.

"Hi, Mrs. Peterson," I say, smiling at the woman in the front office. "I think I need to switch my classes around a little."

"Of course, dear," she says, smiling at me. "What is it?"

"Well, I'd like to take debate next semester, so I'll need to switch my English and science classes around. I've already spoken to the teachers. They are fine with it and have space, if it is fine with you?"

"Let me take a look," she says, putting on her glasses and staring at the computer. "Why yes, yes, I think that makes sense. It shouldn't be a problem. And you said you've already spoken to your teachers?"

"They are absolutely fine with it," I say with a straight face.

Then Mrs. Peterson frowns. "Reiko, this isn't because your grades are slipping, is it? I know everyone says senior year grades don't matter, but they do, my dear. Colleges will look at them."

I didn't realize Mrs. Peterson could see my grades.

"Oh, I've just had a lot going on," I say. "Don't worry, I'll be fine."

"I'm sure you will. We want to see you do your best!"

During break, I pop into Mrs. Tully's classroom.

"Reiko! What can I do for you?"

"I was hoping I could switch into your English class next semester. I've already spoken to Mrs. Peterson about it, and she said it is fine. It is all a bit complicated really, you see. I'm switching my elective."

"I'd of course be delighted to have you in my class again, Reiko, but it is a bit . . . out of the ordinary to switch classes like this. But if Mrs. Peterson has already approved it . . ."

"The changed schedule is right here," I say, presenting her with the green form.

"I'm switching English classes next week," I say casually to Dre after school.

She frowns at me. "Why?"

"It's because I'm dropping photography for debate. My dad can teach me all I need to know about photography anyway." I don't make eye contact with her.

"Debate. Since when have you been interested in debate?"

I shrug. "I just thought it would be interesting."

"Interesting, hmm? You know what *I* think is interesting? That Seth is in debate."

"Is he?"

Dre rolls her eyes. "Come on, Reiko, we both know he is." I'm still carrying the green slip with the new timetable printed on it. She reaches out and grabs it. "You are in every class with him!"

"No, not every class." I snatch the green slip back.

"*Practically* every class! Reiko, this is . . . kind of intense. Even for you."

"What's that supposed to mean?"

"I just mean you're intense. You know you are. But this . . . this is . . ."

"It's what?" I tense, waiting for her response.

"It's just a little weird," she says. "A little . . . worrying." She looks genuinely concerned.

"I'm fine," I say, tossing my hair over my shoulder. "Everything is fine."

More than fine. Everything is good, and *nothing is wrong.*

"It doesn't seem fine," Dre mutters darkly.

"Dre," I say, voice sharp, "I'm fine. It isn't a big deal."

She narrows her eyes at me. "He's not worth it."

"Not worth what?"

"This!" She throws her hands up. "All of this! You!"

"You're just being mean because he's Seth Rogers," I say. "If you knew him like I knew him—"

Dre shakes her head so fast her hair fans out all around her face. "Nope. It isn't about how well I know him. It doesn't matter. No guy is worth this. If you keep acting like this—dressing up in ridiculous outfits, changing your class schedule, being generally shady—I'm . . . I'm going to tell Suzie." She folds her arms and purses her lips, waiting for my rebuttal.

"Suzie who?"

"Suzie your mom Suzie!"

I shrug, but inside my heart is thumping fast. "You know my parents—they let me do things my way."

"Not if I tell them I think you are losing your grip on reality." Her expression matches her grim tone. I know what she is talking about. It's the closest Dre has come to saying that she thinks I was losing my mind when I said I still saw Mika.

My palms start to sweat. "Dre, I said everything is fine."

"You always say that, even when it clearly isn't. And, Rei, you know I'm here for you. Always. But . . ."

"But what?"

"If I was losing my shit like this, especially over some guy, I'd want you to say something. Do something."

"Well, I want you to be supportive."

"I'm supportive of *you*, but I'm not supportive of . . . this. And don't ask what I'm talking about. You know what I'm talking about." She's quieter now, eyes dark and serious. "I'm just worried, Reiko."

I take a deep breath. "Okay, maybe switching classes was a little intense."

"You think?" She raises her eyebrows.

"But it's not a big deal! So please don't make a big deal out of it. I know what I'm doing."

She sighs. "Fine. I'll drop it. For now. But if you show up at school tomorrow wearing a French maid's outfit or some bullshit, that's it, you hear me?"

I laugh despite myself. "All right, all right. You've made your point."

Dre laughs too and rolls her eyes. "As if you thought I was going to let you get away with this. Please. Do you even know me?"

I snort. "I already said you've made your point. You don't need to gloat about it."

"Of course I do. Don't ruin my fun."

"You're ridiculous."

"And you love it."

Whatever tension had risen between us moments earlier has evaporated.

"Come on," she goes on. "Let's go back to my house and watch *Drag Race*."

I link my arm through Dre's and grin at her, hoping that an episode or two of *Drag Race* will be enough of a distraction to make her forget that she even considered blabbing to my mom about my behavior.

Seth doesn't say anything when I walk into his English class the next day. When Mrs. Tully announces that I'll be in their class from now on, he looks up at me and shakes his head, before turning away.

An unfamiliar feeling is unspooling inside of me. It takes me a minute to recognize it.

Embarrassment.

When I get home after school, I reach inside of myself, and yank out that ribbon of shame. I pull and pull, until I'm sure it is all out, and then I cut it into tiny pieces and I flush it down the toilet.

I'm Reiko Smith-Mori, and I'm never ashamed. I'm never embarrassed.

Especially not by Seth Rogers.

CHAPTER 46

I'M SITTING WITH DRE IN the parking lot before school
the following Wednesday when Megan comes up to us.

"Reiko," she says in this weird faux serious voice. "I wanted to
tell you right away. Just so you don't think I'm, like, taking sides.
Seth and Libby are dating."

It's like my heart doesn't know where it is supposed to be
because all of a sudden it is in my stomach, and I think I might
vomit.

"Bullshit," says Dre, but she doesn't say it with much
confidence.

Megan shrugs delicately. "I mean, that's what she told me."

I bite my cheek. It was one thing to see Libby and Seth flirting,
but for them to actually be dating?

"Whatever," I say. I know that the only reason Megan is telling
us is so she can report back to Libby on how we respond. "Good
for them."

"But . . . aren't you still . . . into him?"

"No," Dre and I say at the same time.

"Oh," says Megan. She's clearly disappointed. "Really?"

"Yes, really," I say. "And you can tell Libby I said so."

"Tell Libby what?" Libby has walked up behind me. She was obviously dying to see my reaction for herself.

"Just that I think it is great you and Seth are together," I say. The lie tastes bitter.

"Oh, thanks, hon," she says. "I really appreciate you being so awesome about it."

"Totally," I say. "I mean, it isn't that big of a deal. Although I'll admit I think it *is* a little weird . . ."

Megan perks up at my change of tone, and Dre moves a bit closer to me.

"What's weird?" says Libby.

"Just that you don't seem to be able to date anyone unless Dre and I have dated them first."

"That isn't true," says Libby, flushing a little.

"I mean, it is totally true," says Dre. "But don't worry, we're all good."

"Yeah," I say. "We're good."

My smile says anything but.

"Man, I was hoping you were going to punch Libby or something," Dre says later. "I should have. Should have punched her straight in the boob."

"In the boob?" I say, starting to crack up. "You're kidding, right?"

"It would have been hilarious. And well deserved, if you ask me."

I'm laughing too hard to respond. Laughing so hard that I get the hiccups. And then Dre starts laughing, so we're just sitting in my car laughing our asses off.

"You really okay with that?" Dre says, once we've calmed down a bit.

"With you punching Libby in the boob?"

Dre snorts but then composes herself. "I mean, with her dating Seth."

That chases my giggles away.

"I don't know," I say. I'm surprised how much it hurts.

"That's okay," Dre says. "And it's okay if you are upset about it."

"You've changed your tone since last week," I say, remembering when she called me out.

"Reiko, this is totally different! I still don't especially like Seth, and I definitely don't like how you've been acting, but of course I don't want you to be hurt. And I don't want Libby to be prancing around like she's better than you. Also I don't want you shutting me out because of what I said last week. I still want to know what's going on with you, even if I don't approve. Okay? I don't want you to start hiding things from me."

Again, that hint to things I've hid before, things I'm still hiding now. But despite that, her comment reminds me why Dre is the best. Even if she's annoyed at me, she's always on my side. "Thanks, Dre. I just kind of feel like I *found* him, you know?"

Dre raises an eyebrow. "Reiko, you know he wasn't, like, a lost puppy, right?"

"I know! But you know what I mean. Nobody saw him till I did."

"He wasn't invisible either! Reiko, he was just a regular, normal dude—"

"Exactly! And then I made him into someone cool!"

I expect Dre to tell me off again for that, but instead, she purses her lips together. "You might have a point there," she says. Then she starts to laugh again. "Totally should have punched Libby in the boob."

CHAPTER 47

THIS MORNING, WHEN I OPEN my closet, all my clothes are gone. Instead, there are rows and rows of shining suits of armor. Mika is sitting in the middle of it all, staring up at me. "I thought these would help," she says.

Zach Garcia stares at me during calculus, a funny expression on his face. I wonder if he can see my armor.

"You're pretty messed up over this guy, aren't you?" he says without preamble.

"You mean Seth?"

He leans back in his chair, so far back I'm surprised he doesn't fall. But Zach is the kind of guy who never falls. "Let's blow off history," he says.

I'm not really the kind of girl who blows off class. But I'm not sure I know who I am anymore. I didn't think I was the kind of girl who got dumped either.

"Where should we go?" I ask, looking over my shoulder as we sneak into the parking lot.

We end up going to a Starbucks a few blocks away from our school. "Why are you being so nice?" I ask after we've got our drinks.

"Why wouldn't I be?"

"You don't think that I'm in some kind of vulnerable, damaged state and I'll just crawl into bed with you, right?"

"I don't think you crawl anywhere."

He gets a grin for that. He's right. I don't.

"You just don't seem like . . . the Reiko I know. You seem . . . so keyed up. But fragile, too. I don't know how to explain it." He sees my face and stops. "Sorry."

"It's fine." I take a sip of my iced coffee.

"I can be a friend, you know. I'm a pretty good friend. I mean, I know you've got Dre, and I'm glad you've got her—she's great—but I thought maybe you needed another friend, too."

I appraise Zach with new eyes. I didn't think he was good at anything except football and looking hot.

"Thanks," I say.

"What is it about Seth? Why is he making you go so crazy?"

For the briefest moment, I'm embarrassed that it is so obvious, but then I remember that I've ripped out any embarrassment or shame.

I close my eyes for a moment, asking myself, for the millionth time, what it is about Seth.

"This summer, when we started hanging out all the time, I felt like I'd discovered this person I didn't know I needed," I say, opening my eyes. "I thought that I really knew him, and now it is like

256

he is a completely different person. It is making me doubt everyone. I think I'd feel the same if Dre suddenly didn't want me in her life."

"Rei, I think this isn't just about Seth. Your reaction, I mean."

"Zach Garcia, are you trying to psychoanalyze me?" I kick his foot, grinning. I'm trying for lightness, but I know what he's getting at.

His eyes are serious. "Reiko, I mean it. I've known you a long time"—it's true; we go way back; I've known him since the third grade—"and I've only seen you get this torn up over something once before."

His words are like a slap in the face.

"It's not like that," I say, pushing my chair back, away from him. "Nothing could be like that."

He looks like he wants to say something else, but instead he just nods. "We should get back. But, hey, you better not forget who you are. Seth Rogers has got nothing on you. Hell, nobody has got a thing on you, you hear me?"

I nod. He's wrong, though. Mika was better than me.

But I don't say that.

Zach opens his arms wide. "How about a hug?"

It's a nice hug.

CHAPTER 48

ON FRIDAY NIGHT, DRE COMES over and we make pizza from scratch. While we roll out the dough and put on all the top-pings, we talk about how we're going to decorate our dorm at UCLA, and if we want to rush for a sorority or not and how much we'll come home (*a lot*, I want to say, but instead I say, "Oh, maybe once a month," and Dre thinks even that is a lot), and while the pizzas are in the oven we go out into my backyard and climb up in my hammock. We lie with our arms pressed up against each other, hair tangled.

Dre rests her head on my shoulder. "I'm so glad we're going to UCLA together," she says. Like it's a fact. Like we've already got-ten in. "Who wants to make new friends?"

"We can make some new friends," I say.

"All right. A few," she concedes.

We swing back and forth, our combined weight making the hammock hang so low that I'm surprised our butts aren't scraping the ground.

"Rei," Dre says, hesitantly, and I can tell by the tone of her voice she's going to ask me something I don't want to hear, so I tense.

"What?" I say.

"Are you feeling any better?"

"I don't know," I admit. I think I'm fine but if I wasn't, how would I know? And everyone keeps asking me, so maybe that means I'm not.

"You will be," she says, and kisses my cheek.

I laugh. "Why did you ask me if you were just going to answer your own question?"

"This is the first time that you've . . . admitted that maybe you aren't okay. In a long time. But I think it is good. And I think that it means you are closer to being okay than when you were prancing around like some sort of demented wind-up doll."

"Andrea!" I say, feigning outrage. At least, I pretend to feign outrage. I'm really feigning feigning outrage, because it stings more than it should. So when I shove her shoulder, meaning to be playful, it's a little harder than it should be and we nearly topple out of the hammock.

Dre just laughs her deep, throaty laugh, the one that is so infectious that I laugh, too.

The alarm on her phone buzzes. "Pizzas are done. Come on, wind-up doll."

We take the pizzas back out into my yard, tossing a blanket on the grass, and eat out under the palm trees and the stars.

"I just realized who Seth is like," says Dre, grabbing a slice of her Andrea Special (bell peppers, onions, fresh mozzarella, and ham).

"The guy in *Little Women* who is all obsessed with the family?"

"Laurie?"

"No, the guy!"

I grin. "Laurie is the guy. He marries Amy?"

"Whatever. Yeah, him. Seth is like him. He just wanted to be close to your family. And what you guys represent."

"Dre, what are you talking about?"

"Like, if we were back to *Pride and Prejudice* time, he'd totally be marrying up. To improve his station and all that."

"Yeah, but we're not in *Pride and Prejudice* time," I say. "We're in our time. And it isn't like we were anywhere close to getting married."

"Times change but people don't." She sounds like a talk-show host. I toss my pizza crust at her.

She catches it and takes a bite. "Rei, I don't think he saw *you*. I think he saw some kind of dream girl who represented the life he wanted. And when shit got real, when you got real—when you screwed up—he couldn't deal." She pauses. "I think you both maybe fell for each other for the wrong reasons. Like you fell for him because he was so into you, and there's something pretty potent about that." When I go to protest, she holds up her hand. "It wasn't just that for you, I know. He also . . . took you away from yourself, I think. From things you didn't want to think about."

"That makes it sound like I was just using him or something."

"Well, were you?"

I think about it. "Not on purpose," I admit. "I liked how he made me feel about myself. Or at least I used to. Now he makes me feel like crap. But . . ." I hesitate.

"You were pretty shitty to him sometimes?" says Dre with a wry smile.

"I was getting to that," I say. Dre doesn't even know the half of it. How I made him stay up in my room when Libby came over. Or how I used to tease him, on purpose, over the summer, because it gave me such a thrill. "I didn't mean to be, though. I kind of got swept up in it all—in the fact that he was into me, like you said." In the feeling of having power over him. It strikes me how wrong that was.

"I'm sure you didn't mean to be nasty," Dre says, nodding. "And he's definitely been super shitty to you, too." I know she's letting me off the hook because she's my best friend, and I'm grateful, but I know I shouldn't have treated Seth the way I did.

"I wish you'd talked to me about all of this," Dre says. She pauses. "Sometimes I think it was about more than Seth, Rei-Rei."

I know what she's referring to. *Who* she is referring to.

"Maybe," I admit for the first time, but that makes me feel uncomfortable, too. It makes me think that I was just using Seth to forget about Mika. But it wasn't just that and it wasn't just that I liked the attention. I liked him, too. More than liked him. "It was a lot about Seth, too. Not just . . . about . . . you know . . ." I let my voice trail off because even with Dre, even after all these years, I can't say Mika's name out loud. "I think I really did . . . love him. In a way."

"You loved a version of him. He loved a version of you."

"Isn't that true about everyone, though? We're all only versions of ourselves."

Dre raises her eyebrows. "Getting pretty deep there, Rei-Rei."

I nudge her with my shoulder. "Hey, you started it."

"You know I'm always here to discuss deep philosophical crap with you. Hey! Maybe I'll major in philosophy."

"Dre?"

"Uh-oh, I know that tone. Are you about to get all cheesy on me? I got plenty of cheese on my pizza."

"Just, thanks."

"Rei, baby doll, you don't ever have to thank me for being here. I always will be, all right?"

I smile back at her but feel a sharp twinge inside my chest.

Because nobody is always there.

CHAPTER 49

ONE NIGHT IN NOVEMBER, I'M in my room watching a video on how to do a reverse fishtail braid when there is a knock on my door.

It's my dad.

"Hey, Dad," I say. "Everything okay?"

"Yep! All good. I just wanted to come . . . say hi. See how you're doing. Feels like it's been a while since we talked." He's standing awkwardly in my doorway, so I get up from my vanity table and sit on my bed.

"You can come in, you know," I say with a smile.

He comes in and perches next to me at the end of my bed. "So . . . how are you doing?" he says.

"I'm fine," I say automatically.

"You know, your mom and I are always here, if you need anything."

I nod.

"I also wanted to see . . . if you'd had a chance to apply to Tokyo and Temple?"

"Aha! The real reason you came in here."

Dad holds up his hands. "Not true! I really did want to check on you."

"All right, fine, I believe you."

"But I also wanted to make sure you'd applied. I checked online and the deadline is in a couple of days."

"Dad, I don't know . . . I said I'd think about it."

"Remember, Reiko, applying isn't committing." Then he gives me a big cheesy grin. "And think how happy it would make me!"

I roll my eyes. He knows I can't say no to that. "Fine. I'll apply, okay?"

"Wonderful! Do you want help with the applications?"

"I'll get started and I'll let you know if I need any help," I say, smiling despite myself. He's practically giddy. "This doesn't mean I'm going to go, even if I do get in. I don't want to go to Japan anytime soon, you know that."

He nods, scanning my bookshelf. "I remember when you used to want to go to Japan," he says, taking something out. It's my Japan scrapbook. It was tucked between my old yearbooks. "I think you remember, too." His tone is more serious now. "I think you'll be glad you applied." He puts the scrapbook down next to me.

My initial instinct is to throw it in my closet or under my bed, but I force my panic down and smile at my dad.

He gives me a kiss on the forehead. "I love you, Reiko. And I'm proud of you."

"I love you, too, Dad."

After he leaves, I flip through the scrapbook, remembering what it felt like to want to go to Japan. I expect it to hurt, seeing the dreams that Mika and I had shared laid out in front of me, but instead I'm filled with an unfamiliar, quiet joy. I'd forgotten how much I'd wanted this future. For myself as well as for Mika. And as I keep flipping through the pages, a small yearning begins to bubble up inside of me.

I'm working on the application a few hours later when Mika peeks over my shoulder. "Are you really applying to the University of Tokyo?"

I slam my laptop shut.

"I heard you and Dad," she says, climbing up in bed with me. "You don't have to hide it."

"Are you upset?" I ask.

Mika frowns. "Not upset exactly. Just a little jealous. But, Reiko, I want you to be happy. I want you to go to Japan if you want to."

"But . . . you are always saying that you don't want me to leave you."

"You have to leave me sometime. I just wish I could go with you. Especially if you go to Japan." She sounds wistful, but not sad.

"I wish that, too," I say. "So . . . what do you think I should do?"

"I think you should definitely apply to the University of Tokyo. And Temple! You can do it for me."

"But . . ."

"I'd be proud of you if you got in," she says. "So would Dad."

"Yeah, he would be," I say. And then I laugh. "He's such a dork. Did you see him in here? Pretending he was just casually popping by."

"Dad is really great," says Mika, curling up under my arm.

"I know he is."

"And Mom is really great, too."

"I know."

"And so is Koji."

"I'm sensing a theme, Mika."

"You are great, too, Rei-Rei."

I squeeze her shoulder. "I don't know what I'd do without you, Mika."

She doesn't reply.

We sit together in silence for a long time.

WINTER

CHAPTER 50

BY THE TIME WINTER BREAK rolls around, I can't wait
to not have to see Seth's face every day at school. Switching to the
same classes as him was a horrible idea and has completely back-
fired. I'm stuck witnessing his continued transformation into some
cool guy. Some guy I don't even recognize. And, to make it worse,
he and Libby are always all over each other: making out in the
parking lot, up against the lockers. It all feels like such a produc-
tion. Like a show. It makes me wonder if that is what Seth wanted
from me.

It makes me wonder if we were both using each other all along
and I never saw it till now.

I know there are going to be parties every night of break, but I
can't stomach going. Especially because Dre is going to be in
Mexico with her mom and sister, so I'd be all alone. I notice that
I'm pointedly not invited to Libby's New Year's Eve party. Not
that I expected to be, or even care. Ever since what happened in the
parking lot, we mostly avoid each other. I can't believe we used to
be so close.

I've never felt like this before.

My confidence is molting off of me like feathers on a bird, and I feel naked without it.

I'm in the kitchen the first Wednesday afternoon of winter break, eating pancakes while I scroll through my phone, when my mom storms in. "Reiko," she says, her voice a warning.

"What?" I say, without looking up.

"Your grades came in."

Shit. With everything going on, I forgot that the school sends alerts to our parents when our grades are available.

And mine have slipped.

Seriously slipped.

Part of the reason my parents have always given me so much freedom is because I've always done what is expected of me. I get good grades, don't get into any Trouble (with a capital T, like get arrested or pregnant or something). Another reason is because a therapist told them to let me process what happened in my own way. And then the secret reason is they live in their own bubble, apart from Koji and me. Floating above us.

"What happened?" Mom says.

I shrug. "It isn't a big deal. Your senior year grades don't even matter."

"Of course they matter! They are the last grades schools see!"

"Mom, I've had a four point oh all through high school. One bad report card isn't going to ruin my life."

"Reiko, you've just completely tanked your GPA with these grades. Do you even know how bad they are?"

"It's fine," I say. "I'll pull them back up next semester."

"It's not fine," Mom says. "It isn't the grades, Reiko. It's why they've slipped this much that's worrying me. You haven't been yourself. I thought . . . I thought we were doing the right thing, leaving you be. That it was what was best for you. But now, with this whole thing over this boy—"

"Seth. He has a name." My voice is flat. I don't want to talk about Seth.

"Whatever his name is! I don't know what has been happening to you recently. It isn't healthy, Reiko—how you've been."

"I'm fine, Mom," I say, willing her to stop talking about this. "It's fine."

"No, Reiko, it isn't. We pretend it is, but it isn't." We're teetering close close close, too close to what we never talk about.

I blink furiously and take a big swig of orange juice to distract myself. But there's a lump in my throat, and the orange juice can't get past it so I start to cough, start to choke, I can't breathe—

. . . *another wave smashing my face. Water rushing down my throat . . .*

Mom is there in an instant, rubbing my back, worry etched on her face. Making soft sounds. Holding me.

"Shhh," she says. "You're okay, you're okay. Deep breaths, remember." And then, like she thinks I might have forgotten how: "You can breathe. There we go, in and out. Slowly. You're okay."

I'm okay, I'm okay, I'm okay.

After I catch my breath, Mom sits down next to me. "That . . . didn't go how I wanted it to," she says. "I'm sorry."

"I'm sorry, too," I say, voice small small small. It doesn't sound like me at all.

"You've always done so well in school. I didn't realize how much this . . . *Seth*"—she says his name carefully, like it's a grenade that could go off between us—"I didn't realize how much he meant to you."

"I didn't either," I say.

"I should have noticed sooner. I should have done something." And now I don't know if she's talking about Seth or Mika.

I give her a watery smile. "It's okay," I say.

It's okay, it's okay, it's okay.

"I think we all say that too much." She gives a watery smile. It's true. We're always fine in my family, even when we're not.

"Were you going out?" I ask, noticing for the first time that she has her coat on.

"Yes. Same place I go every Wednesday afternoon. The care home in Palm Desert."

"What? Why?"

She laughs. "Because, Reiko," she says, arching one eyebrow, "sometimes it's nice to do something for someone else."

I feel guilty then because it reminds me of my conversation with Dre, about how I treated Seth, and not just him: how I sometimes treat other people, too. Sometimes I wonder if I do things because I want people to like me, because I want to be seen as a good person, rather than because it's good to do them. I'm suddenly worried I'm not a very nice person.

"Want to come?" Mom asks.

I do.

On the way to Palm Desert I ask my mom what we're going to do when we get to the care home. "Are we going to do arts and crafts? Call bingo?"

Mom laughs and shakes her head.

"I do their hair and nails," she says, gesturing to the back seat. I look behind me and see a box full of curlers and combs, bottles of nail polish. "And you are going to help."

I'm flabbergasted.

"When I first started visiting a few years ago"—she gives me a significant look just in case I don't realize what prompted her to start volunteering—"they asked me what my skillset was. Did I want to bake cookies with them or do craft projects or games? And I thought about it and realized that with my background in the fashion and beauty world, this is what I could do." She grins. "And I've learned how to do a mean manicure, if I do say so myself."

I can't believe that my mom has this whole secret side of herself that I didn't know about. That she does something just her, without my dad.

It makes me feel like I know her better, and like I don't know her at all. It's simultaneously comforting and disquieting all at once.

CHAPTER 51

I CAN'T REMEMBER THE LAST time I hung out properly with Mom, apart from that lunch at Las Cas a few weeks ago. Since Mika died, I've avoided both her and Dad. I always thought that was better for everyone, but now I wonder if they've missed me more than I realized.

When we arrive at the Palm Desert care home, everyone knows my mom. I know I shouldn't be surprised—she did say she came every week—but I am. She's so relaxed and warm here, too, even stopping in the corridor to ask a nurse about a particular resident.

The afternoon passes quickly, and I find myself laughing more than I thought I would. The old men and women in the home are funny and kind. Frank boasts about the prizewinning hens he used to raise, Barbara confides how many lovers she's had ("Sixty-three, at last count," she says with a significant glance at Frank), and Evelyn takes my hand in her own and tells me, without preamble, that she lost her own sister when she was young, and a daughter ten years ago.

"So I know what it is to lose people," she says quietly, eyes wide and clear.

I stiffen and quickly look up to see if my mom heard, but she's laughing loudly at something Frank is saying. I take a deep breath. I'm fine, I'm fine. This is just a sweet old lady. She's not going to make me talk about Mika.

"Your mama is doing the best she can," she goes on. "And that's all anyone can do."

"I know," I whisper.

"I hope you come back with her. You smell like sunshine. It's good for our old souls."

On the way home, I feel lighter than I have in months. Mom turns down the Christmas music that's been blasting out. "I'm going to check in more," she says. "I've let you get too far away. I want to be there for you. That's all I ever want, Reiko. To be there for you."

"I know," I say. And this moment should be special, it should be making us closer, but it's making me feel awkward; it's making me feel claustrophobic. "Today was fun," I blurt.

"You really think so?" A shy hope is pushing my mom's sadness away, like a gentle but persistent breeze.

"Yeah," I say, and I realize I mean it. "It was."

Mom smiles at me.

"Can I go with you next week, too?" I ask.

"I'd love that. And I think the little crew there would, too. They've got each other for company, but I know they love visitors."

She pauses. "It helps me to think of other people. Gets me out of my own head."

It's the closest Mom has come to talking about missing Mika, and I'm surprised by what she's said. I always thought my mom and dad were fine because they had each other and because they always always always reassure me that they are okay, but after today I know Mom isn't . . .

"Hey, dreamy eyes"—Mom nudges me—"you all right?"

"Yeah," I say.

Because for the first time in a long time, I feel like I might be.

CHAPTER 52

WHEN THE NEW SEMESTER STARTS, I feel like I've missed more than a few parties. I'm completely out of the loop, like everyone learned a new language over break, one that I don't know. Libby struts down the hall with Seth by her side and I wonder if I ever looked like that, ever walked like that, was ever that obnoxious in my reign.

I wonder if I'll ever be back on the throne again.

But most of all, I wonder if it even matters. Why did I try so hard to be so popular? It wasn't like it was going to bring my sister back. It isn't like me being as perfect as I could be was ever going to make a difference. One can never be good enough for two.

I'm in the bathroom between classes one morning in late January when I hear someone sniffling in their stall. No, not sniffling. Sobbing.

My instinct is to dry my hands and get out of here as fast as I can.

But.

I wait for a second. Just to make sure.

The stall door opens and I recognize the girl who steps out. She was in my art history class, the one who gave me her Diet Coke. Penny. Her name is Penny.

She's still crying, head down, hair covering her face, but then she glances up.

"Hey," I say. "You okay?"

"I'm fine," she says, voice clogged.

"Are you sure?"

"Yep." She's still facing away from me.

I hesitate. I know what it feels like when you don't want anyone to know you are hurting. I want to do something. I dig around in my bag for my hydrating cream that I use when my skin gets puffy from not getting enough sleep. "Penny?"

She glances over her shoulder. "Yeah?" I can see how red her eyes are now.

"Here." I hold out the cream to her. "Put this on under your eyes. It'll help."

"Thanks," she says.

I smile at her.

Before I go to sleep that night, I tell Mika what happened.

"I thought about what you would do," I say, shrugging my shoulders a bit, suddenly feeling strangely bashful about my unexpected act of altruism. I want her to be proud of me.

Mika shakes her head and laughs softly. "Reiko, that's nice and all, but it's not that nice."

"It's not?" I shrink into my pillows.

Mika climbs up next to me. "I mean, of course it's nice, but it isn't like you deserve a medal or something."

I cringe. She's right. I want a shiny gold star for being a good person. I want the credit.

"I could have just walked away." My tone is more defensive than I mean for it to be.

Mika laughs again and nudges me with her shoulder. "Oh, Reiko." For the first time in a long, long while, I feel like she's the big sister again. Like everything is the way it is supposed to be. "You know what you should do?"

"What?"

"You should go out to lunch with her tomorrow."

"What? She wouldn't even talk to me in the bathroom. She won't want to go to lunch with me."

"Of course she will. Aren't you 'Reiko Smith-Mori'?" She puts my name in air quotes.

"Maybe that is how it used to be, but not anymore," I mutter darkly.

"Reiko! This isn't like you at all. Just because you aren't with that Seth guy and because Libby is being a bitch . . ."

I inhale sharply, shocked at the swear word.

Mika rolls her eyes. "Yes, I said bitch. I'm fourteen, remember?"

Like I ever need reminding.

"Anyway," Mika goes on. "You're still you. They didn't take anything away from you. They can't. And I guarantee this girl won't care that you aren't with stupid Seth Rogers or are fighting with Libby. And plus, it's more than that. She'll appreciate that you are being nice." Mika leans in close. "If someone heard you crying in the bathroom, I'd want them to be nice to you, too."

The next day Dre asks if I want to go and get burgers for lunch.

"I'm actually going to try to find this girl Penny," I say.

Dre scrunches her face up. "Who is that?"

"You know, blondish hair, kind of short?" I realize I don't know anything else about her except that she was in my art history class, likes Diet Coke, and was crying yesterday.

"Reiko, that's, like, half the female population of Palm High. Why do you have to find her?"

I shrug. "I found her crying in the bathroom yesterday and . . . I want to see if she's okay."

Dre's scrunched expression gets even scrunchier. "By taking her to lunch? That's weird." Then she full-on frowns. "This isn't like some sort of friend version of whatever the hell happened with Seth Rogers, right?"

I laugh. "Dre, it isn't like with Seth. I'm not . . . trying to use her to make myself feel better," I say slowly, trying to articulate what it was I did with Seth. I'm still not sure if I even understand it. "I just thought it would be a nice thing to do."

"Still sounds weird, but, hey, I'll take this over you rocking up in a sexy schoolgirl outfit."

"Dre!" I swat her on the arm.

She steps back and laughs. "Go have lunch with your new friend, you weirdo."

I find Penny by herself in the parking lot.

"Hey," I say. "How are you?"

She tilts her head to the side. "Hi . . . I'm fine, I guess?"

"Cool," I say, voice overly bright. "I'm glad to hear it."

"Oh, do you want your lotion back? Thanks, by the way, it really helped with . . ." She gestures to her face.

I shake my head. "Oh, don't worry about it. You can keep it. That's not why I came over."

"Well . . . then what do you want?"

I try to channel Mika. "I was thinking . . . maybe we could go to lunch?"

"To lunch?"

"Yeah!" I say, words tumbling out. "Just because, you know, you seemed upset yesterday, and I thought maybe that would help?"

"Why are you doing this?" she says, looking wary. "It's fine, I'm not some charity case."

"I know that!" I say. "I just . . . I don't know. I thought I'd ask." I feel dumb.

"I mean, that's really nice of you, but it isn't like we're friends."

"I know," I say, starting to feel my neck get warm. "Listen, don't worry about it. It was a silly suggestion."

She exhales, long and loud. "No, I appreciate it. You might actually understand, too." Her eyes are piercing.

Warning bells go off in my brain. This isn't what I was

expecting. This isn't what I was prepared for. I wonder if she knows about Mika.

"My mom's sick," she says. "Like really sick. It's really scary. I haven't told anyone. I don't know . . ." Her voice trails off.

". . . how to talk about it," I say. "Yeah. I get that." I pause. "Well, do you . . . want to?"

"Not really. But I do actually kind of want to go to lunch."

"Yeah?"

"Yeah."

We go to a burrito place near campus. Penny doesn't say anything else about her mom, and I don't say anything about Mika. We talk about random stuff, like what our favorite time period was last year in art history. She tells me she wants to major in art history and maybe study abroad in Paris.

"Do you want to study abroad?" she asks.

"I used to want to go to Japan." The words are out of my mouth before I've thought them through.

"But not anymore?" It's a gentle prying, but still a prying. Like when the dentist is checking for cavities.

I think about the applications I sent to schools in Japan. And I'm filled with a quiet and familiar longing that feels something like being homesick.

"I don't know." My honesty makes my words heavy.

"Japan has a really cool modern art scene," she says, and I nod. She's right. I'd forgotten that.

I wonder what else I've forgotten about Japan.

When we get back to campus, we exchange numbers. "We should hang out again," I say. And I mean it.

"Yeah," Penny says, grinning. "We should."

That night at home, I realize I don't want to tell Mika about lunch, because that would seem like I wanted credit for spending time with Penny. And yesterday, I did. But after actually hanging out with her . . . that seems ridiculous.

And the next morning, when I'm alone in my room, I get out my Japan scrapbook. As I gently flip the pages, looking at the pictures, reading my and Mika's captions, I get that same twinge of strange homesickness. And something else. A tiny spark of wanting.

CHAPTER 53

AS JANUARY TURNS INTO FEBRUARY, I find myself making new routines.

I go to the care home on Wednesdays.

I start studying again, really studying, to bring my grades up.

I ask my mom to take Dre, Penny, and me to an art gallery opening.

I start rock climbing again.

And I barely think about Seth at all.

As I'm heading through the house to my room one night, I hear a guitar playing in the garage. I pause, because it sounds good. Really good. So good that I'm sure it can't be Koji.

But it is. When I go into the garage, he's strumming his heart out and belting a Radiohead song with his eyes closed. I let him finish the song and then wolf whistle and applaud.

He looks up, startled.

"Koji, you sound amazing!"

He puts down the guitar and runs his hand through his hair. His chubby cheeks that I thought he'd always have are gone—all his baby fat has melted away. He's somehow gone from my adorable, albeit pesky, little brother to a confident, handsome teenager. When did he get so grown up?

"Thanks," he says. "I've been practicing a lot."

"It shows. I'm really impressed."

His words come out all in a rush. "Actually . . . I'm auditioning for this thing, this band thing? It is kind of like *American Idol*? But, like, a new show. And I was wondering if you could come? To support me?" He's tugging on his shirt and not looking at me.

"Me?"

"Yeah. You're allowed to bring two people, so I chose you and Ivan." Koji has known Ivan almost his whole life—they are close the way Andrea and I are close.

"Are you sure you don't want Mom or Dad to go with you?"

He shakes his head. "I want you to be there. Like you were for . . . you know, when you used to go to her recitals . . ."

I don't know what to say. I want to support Koji, but I wish Mika was here, too. She loved music so much.

I'm quiet too long and Koji's face falls. "I mean, you don't have to. It isn't a big deal."

But it is.

And I want to be there for Koji. Especially since Mika can't. She'd want me to be a good sister to Koji. Like she always was to me. I have to push aside my own feelings and do the right thing for my brother.

"I'd love to be there," I say. "When is it?"

"Not till March. So I've still got plenty of time to practice."

"I wouldn't miss it for anything."

SPRING

CHAPTER 54

ONE NIGHT IN EARLY MARCH, I'm almost asleep when my phone buzzes with a text message. And keeps buzzing. And then it rings. It's Dre. I pick up, worried that something's wrong.

"Reiko! UC admissions emails just went out! I got in! I got into UCLA! We're going to go to UCLA together!" She's shouting and out of breath.

I can hear Tori in the background. "My baby sister is going to be a Bruin!"

"Dre! That's amazing!" But I must have waited a second too long to respond, or maybe my excitement isn't quite what she was hoping for, because her voice wilts.

"You got in, right?"

"I mean, I haven't checked, but . . ." I hesitate. Old Reiko would have been sure she'd gotten in. But then Old Reiko was sure that Seth would never break up with her, and look how that turned out. I'm not sure about anything anymore. I'm not who I thought I was. No—I'm not who I wanted everyone else to think I was.

"I'm sure you got in," Dre says, but just like me, she waited a second too long to say it.

"But . . . what if I didn't?" I whisper.

"You did, you definitely did."

"But we're celebrating *you*!" I say. This is about Dre. I shouldn't be making it about me. "I'm so proud of you, Dre," I say, and I mean it.

"Thanks, babe. Do you want to come over to celebrate? My mom's making the tamales she only makes for Christmas."

"Dre, it's almost midnight and your mom is making tamales?"

Dre laughs. "She's excited."

"Ah, it's pretty late," I say. I can't face it, and I don't want to think about why. "I'm already in bed. But I'll come pick you up for lunch tomorrow? My treat! To celebrate you!"

"To celebrate *us*," Dre says. "My mama is already cheering for you."

"Go celebrate with your family. We'll have plenty of time to celebrate together."

After I hang up, I check my email, my fingers trembling as I log in.

I didn't get in.

Since the breakup, Seth has taken up so much space in my brain that there hasn't been room for anything else. For the first time I start to wonder what else I've given up by letting him have so much space in my brain, in my heart, in my life. It's like I've been wearing tunnel-vision glasses, and all I could see was him.

Getting Seth back won't fix my not getting into UCLA.

I can't fix that.

Was he worth all this?

"So I didn't get into UCLA," I say at breakfast the next day, trying to keep my voice breezy and light. Part of me hopes my parents don't hear me, that my words are so breezy and light they just blow right out of the window.

They hear me.

"Oh, honey," Mom says, coming over and folding me into a hug. I expect her to tell me that she knew this would happen when she saw my fall grades, but she doesn't.

"They are idiots!" Dad declares, banging his coffee mug on the table for emphasis. Coffee sloshes over the side of the mug. "Absolute idiots!" He's so genuinely surprised that I realize my mom must have not told him about my slipping grades.

"And you," Mom says to him, letting me go and grabbing a dish towel, "are getting coffee all over the table."

"Sorry, Rei," says Koji, looking up for a brief moment from his phone. "That sucks."

"I just . . . can't believe it," I say.

"Holy shit!" Koji says, as something pings on his phone.

"Koji, as much as I appreciate your empathy for your sister, watch your language, please," Mom says lightly.

"No, not that." He looks up at me. "I mean, no offense, Rei. But they've just announced the final date and time for the *Show Us the Talent* auditions! It's next Sunday! I'm scheduled for ten a.m.! It's actually happening!"

"That's wonderful, Koji." Mom beams. It's like I haven't just told them I didn't get into my dream school.

"Are you sure we can't go with you?" Dad adds.

"I've already put Reiko and Ivan down," says Koji. "You still want to come, right, Reiko?"

"Of course," I say. And I do. But I also kind of wish we were still talking about UCLA. But we spend the rest of the morning talking about Koji's audition. And I tell myself that it is because my parents don't want me to get upset. As I've got a history of bottling things up, they probably think that's how I want to deal with everything bad that happens to me.

CHAPTER 55

EVEN THOUGH SETH IS A part of our regular crew now, I haven't spoken directly to him in months. Libby either. So I'm shocked when I get a text from him the following Saturday morning asking me if I want to go climbing.

It's been a crappy week. Koji was right. Not getting into UCLA does suck. A lot. It sucks having to tell everyone that I didn't get in and having to act like it's fine. But I hear the whispers slithering through the halls.

Did you hear that Reiko Smith-Mori didn't get into UCLA?

What I hear instead is *Did you hear that Reiko Smith-Mori isn't that great?*

And then I hear something that makes everything worse.

Seth got into UCLA.

"At least you won't have to worry about seeing him there," says Dre.

I can't help but feel like it's because I told him to apply.

I feel like he took my spot.

But getting Seth's text makes me feel better. I grin at my phone, because it feels like everything is finally going back to how it used to be. How it should be.

We decide to go on a night climb. Like when we first properly met out under the stars. As I drive to his trailer, I'm giddy with anticipation. And then he gets in the front seat like he has so many times before and it feels so normal. It feels right.

"Hey," he says.

"Hey," I say back. And then, because I have to know: "What prompted this?"

He shrugs. "Wanted to see you." A pause. "I got into UCLA. And I wouldn't have even applied if you hadn't encouraged me."

"I know, I heard. Congratulations," I say. And I mostly mean it. Especially if he's giving me the credit I deserve.

"Yeah," he says, smiling his Seth smile at me.

I smile back.

"And . . . it made me realize that I miss you," he goes on.

"Thanks, I guess?" I say. I feel like I should be more pleased than I actually am.

"I should be thanking you. I guess some of your good luck really did rub off on me."

This time my smile is more forced. "So . . . you and Libby. How is that?"

"Ah, she's been kind of a bitch recently. We're not really together anymore."

"Oh, cool," I say.

I knew it. I knew he'd realize that he missed me.

Feeling confident, I drive toward one of our regular climbing spots, or what used to be one of our regular spots, but as we're going down a dark road, Seth asks me to stop the car. "Just pull over here."

I'm perplexed, but I do it. Then I try to remember if Seth ever used to talk to me like this, in this casually bossy way.

Like he just expects me to do his bidding.

The way I used to talk to him.

"Is there something here?" I say, parking on the side of the road.

"You're here," he says, and then leans across and kisses me. Hard.

I'm so stunned that for a second, I don't respond, but then I start kissing him back. Maybe this time we can treat each other better; know each other better.

He pulls back and looks in the back seat. "I thought we could maybe pick up where we left off," he says. "You know, for old times' sake."

CHAPTER 56

HE PULLS ME AGAINST HIM, and then his lips are wet on my jaw, on my neck, on my collarbone. He runs his hand along the curves of my body. "I forgot how great your ass is," he says.

I flinch at his words and his touch.

I remind myself that this is Seth. Seth Rogers. He's happy and celebrating about UCLA. I helped him with that. He needs me. Everything is back the way it used to be. And I'm in control again.

But.

He feels like a stranger. It feels like when I kissed that guy in Morongo.

And I don't like it.

I tell myself that I can do this, I can handle it, I can be in control. And suddenly, he is taking my shirt off, and my jeans, eyes not on my face, eyes on my body, eyes so big that they take up his whole face except for his mouth because his mouth is on me, too. It's like he's nothing but eyes and mouth and hands.

And something else, something in his boxers, because somehow between taking off my shirt and us lying down in the back seat, he's also stripped down to his boxers.

There is something urgent about the way he's kissing me. Something desperate. I feel like he's going to tear my skin off with his fingers, the way he's pawing at me. The way he's clawing at me, it's like he wants to devour me. Like he wants to own me.

I'm in charge, I'm in charge, I tell myself. It's Seth. I'm always in charge with us. That is how it works. But it shouldn't be about power.

I try to straighten and push back, but he's on me like a leech, like he's trying to suck out my soul through my lips. This isn't how people kiss. Or maybe this is how a person kisses when they have wanted something for so long and they are finally getting what they want. But it doesn't feel like I'm in a car with a person. It feels like I'm trapped in the car with a fox or a raccoon, something with sharp teeth and claws. Something that looked kind of cuddly before but has turned into something else entirely.

More pawing. More clawing.

And then. "Stop, Seth," I say, but it's like he doesn't hear me, like he doesn't speak English. Like he doesn't speak human.

He is on top of me, writhing, and I'm under him, and I never noticed how heavy he was until this moment, until he won't get off of me.

His hip bones are digging into my own. I'm sure I can hear our bones grinding against each other, like teeth gnashing. He is the top of the jaw and I am the bottom and we are gnashing gnawing, and this was not how I ever wanted this to be, not how I imagined it would be, especially not with Seth.

He finally takes a breath, and it is then that I shove him, hard as I can. I shove him *off*, and then I reach up behind my head and open the car door and I slip out, practically going headfirst, not caring that I'm barefoot and only in my bra and silk underwear. Flimsy as it is, tonight it feels like my armor.

The sand is rough under my feet. The windows of the Jeep are so fogged up that I can't see Seth. When he comes out of the car, he's wearing his jeans and T-shirt. He's taken the time to get dressed.

"What was that?" he says, eyes searching. "What happened in there?"

"I should be asking you what the hell happened in there. I said stop, Seth."

He blinks, and every time his eyelids flutter closed and open back up again, he is more and more human. More the Seth that I used to know.

"You did?" There is genuine confusion in his voice, undercut by something else that I can't place.

"Yes! Why do you think I shoved you?"

"I thought you were into it . . ." he says, hands in his pockets, eyes on the moon. "And it isn't like we were, you know, actually . . ."

"It doesn't matter what we were actually doing! I said stop!"

"You seemed into it at first," he mutters, staring at his feet. "I mean, you were kissing me back."

"Yeah, at first. Sort of. But then I wasn't."

"Well, that isn't very fair, is it? How am I supposed to know when you aren't into it?"

"When I say stop!" I shout, so loud that my words bounce up into the night sky and back down to our feet and shatter in pieces all around us.

He nods. "All right," he says. But it doesn't sound like he is all right with it. "But it's me," he goes on. Like because of what was once between us, because I'd been wanting him back, I now owe him more than I want to give him.

We glare at each other for a minute.

A beat. "I'm sorry, Reiko," he says. "I'm really sorry." He runs his hand through his hair. "I didn't mean for that to happen. And . . . I should have stopped when you said stop."

I rub my arms. I'm starting to feel the chill now. I don't answer because I don't know what the proper response is when your ex-boyfriend—who you thought you wanted to get back with—has to apologize for getting too aggressive with you in the back of a car. Seth broke my heart, and I'm wondering now if he broke my sanity a bit, too.

"Are you cold?" he says.

"I'm not warm."

"Here," he says, taking his T-shirt off and handing it to me. "Put this on." Something about the way he does it makes me feel dumb, like it is *my* fault I'm standing out in the desert in my bra and underwear. Even though all of this—us fighting out in the desert, him turning feral, him not listening to me, him not getting off of me, me pushing him—is *his* fault. And I know that.

I don't take his shirt. "Let's just get back in the car," I say, opening the door and grabbing my own shirt, wishing that I had never taken it off at all.

Even with my clothes back on, I shiver.

Because it's cold tonight, even in the desert.

I drive him back to his place, even though part of me wants to leave him out in the desert to fend for himself.

"Reiko," he says, as we pull up in front of his trailer where I've dropped him off countless times. "I'm sorry. I don't know who that guy was."

"Yeah," I say. "I don't know who he was either." And as I stare at Seth, I wonder if I ever knew who he was.

"Maybe we can go climbing tomorrow, like actually climbing?"

I shake my head. "I don't think so. But I'm sure I'll see you around at school."

For a second, I think he's going to say something else, but then he just nods. "Yeah, I'll see you."

And as I pull away from his place, I know it's the last time I'll drive out here. But that doesn't make me sad. I don't need his good-byes, or his apologies, or his well wishes.

I don't need anything from him.

I don't know why I ever thought I did.

I don't tell my parents what happened between me and Seth, because I don't have the words. And even if I *did* want to talk about it, it isn't the kind of thing I'd want to tell my parents.

I climb into bed, turn off my phone, and ignore everyone, even Mika.

And I sleep.

CHAPTER 57

THERE IS A PERSISTENT KNOCKING at my locked door.

I open my eyes, wincing in the bright light. The knocking has turned into more of a hammering. I stumble toward my door and yank it open, expecting to see Dre on the other side. Or maybe my mom.

Not my little brother, wearing a leather jacket, with his hair styled, guitar case slung across his back, glaring at me.

"Where were you?" he says.

"What?" I rub my eyes.

"My audition? The one I've been practicing for nonstop for months?"

"Oh no, Koji, was that today?"

"Yes, it was today! And you missed it!" His voice cracks.

"I'm so sorry, Koji, I really am."

"I needed you," he says, and he sounds impossibly young.

"I'll make it up to you. I promise. How did it go?"

"You weren't there. I asked you to be there. I felt so stupid asking you, telling you about it, and then you didn't even show up. You don't even care. All you care about is yourself and what is going on with you."

"Koji, that isn't true. I'm sorry. I just . . ." I can't say that someone I trusted broke my trust again, that someone I thought I knew turned out to be someone different. I can't put into words what happened with Seth, and even if I could, I don't want to tell my little brother that.

But then Koji barrels on. "I should have known you were never going to go. And I know why."

"Koj, what are you talking about?"

"You would have been there for . . ." And he stops just short of saying Mika's name. "I'm still here, you know. *Really* here." And it stings. And suddenly, Mika and Seth are all wrapped up together in a way I never meant for them to be and Koji is right, he's here. He's here.

"Koj, honestly, it was a mistake."

"Everyone thinks that I don't miss her because I was too little, but of course I do. That doesn't mean I don't want to have my own life! I can do music, too, and I can go to the beach. It isn't fair, Reiko. It isn't fair."

I want to say that it isn't about Mika, that something else happened, but everything is always about Mika with me, and Koji knows it.

I don't know when he started to cry, but he is and I go toward him and I hug my little brother as he cries. He's my height now. I don't know when that happened.

"I'll make it up to you," I whisper.

"No, you won't," he says, pulling away from me. "You've never been there for me. I never ask you for anything. This was the one thing. And you couldn't even show up."

"Koji, please, I'll make it up to you. I swear."

He rubs his nose on the back of his hand and for a moment looks years younger. Then he looks up at me, defiantly.

"It's fine," he says. "Don't worry about it."

"Koji, seriously. I will. Just . . . let me figure something out."

He shrugs. "If you say so."

"I will."

And I know something has to change, but I don't know how to do it.

Things between me and Seth are broken, and I don't think they can be fixed. I don't think I *want* them to be fixed. When I turn my phone back on, I've got texts from him, even voicemails. He's finally chasing me again, wanting me again, but it isn't like how I thought it would be. He isn't who I thought he was. He's changed. Or maybe he was always like that and I saw what I wanted to see, like he did with me.

And I find myself weeding him out of my heart like you would weed an untended garden. I didn't realize I'd let him grow so rampantly unchecked in there. I weed until my heart is recognizable again. Until it is completely my own again, with only one big crack down the middle—but that isn't from Seth.

I thought he had broken my heart, but now I know it's been broken for years, and that is why it didn't take much for him to make it crumble.

It's easy to break an already broken heart.

CHAPTER 58

WHEN I GET HOME FROM school the following Tuesday, I get an email from the University of Tokyo.

It's a rejection letter.

I didn't get in.

I didn't get into UCLA.

And I didn't get into the University of Tokyo.

"Oh well," I say quietly to myself. "I didn't want to go anyway." But it's not true. I've been looking at the scrapbook more and more.

I don't know how I'm going to tell my dad. He's going to be crushed.

I wait until after dinner that night.

"Hey, Dad, want to play chess?" I ask, wanting to get him alone. I can't tell him in front of Mom, since she never even knew I applied. It would break her heart to know I'd applied without telling her, and then disappoint her to know that I hadn't gotten in.

"Sure!" he says, beaming at me. "It's been a while." He doesn't know how often I play with Mika.

We go into his study and he gets out his old marble set. The figures are carved like Japanese samurai.

I take a deep breath. "I didn't get in."

He looks up at me, his eyes kind. "I know, sweetie. You told us."

"No, not just UCLA," I say, my voice cracking. "I didn't get into the University of Tokyo." I stare very hard at the chessboard. Just one more thing I didn't do, couldn't do, that Mika would have.

"Oh," Dad says as I move my knight. I wait for him to say what he said about UCLA, that they are all idiots. Wait for him to reassure me.

"Well, it is very competitive," he says.

I blink.

"And they are very . . . traditional," he goes on. "But that's a shame." Then he does this weird fake laugh. "Maybe Koji will get in."

I suddenly realize how much it meant to him for one of us to go.

"I'm sorry," he says, and then all his words come out at once, as if he's just realized what he should have been saying. "I don't know what they were thinking. Rejecting you! My daughter! It's madness, I tell you, absolute madness. Must have gotten stricter from when I went."

"Maybe," I say.

"You'll get in somewhere wonderful. Somewhere great." And I don't know if it is my imagination, but he doesn't sound as confident as he did the last time he told me that.

I'm starting to wonder if I'll get in anywhere at all.

He moves his bishop and looks at me. "Reiko, is everything okay? You've not been yourself this year." He gives me a sad smile. "Don't deny it—your mother and I notice. But we thought letting you do what you need to do is best. But now I don't know."

"I miss Mika," I say, the whisper slipping out like a leaf falling, inevitable and fragile.

If I'd said Mika's name to my mom, it would have been like dropping a bomb, but my dad just sighs deeply, like he's been waiting to let out that breath forever.

"I know, Reiko. I know." He reaches across the chessboard and takes my hand. "We miss her, too." He takes a long breath. "But you can't blame what happened for everything that has happened since then. And"—he squeezes my hand—"you can't blame yourself."

I squeeze his hand back.

"She'd be so proud of you, Reiko. I'm so proud of you." And then: "But I think she'd want you to talk about her. And I think she'd want you to live the very best life you could."

I've been trying, I want to say. *I've been trying so hard*.

But.

I don't know who I've been living for.

Mika knows something is wrong, but she doesn't ask me about it. Instead, she flutters around, rubbing my shoulder, playing with my hair. I wonder if she knows I talked about her for the first time in years with our dad. I look at her, look through her.

I wish I could tell her about Seth and the college rejections and about missing Koji's audition. I wish she was here-here, big-sister-here, instead of here like this. This is the kind of thing I want to tell nineteen-year-old her. A Mika who is older and wiser than me and who would have the kind of advice and the kind of comfort I need.

Fourteen-year-old her isn't much help. But I only have myself to blame that this is the version I have of her. And that makes my heart ache.

She senses that I need something more than she can give me. "I think you should call Andrea," she says.

"Really?" I'm surprised because usually Mika wants it to be just us.

"Of course," she says. "I don't think I can help you right now, and Dre can." She smiles at me. "I love you, Reiko."

So I do what my sister thinks is best and call Dre.

CHAPTER 59

I TELL DRE ALMOST EVERYTHING

I tell her about not getting into the University of Tokyo.

I tell her about letting Koji down.

And I tell her I saw Seth, and it didn't go well. I don't elaborate.

"Oh, babe, I'm sorry," she says. And then after a long pause, she adds, "You know this weekend is the Beach Band Bash?"

"I don't even know what that is."

"It's this big jam session down in Oceanside. Tori's boyfriend is one of the organizers. I bet he could get Koji on the lineup. You know, to make up for you missing his audition."

"Wait, what? Really? That would be amazing!" Then her words sink in. "It's . . . at the beach?"

"Kind of in the name, Rei-Rei."

I think about what Koji said to me, about not making his music a thing, not making the ocean a thing.

I close my eyes.

I want to make it up to him.

And this? Celebrating his music on the beach?

It's the perfect way.

"That sounds great. If Tori's boyfriend really can do that."

"Oh, for sure. But, Rei . . . you'll be all right?"

"Yeah, I think I will."

Koji can't believe that I've gotten him on the lineup for the Beach Band Bash. "This is the first time I'll have ever jammed in front of, like, a real audience!" He's beaming. "This is going to be so awesome."

"I know it doesn't make up for me missing your audition, but I'm so proud of you. I can't wait to hear you play." Then I smile. "Properly play, not just out in our garage."

"Thanks, Reiko," he says.

"Do you want Mom and Dad to be there?" I ask.

"Mom and Dad are in New York this weekend, remember? Dad has some business trip, and Mom is going with him."

"So it'll be just us." I haven't told Mika I'm going back to the beach. I'm scared to tell her. I don't know what she'd say.

"Yeah," he says, grinning. "We'll have to represent for the Smith-Moris."

A slight pang thrums through me, like I've hit my funny bone, but then it's gone.

"Yeah," I say, "we will."

CHAPTER 60

THE LAST TIME I SAW the sea I was twelve. I'm seventeen now. Five years is a long time to not see the sea. But it is a hard thing to forget. Especially when it stole your sister.

It is bigger than I remember it.

We're in my car. Koji is in the back seat, wearing his headphones, humming and bopping his head to a beat I can't hear. I don't think he knows how big this is for me.

I don't think I want him to know.

I keep both hands on the steering wheel, but I can feel my palms starting to sweat.

It's a different beach than the one I last saw, but it's the same ocean.

Dre is sitting next to me, and she reaches over and rubs my arm. "You're doing great," she says. "We'll be way up on the beach. Nobody is going in the water. You'll be fine. We'll all be fine."

I feel like I'm going to throw up, but I nod.

I'm fine, I'm fine, I'm fine.

* * *

We park and then take Koji over to where he needs to be. He's the third act. I thank Tori and her boyfriend for getting Koji on the lineup and go with Dre into the crowd to wait for Koji's set.

I'm surprised how many people are here from our school. Oceanside is a good two hours from Palm Springs, but I recognize lots of faces. Zach Garcia is here, too, and at first, I think he's staying close to me, but then I realize he can't keep his eyes off Dre. And she keeps looking over her shoulder and beaming at him.

Something clicks in my brain. I realize that Dre must be crazy about Zach. And that he must feel the same way about her. How did I not see it before? Just as I'm about to text Dre demanding that she tell me everything, the speakers crackle around us, distracting me.

"Next up, Koji Smith-Mori!" says the host from the small stage set up on the beach.

I cheer as loud as I can.

Koji makes his way onto the stage, and he looks like someone I've never seen before. He looks older, more confident. And when he starts to play, I'm blown away by how good he is.

I wish my parents could see him like this.

I wish Mika could see him like this.

He plays three songs, and then, amid the cheers and applause, he leans close to the mic. "I just want to thank my sister Reiko, who's here tonight, and my sister Mika, who I wish could be here, too."

Dre grabs my hand.

I know Koji means well.

I know he means it with love.

But suddenly, the crowd feels like it is crushing me, and I need to get some space. Need to get some air. But even the air is heavy here, not like dry desert air.

"I'll be right back," I say to Dre, pushing my way past people, out of the crowd. Right as I'm almost through the throng of people, I look up and see Seth walking toward me.

I don't believe he's here.

I stare at him across the sand and he stares at me, and I try to remember that once upon a time, we were friends.

And I pretend for a second that things had gone differently with us and we'd just been friends all summer and we'd never hurt each other.

And then someone runs up next to him and grabs his hand, and it's Libby. And I remember how he called her a bitch and how I reveled in thinking I was better than her, and even though she's been awful, the thought makes me feel icky. All the same, I don't like looking at them. So I kind of wave goodbye at them, and Libby gives me this weird wave back, and I'm mad at both of them but also at myself.

I turn and walk in the other direction.

Down to the sea.

I think I see a figure in the surf.

No . . . it can't be. It's too dark, and my eyes are playing tricks on me.

There, in the moonlight, there.

It's Mika.

It's Mika.

Mika is in the sea.

And I'm worried she's angry that I came back here and didn't even tell her. Is she angry that I came to watch Koji play? I have to explain.

I start to run.

Into the sea, into the waves.

Mika!

Mika!

I hear someone yelling my name from the shore, and I turn back for a second.

And then a wave crashes into me. And drags me down.

Drags me under—

. . . wet coarse sand . . . in my nose . . . in my mouth, and water, so much water . . . my lungs a bubble about to burst . . .

Memory merges with reality, and I don't know which way is up.

This has happened before.

I keep my eyes and my mouth tightly shut, but my lungs are starting to scream for oxygen and then there are arms behind me, around me, pulling me up, pulling me out and then—

Air, sweet starlit air.

I'm shaking all over, and I open my eyes to see Dre and Zach on either side of me, pulling me out of the surf and up the beach, away from the waves. Away from the sea.

"Reiko! Honey, you're okay. We got you," says Dre.

I look past her, and Seth is standing up on the beach, exactly where he was before. He hasn't moved.

"You're shaking! Don't worry, we'll get you warm and dry," Dre goes on.

"Is she okay? Why isn't she answering?" says Zach.

Seth still hasn't moved. He's standing with Libby, and they're just staring at me.

A sob that starts low inside of me rips its way through my heart, and then I'm shaking even harder and sobbing.

Zach's eyes widen, and he looks at Dre for instructions. Jumping into the waves to rescue a drowning girl is one thing; dealing with this is something else.

Someone has stopped the music and people are starting to crowd around us.

"What are you all looking at?" Dre shouts. "I didn't see any of you going to help her!" I don't know if she's specifically yelling at Libby and Seth or at everyone.

"My brother," I gasp. "Where's Koji?"

"He's right here, sweetie. He's right here. He was just packing up his stuff. Hold on." Dre looks over her shoulder. "Koji! Let Koji through!"

And then he's there; my little brother is next to me, fear splashed across his face.

"Reiko, everything is okay, everything is okay," he says in a low, calm voice. "Here, Zach, I've got her." And then my brother loops my arm over his shoulders. "Come on, Rei."

Dre and Koji lead me up the beach and toward my car. Tori runs up with towels she's procured from somewhere and wraps me up.

They lay me down in the back seat, with my head in Dre's lap. She strokes my hair.

"Mika? Where's Mika?" I say. "I saw Mika."

"Oh, honey," says Dre, and her lip is trembling. Then she leans forward toward her sister, who is sitting in the driver's seat. "Tori, she's asking about Mika."

"She's fine," says Tori, with a gentle firmness. "She's just had a shock. She's fine. We'll keep her warm and bundled, and we'll get her home."

I'm still shaking. I can't stop shaking.

Koji is sitting in the front seat beside Tori and looking back at me with wide eyes. "Should I call my parents?"

"Koji! Don't go anywhere!" I say, unable to keep my teeth from chattering. "Don't go."

Dre keeps stroking my wet hair. "Shh, he's not going anywhere. Nobody is going anywhere. We're all right here, babe. We're right here." She looks up at Koji. "Tori's right, she'll be okay. But, yeah, maybe call your parents to let them know what happened."

Koji nods but keeps watching me, watching me like I'm watching him. Like if we look away, one of us might disappear.

"Don't go," I say again, and Dre holds me close.

"I'm not going anywhere," she says. "Koji's not going anywhere. We're right here."

But Mika isn't here. *Mika isn't here.*

I couldn't save her.

I'll never save her.

CHAPTER 61

The Last Time I Saw the Sea

"TAKE CARE OF YOUR SISTER," Mom called out as Mika and I ran down the beach. She was fourteen, and I was twelve, but being at the beach made us act like little girls again. "Don't go in too deep," she warned, but we weren't scared. We were good swimmers. I trusted the sea then.

The waves changed without us noticing. And when I came up for air after diving like a mermaid, I was slammed back into the ocean, and I tumbled around like a sock in the washing machine. I didn't know which way was up, which way was down. Then I felt the sand under my fingers—It got in my nose and in my mouth, and not just sand, water, so much water, my lungs were a balloon that was about to pop. I was trying to fight it, but I couldn't, and then there were hands around my ankle, pulling me up and out. Like I was a fish that they'd caught by the tail. I came up choking, water slapping me in the face.

Mika was there. Breathing hard, tears streaking down her face. "Come here," she said, reaching out for me.

"Mika, I'm scared!"

"You'll be okay, Reiko," Mika whispered in my ear. "Be brave."

And then another wave came and we went down, and by the time the lifeguard got out to us, Mika was exhausted, because she'd been swimming for both of us. As soon as the lifeguard was close enough, Mika thrust me at him and he caught me in his arms and as I let go of my sister, another wave came, and took her.

They told us, after, that we were lucky they found her body at all, lucky that it hadn't been swept away.

Lucky.

The ocean can do that, they said. Change quickly. Too quickly for anyone to notice. They didn't use emotional words. They didn't say that it gets angry. They said things like

rip

tides

currents

words as cold as the sea.

But I know. I was in it. That sea was angry. And it was greedy. And it stole my sister.

And it should have been me. And I have spent every moment since trying to make up for it.

CHAPTER 62

I WAKE UP IN MY bed. Alone.

It's the next morning. My parents are still in New York.

I go downstairs and find Koji making pancakes. He passes me a plate without a word.

"You okay?" he says finally.

I nod. "I think so." I take a bite of pancake and then look at my brother. "What do you remember about Mika? You're older than her now—than she was."

"I know," he says.

"Do you remember what she looks like?"

"Of course," he says. Then he grins. "She looked like you."

"Do you remember her voice?"

His grin fades. "No . . . not really."

"I miss her," I say.

"I know. I miss her, too." He sounds so sad.

"I would do it for you, too, you know," I say. *I'd keep you afloat, like Mika did for me. I'd make the lifeguard take you first is what I mean.*

"I know," he says. And I know he understands.

"Koj, wanna go on a drive?"

"A drive? Where to?"

I smile. "We'll know when we get there."

We go out into the desert, and we talk about Mika. We talk about her until the sun goes down and then we go get tacos and he tells me how much he wants to pursue music and how much he likes this girl Maggie, and I tell him I don't know where I'm going to go to college, and we talk and we talk and we talk, and I realize all this time that Koji has been there, waiting for me to talk to him. Waiting for me to see him.

My parents get home that evening, and Mom rushes in and wraps me in her arms. "Reiko, Reiko," she whispers against my head. "Are you all right?"

I hug her back. "I'm okay," I say. "And, Mom"—I pull back and look at her—"I want to talk about Mika."

Her eyes glisten. "I'm so glad," she says.

Later, after we've been in the living room, looking at pictures of Mika, sharing memories, I take a deep breath and ask what I've been wanting to ask all day: "Can we watch the video from Mika's last piano recital?"

And then, on the screen, there she is. Mika playing the piano. The piano that we still own but that nobody touches.

She walks out on the stage with a straight back and her hair tied back in a severe bun. She's wearing a crisp white collared shirt and black trousers.

"I thought she looked so grown up that day," Mom says, "and I can't believe that anyone would have thought she looked grown up when she looks like a little girl playing dress-up, pretending to be an adult." Mom laughs a little then. "She insisted on doing her own makeup, and it was terrible. I made her take it off and she was so mad at me."

I remember then that Mika and my mom used to argue a lot. And finally acknowledging that she wasn't the "angel sister" doesn't make me sad.

It makes me relieved.

On the screen, Mika goes and sits at the grand piano. It dwarfs her. "Good luck, sweetie." Mom's whisper comes through the speakers.

And Mika begins to play.

The music washes over me like a mist. It seeps into my pores, and it reverberates in my bones. All the hours of hearing that song over and over again when she practiced. I haven't heard it since she died. I had to lock the memory away, because it was too hard to think about it.

Mom is squeezing Dad's hand and I can tell she's trying not to cry.

"I'm sorry," I say, slowly. "I'm sorry I couldn't talk about her for so long."

"We understand, sweetie," my dad says.

"But it wasn't fair, especially to Koji. It wasn't fair to Mika either. She would have hated that." I wipe a tear off my cheek.

"I do talk about her," says Koji. "Just not to you. I talk about her with Mom and Dad, and Ivan and Maggie."

"Is there something wrong with me? Why did it take me so long?" I ask.

"There is nothing wrong with you, darling. You went through something terrible and lost someone you loved very much," my mom says.

My hand is trembling. "But why was everyone else okay so much faster?"

"Oh, sweetheart, we're not okay. And I don't know if we'll ever be, but that itself is okay. For us, talking about Mika doesn't mean we're okay; it just makes it easier. Everyone processes grief differently. You were processing it the only way you knew how. And we thought we were doing the best thing, by letting you deal with it the way you needed to, but I don't know. Maybe we should have done it differently. I worry that being so hands off in our approach only added extra pressure to you. And we never wanted that."

"I wanted to be good enough for both of us," I say quietly. "To make up for losing her."

"Reiko," Mom says firmly, taking my hand, "I'm going to tell you two things that are simultaneously true. You will always be enough, and nothing could ever make up for losing Mika. Does that make sense? I'm so sorry if we ever made you feel differently. We love you. We'll always love you. Just like we'll always love Mika."

"I just want to be okay," I say.

Mom hugs me tight. "You can hurt and still be okay. And we're here for you, Reiko. I know it is hard, I know it will always be hard, and we'll miss Mika every day, but I promise you'll be okay. We all will."

This time, I believe her.

CHAPTER 63

I STAY HOME FROM SCHOOL the next day, and in the afternoon, Dre comes over to check on me.

"Hey, babe," she says, giving me a tight hug. "You okay?"

"Yeah," I say. "I think so. Thanks . . . for everything. To Tori, too. I owe you guys."

"Reiko, don't be ridiculous. You're family."

"Dre," I say. "Can you tell Tori that we can talk about Mika whenever she wants? I know she was her best friend."

"Of course. Tori would love that."

We go out and float in my pool. I'm in a pink flat raft, and she's on one shaped like a unicorn. Then we lapse into silence, and I watch the clouds float by. The one above me is shaped like a rabbit, or maybe a butterfly; they are changing too quickly for me to really make out any shapes.

"Is everything okay, Rei-Rei?" Dre says softly. "You seem a little distant."

"It's just . . . a lot has happened recently," I say. "Like, the whole going into the ocean thing was obviously a huge deal, and so is talking out loud about Mika, but something happened recently with Seth, too. Something I haven't told anyone about."

And I tell her what happened in the back of my Jeep. I tell her how it was like being trapped in a small space with a fox, with an animal, how I had to grow my own claws to push back.

Dre is livid. "I hate him. I already hated him, but now I really hate him. I despise him. What a disgusting shit. He is so lucky I didn't know about this when I saw him at the beach. I would have eviscerated him." And then her face softens, and she swims toward me. "Why didn't you tell me right away? Like, why didn't you call me?"

"There was nothing to tell," I say. "Nothing actually happened. Not really. I didn't want to make a big deal out of it."

"Rei, I love you, but that is a big deal. If you tell someone stop, and they don't stop, that is a big deal. That isn't nothing—that is something. And this is the kind of thing you tell your best friend, okay? I'm sorry. That's a super shitty thing that happened."

"I just felt stupid, you know?" I say, trailing my fingers across the top of the water. "I thought I knew him." I thought he was someone I could trust. I thought he was someone I could feel safe with.

Dre picks up my hand and squeezes it. "First of all, you have nothing to feel stupid about. If Seth made you feel uncomfortable and unsafe, that is *his* fault. He's the stupid one. Hell, do you want me to get Tori involved? I can, you know."

I smile at her. "Thanks, Dre," I say. "I'm fine, I was then and I am now, but I feel better talking to you about it."

"You just remember he's a total shithead, and not worth you at all. Not even worth your pinkie. Not even worth your pinkie nail. Not even worth a clipping of your pinkie nail! Okay?"

"Got it," I say. "I guess, even after everything, the breakup and all that, part of me thought he still cared about me. At least a little. And he clearly doesn't. And it made me wonder if he ever cared about me. Or if . . . if none of it meant anything. And then seeing him unexpectedly at the beach band thing . . . it kind of brought up all the hurt again, you know?"

She squeezes my hand again. "I know," she says. "I know."

I take a big breath. My mom is always telling me to be mindful of my breathing, especially when I'm overwhelmed, and you know what? It helps. I do it again, this time in through my nose and out through my mouth, and I feel like I'm not only breathing out air but I'm breathing all my hurt out.

"You all right?" says Dre. "You are huffing and puffing like you are the big bad wolf getting ready to blow a house down."

I snort mid-exhale. "Dre!" I say in between laughs. "I was being mindful. It's a thing."

Dre's brows furrow. "If you say so. Okay, other than breathing in and out like a lady in labor, what else would make you feel better?"

I shade my eyes and look up into the blue sky, watching the clouds again. One seems to grow wings before my very eyes and in the light breeze, it almost looks like a flying bird.

A flying eagle.

I turn toward Dre. "Can you go somewhere with me tonight?"

"Sure. Where to?"

"I'll tell you on the way."

CHAPTER 64

WE GO ON OLD ROUTE 66 and for a moment, I feel that old familiar pang of hurt that Seth isn't with me for this adventure. Even after everything that has happened, I miss the version of him that I knew last summer.

"I don't believe we're graduating so soon," I say from the passenger seat. Dre is driving and I'm navigating.

"Me either," she says. And then: "I hate that we aren't going to the same school."

"Me too," I say. And quieter: "I hate that I don't even know where I'm going. If I'm going anywhere. Maybe I'll just stay here forever."

"Don't say that, Rei. It'll all work out."

"Thanks," I say. "I wonder who we'll keep in touch with. Do you think we'll keep in touch with, like . . . Zach Garcia?" I look pointedly at her.

If I didn't know Dre so well, didn't know every feature of her face and all of the expressions it can make, I would have missed it:

the flash of wistfulness that flies across her features. But I know Dre's face better than my own. Even in the dim evening light.

"Oh my God! Andrea Torres! Have you been keeping secrets from me?"

Dre squeezes her eyes shut for so long that I smack her on the arm. "Eyes on the road, Dre. Eyes on the road! And talk."

"Okay, fine. You can't get mad at me for not telling you. Do you promise?"

"I promise!"

Dre takes a deep breath. "Zach and I have kind of been hooking up for a while."

"What?" A while? They've been hooking up for a *while*? A memory stirs in my brain. Zach saying that he was glad I had Andrea when he took me for coffee. And I thought he was hitting on *me*. Because that's what I always think. But really, he must have been checking in on me to be nice to her. Oh my God, I can't believe I've been so self-obsessed. I didn't see what was right in front of my face.

"I didn't want to . . . rub it in with everything going on with you . . . and plus, we don't really want people talking about it. You understand, right? You have to understand that."

I understand, but it still hurts that she didn't tell me. It hurts more that she didn't tell me because she thought I wouldn't be able to handle it. And I hate that I was too wrapped up in myself to even notice something so major happening with my best friend.

"That's . . . awesome," I manage. "So . . . do you really like him?"

"I don't know. He's going to Oregon State and I'm going to UCLA . . . It isn't like either of us wants to start college in a long-distance relationship." She grins at me. "Plus, I'll already be in a long-distance relationship with you. I hope my roommate is okay with you visiting all the time."

I know she's trying to make me feel better about not getting in, but it stings anyway. And I'm not letting her get away with changing the subject. "Nope, no changing the subject, Andrea Magdalena Torres. I want to know more about you and Zach."

"Well, since you brought out the Magdalena . . . Promise you aren't mad?"

"Promise," I say, and she holds out her pinkie and I link mine with it.

"Well," she says, lowering her voice and settling back into the driver's seat, and I know she's getting into story mode. "Do you remember that party at the track over the summer?"

"Of course," I say, and then I smirk. "But I'm surprised you remember any of it. You were smashed."

Dre shushes me. "Ahem. I'm telling this story. I was just setting the scene for you. So that night on the track . . ."

As she tells me how Zach kept coming up to her that night and then showed up the next day at her place with donuts and how later they snuck into one of the big hotel pools and then he took her to meet his moms, I start to realize that there wasn't anything all that special about the adventures that Seth and I were having. Here I was, thinking that nobody could understand, and that nobody else could be having adventures like us, living life like us, and Dre and Zach were off on their own adventures, in their own world, keeping their own secrets, too.

And it makes me realize something else.

That the things I miss about Seth—our adventures, and how I felt when I was with him—have less to do with him, and more to do with me.

I made Seth into someone I needed him to be, in the same way he made me into someone else. He was an escape from my grief, and I was an escape from a world he didn't want to be in.

I don't think love should be an escape. And I don't think it should be about power either.

I think love should make you stronger. A better person, not a worse one. And even though my love for Mika broke my heart, I think it made me stronger, too.

Seth didn't break my heart. It was already broken.

But I think it's healing now.

And maybe someday I'll be able to go on adventures with someone else.

CHAPTER 65

"WE'RE ALMOST THERE," I SAY.

We've passed the date farm and the ghost towns. We're almost to Ruth Setmire's house.

"This is . . . weird," Dre said when I told her about Ruth Setmire and how she made me promise to come back and tell her what I'd learned about myself. Then she laughed. "I mean, when I used to ask you what the hell you and Seth got up to . . . I didn't think it was visiting little old ladies."

"Don't let Ruth hear you call her that," I said. "She's fierce. Also old ladies can be fun," I add, thinking of the women at the care home.

"Does she know we're coming?" Dre asks now.

I shake my head. "She didn't know last time either."

"What if she isn't there?"

"She'll be there," I say, with more confidence than I feel. She has to be. "She asked us to come back."

"So . . . is she expecting . . . Seth? Is she going to be confused when you rock up with a hot Mexican babe instead of an ugly white guy?"

I laugh and elbow Dre. "Andrea!"

"What? It's true. I'm hot and Seth's . . . not. No matter what you say. Or Libby. Speaking of. Who knew she would be such a snake?"

I shrug. "Probably should have seen it coming." Then I recognize the street we're on. "Oh, turn in here. I'll buzz."

"Is that Gloria's granddaughter?" Ruth's voice crackles through the intercom. "Well, I'll be . . . You came back!"

"A deal is a deal," I say.

Ruth's living room is littered with cards and unopened boxes and flowers. "It was my eighty-eighth birthday last week," she says.

"Looks like you got spoiled," I say, reading the card on a bouquet of a dozen red roses. I make a mental note of the date for next year.

"Oh, those are from my nieces who live out in New York." Then she cackles. "I think they can't stand it that I'm still around and kicking. They wanna know what is in my will! Or, I should say, who!" She winks at us. "Little do they know I plan on living forever."

Dre nods. "Sounds like a good plan. I'm Andrea, by the way. I'm a friend of Reiko's."

"Last time she was here she was with a 'friend,' too," says Ruth, putting the word in air quotations. "What happened to him?"

"We're not friends anymore. And I don't know if we ever really were," I say, and it is the simplest and the hardest truth for me to say.

"Ah, I see," says Ruth. "Well, I'd say that's a shame, but I don't think it is."

"That is some dope wisdom," says Dre, nodding approvingly.

"You don't live to be my age without getting a little bit wise," says Ruth. Then she gives us a wicked grin. "You either get wisdom or you lose your marbles. Now come sit down; we've got a lot to talk about."

Ruth is just as vibrant and irreverent as I remember her, but even in the past few months I can see she's aged. For all her big talk about living forever, she seems older, and more fragile.

She takes us out to see her studio. It is in what must have once been a garage. There is a huge kiln in the corner and a fine coating of dust on everything. One whole wall is covered with easels, and the other has shelves and shelves of pottery.

"Did your mama ever spot the difference in the eagles?" Ruth says.

I shake my head. "I don't think so. Thank you again for that."

"It wasn't a gift, remember? It was a loan. A conditional loan. You've got to show me how you've grown." Her eyes are bright.

"Whoa," whispers Dre. "This is some deep shit."

"Deep shit is right!" Ruth declares. "Now go on, Reiko."

"I guess, I want to live my best life, but for me. Not for anybody else."

Ruth is beaming. "That sounds pretty good, my girl. I think you've earned that eagle. So what do you think of my studio? I don't use it much anymore. My hands aren't what they used to be. But this is where I used to make everything. Where I made the eagle." She shows us various pieces and tells us when she made them, and why. Dre is fascinated.

"Dre, I didn't know you were so interested in art," I say.

"This one has an artist's soul, I can tell," says Ruth.

Dre glows.

I smile at her, but part of me is jealous. I want an artist's soul.

"And you"—Ruth turns to me, as if I'd spoken my uncharitable thoughts out loud—"you have a wandering soul."

I shake my head. "No, I don't . . . I don't like to travel." Swimming in my pool is one thing. Flying across a wide-open ocean is another.

"I don't believe that for a second," says Ruth. "You need to spread these wings of yours and fly. For you, you hear me? Not for anyone else. I'll do another deal with you," she goes on. "Both of you, pick out something from my shelves. Another loan. Then come back in a year, and you"—she looks at Dre—"tell me what kind of art you've made. And you"—her eyes dart back to me—"tell me how you've flown."

"Ruth, we couldn't take something from you," I protest. "You've already been so kind, and the eagle was a unique circumstance."

"And it worked, didn't it? Look at you! And don't tell me what to do. I'm eighty-eight and I'll do what I want and what I want is to make a bargain with you two. What do you say?"

I look at Dre, who smiles and nods.

"I say, you've got yourself a deal."

"Damn right I do! And I think I'm getting the better end of the bargain. It does my old soul good to see Gloria's granddaughter. So if I have to use a little bribery, well, I'm not above it. The stuff in here"—she waves her arms around—"it's just collecting dust. I like knowing that it has a new home. Especially if it means I'll get a guaranteed visitor. One I actually like, mind you!"

My eyes prickle unexpectedly, and I lean over and kiss Ruth on her papery cheek. "It isn't bribery. We'd come see you anyway," I say, but Ruth is shaking her head.

"I don't need charity, but what we've got here is a deal. Now come on, pick something out and hit the road so I can go to sleep. It's past my bedtime."

Dre picks out a tiny wolf, frozen in mid-howl.

I find a small cactus, re-created in perfect detail. It even has a little owl hidden in a hollow.

"Now you've got a little piece of the desert you can take with you wherever you go," says Ruth, pressing the cactus into my hand.

CHAPTER 66

THE DAYS ARE GETTING WARMER and longer.

I barely think about Seth anymore. He still hangs around our group of friends, but he's easy to ignore. His relationship with Libby is on-again/off-again and even that doesn't bother me. I spend most of my time with Dre and Zach and our other friends. I'm not worried about who I'll go to prom with, or how they'll ask me. I just want to enjoy the rest of high school.

One Saturday morning in April, I'm sitting having cereal next to my mom while she is going through our mail. We've been spending more time together now, and not just on Wednesdays when we go to the care home together.

She stops suddenly, holding up a fat white envelope. "Reiko? What's this?"

It's got a ton of stickers and stamps on it, like it came from far away.

Like it came from Japan.

I steel myself for another rejection, and this one will be worse because it will be in front of my mom, too, but my dad is already taking the envelope out of my mom's hands. It is more than an envelope, more like a parcel.

"Reiko! I think you got in!" he says.

"Got in where?" says my mom, peering over his shoulder.

My dad isn't listening. He's ripping open the envelope, and I want to disappear, because it is painful enough to get rejected without it being so public . . .

"You got in! You got in! Reiko! You got into Temple University!"

"Temple University in *Japan*?" Mom's voice is tight.

I take the parcel from my dad. "I thought . . . I thought when they never emailed me that I hadn't gotten in. I didn't think that they'd send it in the mail-mail, especially not this late."

Dad is grinning and practically bouncing. "They must have sent out their acceptances late."

"But . . . it's so far," says Mom.

Dad puts his arm around Mom's shoulders.

I close my eyes, so I don't have to see her face.

"She isn't going to stay at home forever. If it isn't Japan, it'll be somewhere else," Dad says softly.

I think about the other schools I got into. My dad was right: I did get into other schools. Good schools, too, but nowhere that I was that excited about.

Going to school in Japan.

On my own.

The tiny spark of wanting that is always hidden deep inside of me flares to life, warming me. Encouraging me.

"I want to go to Japan," I say. Mom looks stunned and sits down. Dad looks a bit teary-eyed. "But, Dad, it isn't for you. I mean, I'm glad you'll be happy, but . . . I've always wanted to go. I think I just . . . hid it. Because I felt bad. I felt guilty. And I didn't want to fly across an ocean. But now I think I can." I take a deep breath. "Even without Mika."

"It's what she would want," Dad says.

"I know," I say. "But that isn't why I want to go. I can't live for her forever. I can only live for me."

Mom envelops me in a hug. "That's really what she would want."

I haven't seen Mika since that day at the beach. I need to talk to her about this, I need to tell her.

I think I know where she is.

I know where I have to go.

CHAPTER 67

I GET IN THE CAR alone.

And then I drive west. I drive and drive and drive. I drive out of the desert. I drive until all of a sudden, the ocean rises up next to me. I have the beach all to myself. I take my sandals off and hold them in my hand as I step out onto the sand. It burns my feet. It is softer than desert sand. Softer and finer.

Reiko, Reiko, calls the sea. *Reiko, Reiko* . . .

I follow its call. I walk through the sand, eyes straight ahead, fixed on the horizon.

I gasp as the cold water kisses my feet. And for an instant, I am filled with fear, but then I take a deep breath, and I take another step, and another, until the water is up to my knees. There are seagulls screaming above me, and the water is so cold and the sun is so hot and my heart is so heavy it is going to burst. It has been so heavy for so many years, and it is like this cold water is piercing it because my heart is finally bursting, but it doesn't hurt, it feels like relief. Maybe it isn't bursting; maybe it is putting itself back together.

And Mika is there.

It is just us. Next to each other with our feet in the sea.

"I've missed you," I say.

"I miss you, too," she says.

"I got into Temple University," I tell her.

"I know," she says. "I'm so proud of you."

"Japan is too far. It'll kill Mom."

"No, it won't. She'll be okay. You'll be okay."

"Do you think I should go?" I ask.

"Do *you* think you should go?"

"I miss you, Mika," I say again.

"That isn't a reason not to go to Japan," she says. "Not a reason to not live."

"But Mom and Dad and Koji. What if something happens and I'm not here?"

"You staying here won't stop bad things from happening. And you can always come home. It's just a plane ride away."

"A plane ride across an ocean."

"I wish I could come with you."

"I wish you could, too." I put my head on her shoulder. "I'm scared, Mika." Because this is what I want.

"I know," she says. "But you'll be okay. I promise."

"What about you? I can't leave you here. I can't leave you behind."

Mika smiles, and it is the saddest smile I've ever seen. "I'll always be here," she says, and she puts her hand on my heart. "You know that."

"But I need you, Mika."

"You'll be okay," she says, and it is with just as much of a fierce determination as when she said it that day in the ocean. "You can't be scared forever." She takes both of my hands in hers.

"Where . . . where will you go?" I ask.

"Don't worry about me, Reiko. I'm the big sister, after all."

"I love you, Mika."

"I love you, Rei-Rei."

She lets go of my hand, and she fades away until all I can see is the infinite blue sky.

Finally, finally I say the words that I haven't said, the words I need to say.

"Goodbye, Mika."

EPILOGUE

IT'S THE SAME SEA IN Japan. And the same sky. And the same stars. And the same moon.

Japanese sounds familiar and strange. Sometimes it makes me feel like I'm listening to the words underwater, but then I always make my way to the surface.

Among all the blinking, blinding Tokyo lights, I can still see the stars shining down on me. And I can hear them singing. *You are beautiful*, they sing. But I know I am more than that.

I am whole.

ACKNOWLEDGMENTS

This book would not exist without the help and support of a lot of incredible people:

The first thank you goes to my agent, Claire Wilson. Thank you for being a fierce and brilliant champion, for your steel spine, sharp mind, and kind heart. Signing with you was without a doubt the best decision of my career, and it has changed my life in the best possible way. Here's to many more books and adventures!

Huge thanks to everyone else at the RCW Literary Agency, especially Sam Copeland and Miriam Tobin. Thank you as well to Emily Hayward-Whitlock and Sarah Lewis at the Artists Partnership for your continued support.

Fun fact: In 2015 at my wedding in Palm Springs, one of the ceremony readings was from David Levithan's book *Every Day*. And now David Levithan is publishing my book set in Palm Springs. David, thank you for your support for this book and for your excellent editorial insight and feedback. It honestly is a dream come true to work with you.

Thank you to the whole team at Scholastic, specifically Josh Berlowitz and eagle-eyed copyeditor Jody Corbett. I'm very proud to be a Scholastic author.

To the designer Baily Crawford, thank you for creating such a stunning cover. I couldn't have asked for a more perfect cover for this book.

Thank you as well to the team at my UK publisher, Walker Books, but especially my editor, Annalie Grainger, and my publicist, Rosi Crawley. Annalie, thank you for reading this book at least a million times and for never giving up on me and Reiko. I'm so lucky to have an editor who is as brilliant as she is kind.

And thank you to Patrick Ness for coming up with the excellent title and for all the solid author advice.

A standing ovation thank you to all the booksellers and librarians and bloggers who have supported me. You make the book world and my world go round.

I'm forever grateful for the generosity of Katherine Rundell and Laini Taylor for giving me the book blurbs of my dreams for my debut novel, *The Heartbeats of Wing Jones*. Thank you for your kind words, and for inspiring me as a reader and a writer.

This book was edited over almost two years—at home, in libraries, and at multiple writing retreats. One was in a charming English cottage, where Anna James, Mel Salisbury, Sara Barnard, and Cat Doyle all helped me figure out who Reiko really is, made me laugh till I cried, and also gave me a whole new appreciation for Eddie Redmayne. The other retreat was in a magical French castle, where Alwyn Hamilton, Ryan Graudin, Laure Eve, and Laini Taylor offered wise counsel, excellent company, much-needed encouragement, and copious amounts of French cheese. Thank you all for making my life feel a bit like a fairy tale.

I'm incredibly grateful to Cynthia Hardy Maasry for being an early reader and helping with specific details of Reiko's heritage.

Also thank you to Caesar Maasry for his enthusiasm, and baby Victoria for just being adorable.

I am so lucky to be part of such a joyful and supportive writing community. I honestly know the best people. Special thanks to Samantha Shannon, Laure Eve, Alwyn Hamilton, Anna James, Kiran Millwood Hargrave, Mel Salisbury, Sara Barnard, Anna McKerrow, and Katherine Woodfine. Thank you, too, to the super babes on the other side of the Atlantic: Ashley Woodfolk, Nic Stone, Angie Thomas, Zoraida Córdova, and Dhonielle Clayton.

To Krystal Sutherland, who has been chasing the writing dream with me: We did it, and we are going to keep doing it. Proud of you, and proud of us.

Thank you to Jessica Blair Herman and Allen Leech, who came to not one but two of my book launches on different continents and are incredibly supportive of my career as an author. I owe you guys Escuela tacos.

Thank you to Jennifer Ball for being there for all things bookish and for everything else. I'm so glad to have you in my life.

To Cat Doyle—who has become like an actual sister to me— thank you for all the calls and chats and cheerleading.

To my girls who have all held my hand and gotten me through various heartbreaks over the years: Courtney, Cat, Jessica, Chloe, Jeni, Dyna, Fay, and Janou. I don't know what I'd do without all of you in my life.

Huge thank you to my amazing and far-flung family. To all my Webber, Hopper, and Tsang aunts, uncles, and cousins—thank you for all your support and enthusiasm. Special thank you to

Mimi and Pop-Pop, and Grandma Kay and Grandpa Bob, for giving me a love and appreciation for the desert. And a shout-out to Stephanie Tsang and Ben Puckett for their continuous support, and welcome to the world, Cooper Puckett-Tsang!

Thank you to my wonderful in-laws, Louisa and Paulus Tsang, and my amazing parents, Rob and Virginia Webber, for always being there for me.

This book is dedicated to my brother, Jack, and my sister, Jane. I'm so lucky to be your sister, and I'd do anything for you. Thank you for being so awesome, and for making me laugh so much.

And to my husband, Kevin . . . I'm a better writer, and a better person, because of you. Thank you for all of your help with this book. Thank you for everything. I love our life together. I love you. Here's to our next adventure.